LYNN VROMAN

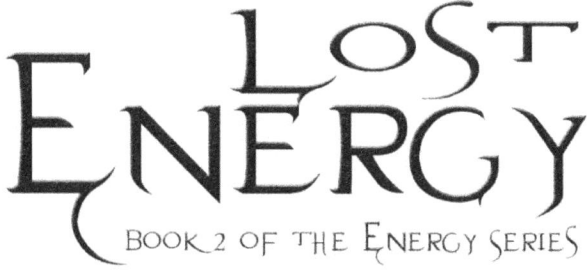

LOST ENERGY

BOOK 2 OF THE ENERGY SERIES

Untold
Press

LOST ENERGY

Published by Untold Press LLC
114 NE Estia Lane
Port St Lucie, FL 34983

ISBN: 978-0692403068

PRODUCED IN THE UNITED STATES OF AMERICA

10 9 8 7 6 5 4 3 2 1

DEDICATION

Victoria, Katherine, Olivia, and Rhys,
always everything is for you.

Acknowledgements

First, I have to thank Jen Wylie and Sean Hayden. You two…there are no words. Thank you.

I have to give a huge shout out to Winston Campbell. You're probably the coolest person I've ever met, not to mention one of the most genuine. Thanks for wanting to be part of this crazy ride.

Angela McPherson, you've become such an amazing friend and supporter. I love our late night conversations and your knack for making me laugh when I'm at my most frustrated. Not only are you a great writer, but a compassionate person who always knows exactly what to say. I'm so lucky to have met you!

As always, thanks to my awesome critique partner, Jadah McCoy, and one of my best friends on the planet, Jenn Wescoat, who read whatever I send them.

Most of all, thanks to my husband and four awesome kids (and you, too, Kody and Mac!), whose support and encouragement drive me to keep going. This wouldn't be possible without you, and I love you, even when I hide away in my writing dungeon.

CHAPTER 1

LENA

THE FAMILIAR

Sweat stung my eyes as my head bounced off the mat.

Stay down, dumbass.

I crawled up the ropes, chest heavy and gasping for breath, until I stood on wobbly legs. It didn't take long for him to come at me again, his cushioned fist slamming against my jaw. The mat met my face for the tenth time, becoming good friends with it. When blood dribbled from my lip to the canvas, I decided to listen to my inner baby and stay down. An ass kicking a day for the last six weeks didn't make defeat any easier, though. If I could catch his chin with one hard hit, it'd be him on the floor mopping up blood with the edge of a T-shirt.

"Get up and try again." Farren wiped his brow and danced around the ring, smacking his gloves together. "An old lady could whoop your ass."

We'd been at this every morning, him beating me up under the guise of training. Running was my thing, not getting into a roped-off square to let a Protector treat me like a punching bag. A man, I might add, whom I once thought a traitor for shooting Tarek, but now considered family. Funny how life worked out.

But Wilma, my former lunch lady/ Protector, insisted on the training. What Wilma said these days was law– unfortunately for my poor face.

Small price to pay for knowing about my past lives as a Guide in Exemplar, I guess. The benefits, Tarek, Wilma, and Farren being the most important, far outweighed the aggravations, like allowing a big, redheaded jackass to thump the shit out of me.

I moved to lean against the ropes, heaving as I spit out my mouthpiece. "I need a break."

He danced around me some more, shadow boxing. "No, you don't. We just started."

"Yeah, an hour ago." I threw off my gloves and gave Jake, who watched from outside the ring, a sneer. "What're you smiling about?"

"Nothing, Lena girl. Love watching a good butt-kicking, is all." Jake. My boss, friend, pseudo-dad, landlord, and mother's boyfriend, all labels he earned. Loyalty had rewards in my book. But his wiseass remarks? So not nice.

"Whatever." I left the ring and stormed by him to hit the showers, needing to wash away some of the sweat and humiliation. "Why don't you get in there with him? Guarantee you won't be smiling for long."

"Hey, I was middle-weight state champ two years running." But Jake took my invitation, the usual routine when I'd had enough. He got his ass handed to him by Farren every time, but it took a while longer as the weeks went by.

I shot him a smirk over my shoulder. "Wasn't Elvis still doing Vegas then?" Wiseass cracks deserved a few verbal jabs.

Jake shoved on his gloves with a scowl that didn't reach his brown eyes. "You got jokes, huh?"

Farren laughed, jumping from foot to foot. "Come on, old man, at least give me a few minutes of a real workout."

"Old man? Aren't you like a hundred?" Jake pushed through the ropes.

"And can still beat the shit out of you." Farren's handsome face split in a grin as Jake stuffed in his mouthpiece.

As the grunts and thuds took over the gym, I pushed open the locker room door.

Testosterone.

Had to love it. Had to put up with it, at least.

I dug in my bag to grab soap and shampoo, spotting a new message on my phone. When I slid the bar over to unlock my screen, Belva's pretty face sat next to the message, *don't forget the picture! See u at 4.*

Smiling, I threw it back in my bag and hit the shower.

Twenty minutes later, I headed out of the gym, shaggy hair still wet, in a pair of shorts and red tank top. Before leaving, I held my phone up to the ring. "Hey, Farren!"

The Protector stopped pounding on Jake long enough to glance my way, and I snapped his picture. "Belva asked." I took a couple—one sweaty and big muscled photo for my friend and one for me when Jake managed to get in a good jab to Farren's chin.

Since Farren was a ginger, his skin always matched the stark red of his hair when he was embarrassed. If fighting Jake and me didn't make him red from exertion, the next best thing was my friend's crush.

He spit out his mouthpiece. "Knock it off, Lena. Don't encourage her."

I stuffed my phone in my back pocket. "You know you like it."

Didn't know it was possible, but his face turned a shade darker. His full lips curved up at the corners, though. "Hey, I'm used to the ladies drooling over me." He wriggled his brows. "But I like them a few more years out of their diapers."

Jake punched him in the jaw.

"Ouch, man! Not fair."

I hiked up my bag, laughing. "She's nineteen, Farren, plenty old enough. If you're trying to find someone closer to your age, maybe you should stop by Sunset Manner. Hear the blue hairs there are pretty hot."

The door closed on Jake's cackling as I headed toward Zander's old car. Since he was now living in Empyrean, I figured he wouldn't mind if I took it over. It was the least he could do, even if he would. Zander owed me for pretending to be my best friend while he conspired to get me and Wilma killed with his Protector, Mateusz, who took over guard dog duties after Zander's original Protector was killed in Arcus. Granted, I understood why Zander tried to send us to Casimir, Arcus's prior Warden. The bastard had held the energy of Zander's dead Protector hostage, and the only way he'd give it up was in exchange for Wilma's energy—and the only way to get to Wilma was through me. Like Zander, I'd do anything for my Protector. Thank God, Wilma never put me in that position, though. Anyway, if he wanted to hide away in a different world, fine. But his car was mine.

I dumped my bag in the passenger seat, hopping in the driver's, yelping when the scorching leather seats burned the backs of my legs. After starting the motor, I flicked on the AC, enduring the first gush of hot air, and turned up the radio. Summers on the mountain were awesome. I couldn't deny it–even with all the city tourists wanting to experience the "wilderness" of the Poconos.

When I pulled into my driveway, I rolled the windows down before climbing the steps leading to my apartment.

I opened the door to find Mom sitting on the couch, reading a book in a new yellow sundress. "Hey, Mom."

"Hi, baby." She bounced off the couch and gave me a hug. Always smiling now, and with an added fifteen pounds and sun-kissed skin, she looked like a twenty-five-year-old.

"Nice dress. Going in early?"

"Yeah, I want to make sure everything is ready for the new menu. If the advertisements worked, we should have a pretty good crowd tonight."

We had a full house every weekend now that it was tourist season and we served dinner. Mom made some cosmetic adjustments to the lobby, too, adding a few small tables, fresh paint, and talked Jake into a couple of video games. Out went all the boxing stuff. I'm sure all the pictures and trophies were sitting in some closet graveyard. My boss couldn't be happier–but I'm almost positive it was because he finally had Jacie Tulman all to himself.

"Me and Belva'll be there around six. She wanted to go shopping first." I shook my head, a smile playing on my lips. "Farren's coming in to help out."

"Well, he is a handsome boy. I don't blame her."

Even though Mom knew Farren wasn't anywhere near a boy, she never failed to see him any different. He looked about eighteen, with a face as smooth as marble. He also had a body that convinced anyone who wanted to cause trouble to reconsider.

"If you say so. I'm gonna get dressed, go for a run before she gets here."

She grabbed her purse. "Sounds good. Oh, yeah." Mom stopped at the door, holding it open. "Wilma came over, said she'd be back in a day or two."

Anger, a step up from the raw pain I used to feel, coursed through me. Wilma always performed the same tactic: come by to tell Mom she was leaving, making sure I was nowhere in earshot to beg her to take me with her. Her little trips consisted of going to Empyrean to talk with Teenesee, Empyrean's Warden, to see if Zander was behaving. I didn't mind that, but she'd also go to Arcus– where my soul mate was Warden.

"Wish she had the nerve to tell me herself." I looked up at the ceiling to keep the angry tears from falling.

"She's watching out for you, honey."

Wilma said the reason Exemplar, specifically Casimir's sister, Cassondra, didn't come after me was because I stayed in my dimension, lived my life. Guess the Synod deemed what happened in early spring, with Casimir and Mateusz trying to disrupt the dimensional lines, wasn't my fault. By law, they had to leave me alone, but only if I played by the rules.

I didn't much care about the rules.

"Maybe she should stop treating me like a child and let me make my own decisions."

Mom left the door to give me another hug. "Love makes us do things that aren't always easy."

I returned her hug, not at all feeling the lecture. "Yeah, like killing Arcus's Warden."

A warden sounded like a jailer to me, but in reality, Wardens were the ones in prison. They had to stay in one dimension and live forever until some power-hungry person came along to kill them, all the while controlling the flow of energy.

Lonely. Miserable. At least, it was for my giant. The world where he'd become Warden when he killed Casimir to protect me didn't have a population of actual people he could talk to. Just those damn squid that climbed the trees squealing all the time.

Mom rubbed my back. "From what Wilma said, Tarek did an honorable thing." She stood on her toes to kiss my cheek and went back to the door. "Look, in a couple months, you'll be in college, out on your own…around other boys."

Yeah, like what Tarek and I had was so small I could move on with some idiot frat boy. I'd keep that to myself. She didn't deserve an attack, verbally or otherwise. Dad did enough damage to last her a lifetime. "Sure, ah, see you later."

"Love you, baby."

As soon as she left, I went to my room to change into running gear, throwing my bag in the corner. Thick, plush carpet felt good on my bare feet. Wilma had given me her memory foam mattress after she moved. She insisted, saying she needed a new one, and I didn't put up too much fuss. Falling into the bed every night, especially after the tough workouts with Farren, felt like heaven.

The dress Teenesee gave me hung in the back of my closet. Every time I reached for my running shoes, it was a reminder of the last night Tarek and I spent together. The most beautiful–and revealing–article of clothing I owned. I had plans for that dress, plans that required Tarek.

Not wanting to dwell–because that led to an embarrassing amount of tears–I laced up my shoes and went outside.

The path I ran hadn't changed since school let out six weeks ago. I'd head two miles east until I was able to cut through the school's backyard to the woods, heading straight to the trailer park. As I delved into the shaded woods, my breathing relaxed and my heart skipped. The spot by the stream, where I spoke to Tarek the first time, crawled with kids from the park. The music was loud and the chatter louder. A few kids waded in the water. Others sat around the unlit fire pit, talking, making out...staying as far away from their parents as possible.

Some waved my way, and I returned the gesture, no longer feeling animosity for kids who were always in survival mode. I used to be one of them. Now, I considered myself reformed since I escaped. Guess I could thank Casimir for some of that.

When I reached the rusted mailboxes, I went to Dad's. Pulling the key from around my neck, I opened his box and checked the contents: a few bills and a grocery store flyer. I jogged down the hill, ready to have another non-conversation with the man whom I used to think was the scariest being on the planet.

As I climbed the cement blocks and turned the knob, a strange but too familiar cloud dulled my brain. I let go of the door and searched for the sole person who had ever caused my mind to go lazy. The only people around were the usual inhabitants, sitting out front, batting away flies, and smoking cigarettes.

The fuzz stayed on my brain for another few moments before it cleared.

What the…?

Rubbing my forehead, I opened the door to find my father in his wicker chair, watching his Indian wall. He gave a slight wave before tucking his hand back inside a thin blanket.

I waved back on my way to the fridge, not even pretending to show any affection. Still hated him, but like any other unwanted pet, I had to feed and water him or guilt would keep me awake at night. From spending six days in Arcus, Dad broke. His pieces would never glue together again. Not many others could return whole from that place. I left a part of me there, too.

After I put his grilled cheese in a frying pan and crammed clothes in the washer, I started the coffee pot. Still, not a word floated between us. I stood by the counter, watching the sandwich cook, my mind drifting to what I used to call Zander heroin. If he found a way to come to Earth, I'd leave it up to him to gather the nerve to confront me. I wouldn't search for him.

Unfortunately, Zander wasn't the only one who could force my common sense to take a vacation. A dimension existed full of Guides whose energy had a magnetic connection with mine. From what Wilma let me know about my prior research, a few didn't like me very much. A list hiding under my bed had a bunch more Exemplians on it who might not find my company welcome, either. The list. A souvenir, Wilma called it, a reminder of those who had to escape Exemplian rule.

I flipped the sandwich, pressing all my tension into the spatula smashing the bread.

Nothing like having an entire world pissed at you.

Lynn Vroman

CHAPTER 2

LENA

COMPANY

Belva sat on the porch steps, glaring at me as I walked up the sidewalk. Five months' experience being her best friend told me she hated waiting and my ears would more than likely be in for a good ten minutes of crap.

I climbed the steps, and her pretty face went from glaring straight to scowling while she tapped her red-lacquered fingernails on her phone screen. "Just once, I'd like you to be on time. Nice lip, by the way."

I touched my tongue to the little gift Farren gave me this morning and smiled. He usually left my face without evidence, but not today. Saying nothing, I pulled my cell from its armband and scrolled to his picture. When I handed it over, her face brightened as her hazel eyes shined on the sweaty, muscular Protector looking right at the camera.

"I swear he's the hottest guy on the planet." She started clicking buttons. "I'm sending this to my phone."

"Go ahead, but if you keep nagging me, that's the last sweaty picture you're gonna get."

Belva, my one-time nemesis, followed me to the door. We hated each other in high school, until Belva...well...had an accident. Ever since, we were inseparable.

"Fine, fine, but hurry up. I don't want to be late for work." Belva had managed to slip perfectly into Zander's spot. Bonus, Jake actually liked her, too.

I snorted. "You mean you don't want to miss a second with Ginger."

"You'll understand when you find *the* guy, Lena."

A small sting zapped my heart. Belva had no idea Tarek existed, had no idea anything outside Earth existed, really. Our discovery of dimensions and the juicy details remained between Mom, Jake, and the two Protectors hovering around me all the time.

Tarek was my secret. My beautiful, painful secret.

"Whatever you say, pal. Try not to salivate when he flexes his muscles."

She laughed, her face turning a sweet shade of pink, and went to sit on the couch to stare at Farren's picture while I got ready.

If Ginger realized how lucky he was to have someone as great as Belva interested in his annoying ass, we'd all be happy.

∞ ∞ ∞

Belva and I pushed through the front doors to a full house. All five little tables had teenagers crowded around them or couples laughing while a bunch of people talked by the concession counter. Everyone ate the food Mom put on the menu and what Farren currently cooked in the kitchen. Belva gave me a quick hug before heading straight to her man, willing to get the new black strapless stained with grease. She swung the door open, and Farren glanced up, his eyes going wide when he spotted my friend. The stove wasn't the only hot thing making him turn red.

I shrugged and blew Mom a kiss before going to the front to help Jake. She grinned, making a show of catching it as she took orders from the counter. By the time I reached Jake, he was knee-deep in loud teenagers and frustrated parents. He smiled, though, even with the nice swell on his cheek.

"Ginger get in a good hit?"

He handed off some tickets, his crooked nose slanting to the right when his grin grew wider. "Can't complain. Got a couple good hits in this time, too." He glanced up, raising a brow. "Thanks for the distraction."

I winked. "No problem."

The crowd didn't thin out until the last minute, with people still buying tickets as the previews started. A couple months ago, Jake broke down and fixed up the back theater–a little gentle coaxing from the pretty Jacie Tulman helped–and so it stayed open all the time now. The added room paid off. Jake even thought about installing a 3-D screen with the extra income. When he told us, Farren smirked, saying he wouldn't be impressed until technology left the Stone Age.

"Why don't you go help Mom finish up? I'll handle the register."

"I like the way you're thinking." My boss' face brightened, and like a kid on Christmas, he nodded with a sloppy grin.

When Jake made it to the concession stand, Mom lifted a hand to his bruise, concern clouding her bright green eyes. He pulled her close and kissed her lips. The guy was in heaven.

Man, all the romance circulating through my little bubble… Wilma and I spent a lot of time rolling our eyes. At least I could admit I was jealous. Wilma got annoyed.

Once the last few people in line bought tickets, I locked up the computer screen and turned toward the kitchen.

With more punch than at the trailer park, the dull haze slammed into my psyche. The magnetism caused my feet to head back to the front door, a pull way stronger than Zander heroin. When I opened it, the fuzz faded, and then disappeared. I shut the door with more force than necessary, blood draining from my face and pooling at my toes, and made a beeline for the kitchen. No way did I imagine that.

The swinging door banged open with a thud against the kitchen wall, making Belva jump and whip her head in my direction.

The grin Belva always put on Farren's face vanished when he looked up from his grill. "Shit."

I nodded, giving him the signal his assumption was correct, and painted on a smile. "Hey, Belva. Could you see if Mom needs some help?"

She hopped off the counter. "Everything okay?"

"Yeah, yeah, fine." I took a deep breath, trying to control the shaking in my knees. "Just need to talk to Farren for a second."

Belva didn't ask any more questions. Over the past five months, she'd gotten used to our secretive behavior. Since she realized that first month nothing romantic went on between her future man and me, she didn't take our little powwows to heart.

"Sure, okay." She squeezed my shoulder on the way out.

As soon as the door shut behind her, Farren grabbed my shoulders. "Tell me."

"I felt someone."

He knew exactly what I meant, seeing as he had the same dull fuzz enter his brain every time a Protector came within a thirty-foot radius.

"You still feel them?" Farren moved me to open the kitchen door, scanning the lobby. "I don't feel anything."

I hustled passed him, stomping to the front door, the lobby a lot quieter now that all the movies started. "No, but it was strong here and faded when I opened the door to look outside."

Almost growling, he grabbed my hand and led me to the first showing room. I gave Mom and Belva an all-good smile, but the way Farren's face transformed to make him look like the warrior he was, caused them both to pale. Jake stood behind Mom, his hands on her shoulders and face tense. He knew from experience not to ask too many questions until the danger passed. Farren would have ignored him in his Protector mode, anyway.

When the doors to the room opened, letting in a flash of light, people grumbled. Farren kept a tight hold on my hand while we made a path around the entire room, reaching the opposite exit door.

"Anything?" His dark eyes, hard and intense, searched mine.

"No." I dragged him to the next room.

We repeated our intrusion in the second and third room, both with the same results. We walked to the counter, and Mom left Jake's arms to hug me. I patted her shoulders, tension squeezing my stomach. Guides didn't make me nervous–their Protectors were another story.

I pulled away. "Can you and Belva maybe go in the kitchen, clean up Farren's mess?"

Mom nodded, understanding on her face. "Sure, baby." She turned to Belva, who had worry scrunching her delicate brow. "Come on, sweetie. I'll wash, you dry."

Belva took Mom's hand after she glanced at Farren.

He managed to drop the warrior face to smile at her. "I'll see you in a few."

"I'll be waiting." She raised a brow. "But…it'd be nice if all of you would trust me a little more." Belva stormed into the kitchen, Mom following.

As soon as the kitchen door swung shut, Jake turned to us. "Is it happening again?"

Damn, Belva had no clue what she asked for. Sometimes oblivion was better than the truth. That said, I put my hands on Jake's chest, and not wanting him to worry, prepared to lie.

Farren wasn't so worried about Jake's worry. "Lena felt someone."

"Shit." Jake pulled me into a bear hug.

"My sentiments exactly." Farren scrubbed a hand through his grown-out buzz cut.

"Listen, guys, let's not get crazy, okay?" I tapped Jake's back, a let-me-go signal he ignored. "Could be a curious new energy. Our story had to have spread like fire. Maybe they wanted to get an up-close look."

Farren shook his head. "Want to explain how a new Guide energy got here? Only one way to cross the lines."

"Yeah, well maybe the Protector's new too." With a little more force, I pushed away from Jake's vice-like hold. "It makes sense."

Jake looked to Farren, hope lighting his brown eyes. "That possible?"

"I wouldn't count out anything right now, but to be on the safe side, I'm going to bunk with Lena and Jacie until Wilma gets back."

Jeez, even he knew she left! But I did like the idea of Farren couching it at my place.

"Yeah, good. That's good." Jake headed to the kitchen. "You two stay out here with Belva for the second showing. Me and Jacie'll take the kitchen." Before he opened the door, he gave Farren one last pleading glance. "Keep her safe."

∞ ∞ ∞

24

By closing time, the whole episode barely won a thought from me, though Jake and Farren were on edge. Jake took Mom home, keeping an arm wrapped protectively around her waist on the way out the door. Farren and I dropped Belva off before heading back to the house. Farren's attention darted toward every movement to and from the car. He even walked Belva to her front door, much to her delight.

But once we pulled into the driveway I shared with Jake, I raced up the steps without waiting for Farren's little recon act. He didn't holler for me to stop–he knew why I ran.

With an urgency that had me fumbling with my shorts' zipper, I stripped down, changed into my halter nightgown, used the bathroom, and dove under the cool sheets. Closing my eyes, I struggled to relax as I sunk into the bed. The fight was useless–the excitement I felt every night at this exact moment never abated.

Like clockwork, I heard him.

So, I'm saddled with Wilma for a while.

I smiled, Tarek's rich voice swelling my heart, tingling my spine. Didn't matter what he said; he could've been talking about the hibernation practices of snails.

She's not all bad, bitching about the animals, mostly.

A gap wedged into the conversation after that– something he had a habit of doing. How I missed those annoying pauses.

She said you're doing better against Farren. Remember what I told you about him. Don't forget the bum right knee. Play a little dirty, and you'll get him on the ground in no time.

I snuggled deeper under the covers, hugging the same pillow I held every night–the one that still wore his shirt– thinking about apples and lilacs.

Wilma said you're happy. He chuckled. *Complain too much, but happy.* I could almost feel his sigh against my ear as it echoed in my brain. *I miss you.*

"Miss you, too." That part of the one-sided conversation I always said aloud, willing him to hear it, know it.

As usual, he changed the subject to something lighter. My giant always made me smile...even when he was worlds away. *I guess Zander's still driving Teenesee crazy. He won't stop asking questions. Wilma avoids him when she goes. She says he complains more than you.*

The tears started to well, and no matter how hard I tried to stop them, they'd come. They came every night.

The river hasn't raged in weeks. Even the squid are behaving for the most part. Wilma only had to kill one this time.

Tarek told me once that his mood controlled the environment. He'd spent the better part of his time trying to rein in his emotions to make the place better. Wilma said our midnight talks helped.

It's cold as hell in the castle, regardless how high I build the fire. Pause. *But I finished the place in the woods, close to the bank. I'll sleep here tonight; Wilma can sleep on the floor.*

I imagined the cabin by the bank, imagined us there together, surrounded by the vibrant colors.

I'm going to let you sleep now. Wilma's banging on the door. She's not finished harassing me, I suppose. Be safe... I love you.

Tears dripped on the pillow as I hugged it closer to my heart.

"Love you, too."

CHAPTER 3

LENA

DAD

Bright sun welcomed me to the morning. I curled deeper into the memory foam, my arms still wrapped around my Tarek shirt-pillow. The thing could probably use a washing, except that'd take away the memory of his scent. Stupid reasoning, but it kept me going.

I closed my eyes. Drifting back into dream world was too appealing to pass up. Fifteen more minutes and I'd face the day, starting with getting my butt kicked in the ring.

And two hours later, I rolled out of bed and tugged on shorts and a T-shirt before heading to the bathroom.

When I stumbled out to the living room, my gym bag stuffed and ready, I found Farren sitting on the couch reading the paper with a mixing bowl full of Fruit Loops. I bought that stuff because of Tarek. Another stupid thing, but the smell reminded me of how his mouth tasted after we ate a box together on the very couch Farren had his butt parked.

Mom was nowhere in sight, already showered and at Jake's, as per her usual morning routine. She and my boss acted like teenagers. Sweet, but it didn't stop me from making gagging noises every time I caught them making out on the couch.

I went to sit with Farren, pointing at his breakfast. "Sure you're not ten?"

He answered by taking a huge bite, milk dribbling down his chin, and continued reading the paper. The way he kept up on current events drove me nuts. He'd have the news on at the gym, in the car, and never failed to read the *New York Times*, the *Pocono Record*, and the *Post* as often as possible.

I went to grab a banana off the kitchen counter and sat back down. "You ever get tired of all the chaos?"

"Are you kidding? What I don't get is how you can ignore it." He took another sloppy bite of cereal.

"Pretty simple, really."

"Not for me," he said around a mouthful. "All the passion in this dimension… It's perfect."

"Don't know why you keep saying that. Exemplar sounds like it has perfect down to a science."

He folded the paper, giving me the same annoyed frown as usual when we ventured into this conversation. "Without a little chaos, life's not worth living." Brown eyes lighting, he smiled as he tweaked my nose. "You all are so…impulsive, unpredictable."

Impulsive. Nice way to put it. "Yeah, well, nothing like getting addicted to stupidity, big guy."

"Hey, I'm not addicted." He slurped the milk left in his bowl and swiped a hand across his mouth. "Trust me. Old Lena would've appreciated it." He scraped another spoonful to get every piece of cereal before putting his dish in the sink.

Old Lena. His nickname for my past lives. I didn't mind. The only time I ever hated hearing about my past self was when Tarek mentioned her. Jealousy slithered into my gut every time. Nothing like hating…ah…yourself, I guess? She had so much time with him. I had moments.

Farren clicked off the television and shot a thumb at the door. "I have to stop by my place and grab some stuff before kicking your ass."

Oh, the way he said it, as if beating me was inevitable. It was, but he didn't have to say it all the time.

∞ ∞ ∞

The gym routine went…well…routine. I almost got his knee after about fifteen minutes, but made it too obvious.

A smile appeared on Farren's stupid face. "Ah, so Tarek's been giving you a few pointers, huh?" He danced around the ring.

Grunting, I lunged again, trying to make contact with his even, white teeth. He dodged and tapped me on the right cheek hard enough to have my head flinging to the side. "Keep your arms up; watch my face. Don't let your eyes follow your swing." He jabbed again, but when I listened to him, his advice actually worked, his gloved fist swiping air. "Good, keep it up."

After another hour dodging fists and getting hit in the face, I spit out my mouthpiece. "Enough." I gave Jake the go-ahead on my way out of the ring. "Your turn."

I didn't hang out for their normal banter, my mind already on the afternoon's run. But Farren's voice followed me to the locker room. "You're running with me today, kid."

I opened the door. "Whatever. Then you'd better finish him off quick, 'cause I'm ready to go."

Jake's wounded voice chased me to the showers. "Not nice, young lady."

∞ ∞ ∞

By the time we ran into the woods, gray clouds rolled in and thunder clapped the sky. The run continued, though. A few streaks of lightning and a little downpour wouldn't deter me from what I loved to do most. So what if Ginger tagged along? In my ring, he had to fight to keep up with me. Felt pretty good watching him struggle when I let loose in the high school's backfield.

The rain didn't stop the congregation at the burn pit either. A few blue tarps hanging on tree limbs and they had shelter–and for an almost naked couple, an illusion of privacy. Everyone could see them, including us as we jogged by. No one bothered to pretend to look away. All the perverted peepers needed was some popcorn.

By the time we broke through the woods, the rain was a warm sheet pounding on top of our heads. The warmth felt good, and by Farren's smile, he seemed to enjoy it, too.

Bypassing the mailbox, we went straight for my old trailer. When we got to the front door, I had to yell over the storm. "Wait out here. You'll spook him if you come in."

Farren wiped the water from his face and nodded. "But make it quick, will you? As much as I like the rain, wet shorts aren't fun to run in." He scrunched up his cheeks and puckered his lips. "Chafing sucks."

"Whatever. Fine. Ten minutes." I pushed through the door.

Dad sat in his usual spot, but fear crept in his watery eyes. The rain slapped the roof, and with the sun hiding, the place had a dark, ominous feel. Guess I would have been a little freaked out, too.

"It's fine, just the rain," I said when his scared eyes followed me into the kitchen. "It'll be over soon."

He didn't answer, rarely did when I actually had to talk to him. *How the hell did this guy scare the shit out of me?*

I left puddles from my drenched sneakers on the thin carpet as I went to take the load from the dryer, throwing it into his room. His terrified gaze followed me into the bedroom and across the small path through the living room to the kitchen.

"Trust me, you're fine. It's. Just. Rain."

When he refused to answer with anything but fear, I ignored him to make coffee before pulling out the stuff for a sandwich.

He wrapped his thin blanket tighter around his frail shoulders, his fingers shaking, along with his lips. "Is the floor gonna eat me again?"

I dropped the butter knife, mustard going all over the faded linoleum. That was the first I'd heard him speak in a while. More, this was the first time he'd ever brought up his trip to Arcus. After a deep breath, I picked up the knife, set it in the sink, and poured him some coffee. I went to squat in front of his chair, handing him the cup. "No one's gonna ever take you from this place again."

Dad wasn't convinced. "Can't sleep, can't eat when you're not here…a-and there's been people walking around the trailer at night, lookin' through the windows." He pulled the cup to his chest, leaving the contents untouched. "They don't think I see 'em, but I do."

My skin prickled. "Are you sure? Maybe it's the neighborhood asshats messing with you."

His muddy eyes rounded, the whites shining. "It ain't though. I hear that wind, you know? And see the sky open up out the front window. Why they wanna get me, girl?"

Oh, shit. "Listen, how 'bout I come over tonight, check it out? Would you like that?"

He nodded so vigorously, coffee sloshed over the rim of his cup. "Yeah, I'd like that, like it a lot. Could you maybe ask them to go away? I won't tell no one, I swear."

Wilma's threat still had an effect, I see. "Sure, Dad. I'll tell them." I left to grab his sandwich, putting the paper plate on his lap. "Eat your lunch."

It took a while to calm him down and make him eat. My ten minutes were long over by the time I went outside to meet irritated Ginger.

"That wasn't ten minutes." Farren wrung out the bottom of his saturated muscle shirt.

I tilted my head to meet his eyes. "Stop crying. We got bigger things to worry about."

He gave up on the shirt and pulled it off, giving the old bitties sitting on their porch next door a peep show. Their whistles and suggestive offers went unnoticed. "Like?"

"Looks like my Exemplian stalkers are camping here at night."

"You sure?"

"The old man says he sees people looking in the windows, even heard the wind and saw the sky open." I shrugged. "We should at least check it out."

Farren's eyes shined. "Well, why don't we come crash the party?"

Crazy Ginger. I ran up the hill. "Sounds like fun."

CHAPTER 4

LENA

CONFRONTATIONS

The storm calmed from a frenzied temper tantrum to a whimper, and the sun beat down on our backs during the run home. No surprise, when we reached my steps, Belva sat on the porch scrolling through her phone. Her headphones blared so loud I heard the beat of her hip-hop from three feet away.

I stood in front of her and waited until she noticed.

Finally, she pulled her earbuds out with a smile. "You're kinda wet." Her gaze drifted around me to shirtless Farren. "And you're kinda hot all wet."

Didn't that create a raging blush on poor Ginger's face?

Shaking my head, I step around her, unlocking the door. "You got a key, pal. You should use it some time."

"And miss the free show? Don't think so." She whistled as she stood.

I happened to turn my head to investigate when Farren stalked up the three porch steps, a feral look gleaming in his dark eyes, despite the blush. He slowed his momentum, never taking his eyes off my shocked friend, who no longer smiled, but worked hard to pull in air, clutching her phone to her chest.

Ha! Not feeling so in control now, are you?

He stopped when their bodies touched, strong bare chest against heaving tank top. A long finger trailed down her cheek. "You're playing dangerous, little girl." He bent to whisper loud enough in her ear that I heard every word. "Don't start the game if you're not ready to follow the rules."

His smug face–one eyebrow raised as if saying *she asked for it*–met my surprised one as he circled me and headed up the stairs. I turned to Belva with mouth wide open and an *oh, my God* on my lips.

Her trembling hand followed the path of his finger, but as quick as any professional player, her poker face slammed into place. "Well, then let the games begin."

∞ ∞ ∞

Saturday was as busy as Friday, with people lined up down the sidewalk to buy tickets, ignoring the dark sky threatening a repeat of the afternoon storm. As soon as we made it inside, Jake rushed us all into our places. He signaled for Belva to go in the kitchen with Farren, but she shook her head. "Can you switch with me tonight, Jake?"

My boss opened his mouth, probably to say no, but then Farren joined in. "I like that idea, man. Need to talk to you, anyway."

Jake's face tensed. "Ah, yeah, sure." He pointed to Belva and me. "You two hit the registers."

Belva grabbed my hand, leading me up front. Once we punched in our codes, I nudged her shoulder. "What was that all about?"

She shrugged, smiling. "I need to give him space, make him miss me."

I swiped a credit card and handed tickets to a couple teenagers. "Make him crazy, you mean."

Belva turned on the charm for some interested college kids, taking their money and rejecting their cell numbers. "Hopefully."

After a good forty-five minutes, and about three cell number refusals later, the herd thinned out enough for us to talk a little more. I cleared my throat, trying to find a good reason to give for leaving before the late showing when Belva gave me an annoyed glare.

"Jesus, Lena, spit it out." Subtlety and patience were not virtues my gorgeous friend had.

"I...um... Farren and I are gonna be heading out soon. Some...yeah...some kids have been messing with Dad the past few nights." Close enough to the truth for me not to feel too guilty.

She raised a perfectly waxed brow. "So? Maybe they'll give him a heart attack. He deserves it."

"He's broken now, nothing like before. Harmless." A trip to another dimension where a sadistic jerk ruled over squid did that to a person, but I kept that little ditty to myself. "Can't let any predators swoop in on vulnerable prey. It wouldn't be right."

Her cheeks reddened some, making me regret my words. My little nickname for her in school was "pretty predator." She didn't like it all that much.

Straightening her tank top, Belva tilted her head. "You know what I think?"

"Not a clue." I punched the lock code on the register when the last in line straggled in and waited for the "don't rub it in my face" lecture.

Surprised, she instead pulled me in for a hug. "I think you've got to be the most amazing person on the planet."

"It's a pretty big planet." *If she knew how big...*

"Stop it. You forgave me, and you take care of that bastard. I think you're in at least the top ten."

Wanting awkward intimate time to go away, I headed for the counter and my mom. "Maybe the top one hundred. Top ten's pushing it."

She came up beside me, smoothing her hair. "Nah, top ten–at least you are in my world. And as far as I'm concerned, my world is all that counts."

Had to give her props; she was honest. "Don't I know it."

We sat around the counter, talking to Mom and ignoring the drooling-Belva leers from a couple cute boys at a table, when Farren and Jake walked out from the kitchen. Both men seemed relaxed, which was surprising if the conversation about leaving early was an honest one. But when Belva spotted Ginger, she switched gears from ignoring the idiots at the table to sauntering over, pulling up a seat, and giving the cuter of the two her undivided attention.

Yup, that cured all the calm off Farren's face. The way his jaw tightened when he glanced in my friend's direction gave me a distinct feeling he was the one who would have some trouble with the rules. Belva's eyes stayed on the guy, who leaned in closer. If I knew her at all, I'd bet my secret cash stash her entire focus was on Farren's reaction. Her deep smile and sexy lip bite when angry Ginger took a few steps closer to the table proved my theory.

Here we go. I turned to Jake. "He tell you what's going on?"

He pulled Mom close, kissing the top of her head. "Yeah, he did. Be careful, all right?"

"Wait, what's going on?" The worry flooding Mom's eyes had me contemplating lying, but I'd decided after my second Arcus trip, she'd always hear at least an outline of the truth.

Squaring my shoulders–and moving to block Farren's view of Belva–I answered with complete honesty. "Dad saw Exemplians outside his place last couple nights. Probably the same Guide I felt yesterday."

Mom's bottom lip trembled, but she lifted her chin. "Remember what Farren's been teaching you, and…and actually, why don't you stay behind him when you find the jerks."

I bent to kiss her cheek. "Thanks for the advice." I turned to Farren–and the steam coming from his ears. "Let's go."

He didn't respond, his body tight. When Belva snatched the guy's phone from his hand and plugged in her number, Farren's fists clenched. I punched him in the arm. It probably hurt about as bad as a feather whipping, but it got his attention.

"What?" His tone would've had a lesser person cringing.

"Let's. Go." When he still didn't budge, I grabbed his arm, attempting to drag all that muscle out the door.

A death stare targeted my invading hand. "Wait a second." He pried my fingers off his forearm and stalked to the table...and the unfortunate guy who was busy with Belva's phone.

Farren snatched her phone from the guy's hands, handing it back to her. Then with the lethal calm of a sociopath, Farren picked up the scared kid's phone from the table and squeezed until it fell on the thin carpet in pieces.

"She's not interested, clear?"

The guy couldn't nod fast enough, his once tan face as white as snow.

Farren held out his hand to Belva. "Time to get up."

I turned to Jake, shocked as hell, and motioned for him to do something. My boss shook his head, smiling.

Belva ignored Farren's hand as she stomped to the kitchen. She yelled over her shoulder before pushing the door open. "You better make up your damn mind, 'cause I'm not gonna wait forever!"

Pretty sure the entire lobby felt the heat from those words and the ice from the kitchen door slamming in Farren's face when he tried to follow her. His huge back heaved a few times as he stood at the frame, hands on either side, squeezing the wood until it creaked. By the scrambling in the lobby, I'm sure everyone heard the wood splitting, too.

Damn. Belva didn't understand how dangerous a Protector game was.

CHAPTER 5

LENA

UNWANTED VISITORS

"Want to say something, or am I gonna have to invest in a new steering wheel?"

Farren answered by gripping the wheel tighter, his cheeks flaming. I probably shouldn't have let him drive, even if the deep scowl on his face indicated he'd have taken off my head if I refused to hand over the keys.

I let the silence, flashing lights from other cars, and stoplights fill the space between us for another block before trying again. "Why don't you give in already?"

He laughed until he yelled, stabbing me right in the eardrum. "You think I don't want to be with her?"

"Well…not after tonight." I kept my tone neutral, practicing the same calm skills Tarek always had.

He smacked the wheel and yelled one more time. After another red light, Farren's softer voice filled the car. "I used to work for the authority, Lena."

I really believed this was going somewhere. But…damn. "I got that when you tasered Tarek, remember?"

"Okay, and so I know how they operate, what they do to defectors and rogues…traitors."

Shit, this didn't sound good.

"When Guides stray, they're easy to kill, especially if their Protectors don't stick around after transport." He took a deep breath and continued on the exhale. "Someone always knew something, and willing or forced, they'd end up telling us where the traitors went."

"Farren, you don't have to—"

"I've ended more Guides' cycles than I care to remember." He shrugged, his fingers still white on the wheel. "Always a one-man operation. Get in, get out, careful not to disturb the dimension when you're butchering somebody. Killing a traitor, well, that was honorable, right? They'd recycle somewhere else, pay for their sins."

Yeah, like me...

"Farren—"

"But Protectors are a different story, not so easy to kill them." His eyes, a little wild, glanced my way before focusing again on the road. "They still had to pay, though."

He didn't have to finish. The conclusion to the story was obvious. A savage urge to protect my best friend settled in my gut. "I get it now, really."

He pulled into the trailer park, shaking his head. "I see all their faces every time I close my eyes. Every single person I..." He killed the engine when we pulled behind Dad's place. "I believe in karma, Lena, and it's waiting to bite me in the ass. Can't take the chance with her. Won't."

I sighed. "Maybe you should let her go, let her talk to other people without scaring the shit outta them. Stop giving her hope."

He rubbed his smooth face and let out a half-groan, half-growl. "She doesn't make it easy."

I opened the door, ready to let him off the hook. "No, no she doesn't."

Farren got out, pushing the lock button on the keychain, and headed toward the front of the house. Before I opened the door, he grabbed my arm. "I'll control myself next time, promise."

I palmed his cheek. "Someday, all this, it's gonna be over. They'll get tired of bothering with us. But until then, you've got Wilma here to help you." I gave him a light slap on his red cheek before things became too emotional. "Maybe you should trust Belva, too. She's stronger than she looks."

He tilted his head. "Always the optimist, aren't you?"

"Somebody's gotta be." I lowered my voice before opening the door, more than ready to change the subject. "Look, he spooks easy. Try not to act so, ah, scary, okay?"

Farren smiled, or rather gave a sneer that curled the right side of his mouth. "No problem. I'll stand in the corner…make sure he knows I'm there."

"Yeah, that won't terrify him." I went inside.

As usual, Dad sat in his chair. His happy relief turned to horror when we walked in and his eyes shifted from me to Farren, who closed the door and stood there as promised. With his arms crossed and looking like a menacing biker without the hot tattoos, angry Ginger made a point to give my shaking father a stare-down.

Before I had a yellow puddle to clean up, I scowled at Farren and went to kneel in front of the wicker chair. "Hey, look at me." My voice didn't get his attention, and so I grabbed his jaw, forcing him to look. "He's here to help, okay? No need to be scared."

Dad's body quaked so hard, I feared the chair might collapse. "He's almost as big as the other one. They ain't human, girl."

A snort came from the Big Red peanut gallery. "Almost, huh?"

I whipped my head around and mouthed for Farren to shut up, and then made an effort to soften my face before turning back to the shell in the chair. "He's human, and so is the other one. But he won't hurt you; I won't let him."

"How you gonna stop him?"

Ugh! Dammit! I turned to Farren. "Don't hurt him."

Farren scratched his head with a grin. "Ah, yeah, whatever."

Patience wasn't one of my virtues either. A groan escaped my lips when Dad whined and pleaded for me to make him leave, but I cut him off. "He stays, and you're gonna stop acting like a baby, got it? We'll need him if those people show up again."

I stormed into the kitchen, rinsed out the coffee pot, and started fresh. Farren stayed at the door while Dad hunkered under his blanket, never taking his eyes away from the *almost* as big guy in the corner.

Yeah, not the most ideal way to spend the evening.

∞ ∞ ∞

An hour, and another, ticked by. Farren and I eased into our usual banter, him saying something stupid or annoying and me calling him on it. We laughed a little, argued a little more, and didn't bother to acknowledge the trembling sack of bones in the wicker. After a while, Dad reverted to the silent Indian-wall observer, ignoring us, too.

"...and it's not funny. She did say–" Farren's passionate defense of some starlet's recent brush with the law using his tabloid research stopped. "They're here."

He went for the window, all traces of relaxed gone. Thirty seconds later, the fuzz entered my brain, too. I moved from the kitchen counter to join Farren at the window.

"Dad? Go in your room and be quiet. Don't come out." I could fake calm with the best of them. But when he didn't get up, I dragged him from his chair and heaved him in the room. "Stay here." Not waiting for a reply, I shut the door and went back to Farren.

Two figures who definitely didn't belong to the white trash mafia strode down from the graveled hill leading into the park. Both were female. The smaller one sporting a less obvious leotard-like outfit Tarek used to call his warrior suit walked in front of a taller, thin woman wearing a flowing dress that didn't look comfortable in the sweltering July heat.

By the tension in their faces, they knew we were there, too.

"I'll be damned." Farren scrubbed a hand through his hair. "This isn't good." He met my questioning face. "Looks like the Synod decided to make a personal visit."

"This is an 'oh shit' moment, isn't it?"

Farren's attention went back to the window. "I'd say it's *the* moment. You see that Protector?" *Like I could miss her...* "She's five-cycled and ruthless as hell, and her Guide's been a Synod member since before my first cycle."

"What do you think they want?" As if I didn't know that.

The "you have to be kidding me" glare Farren threw showed he thought the question just as stupid. He closed the curtains and went to the door. "The best thing we can do is go out there, confront them."

I stumbled into the kitchen. "Ah...disagree. Going out the back window and getting in the car sounds better."

Farren stomped over, grabbed my hand, and went to the front door. He stuffed the car keys into my front pocket. "In case..."

He tugged on my hand, but all he got was a no-go, my feet planted on the floor and sprouting roots. "No."

Farren bent down to my ear. "Running won't work; they'll keep coming back."

"Shouldn't we wait for Wilma?"

"Love to, but I don't think they'd be willing to wait with us."

I really hated when he made sense.

"Stay behind me. If shit goes down, take off. Avery won't do anything to you."

"And Avery is?"

"The Guide. She's the Synod's Creation Lab overseer, the person who controls in-coming and out-going energy. A fucking big shot. But you Guides aren't known for your strength," he tapped his temple, "just this."

"What are you gonna do?"

"Try not to let Nicolette kick my ass too bad."

Well, what could be said to that?

We stepped off the cement blocks as the women approached. Nicolette stopped short. Her clear blue eyes shot to Farren then behind him, past me, and into the house. "Where's Wilma?"

"Around." Farren sauntered over to face her, all arrogant with confidence I really hoped he had. "Better question is why are you here?"

Her eyes narrowed as she widened her stance. "Doing my duty, *Protector*."

Farren rolled his shoulders. "Sticks and stones, Nikki. But let me make something clear." He stood two inches from the woman, cocking his head to the side as he looked down at her. "You're not getting anywhere near the girl, got it?"

When she spoke, I looked down to make sure my shoes were tied–didn't want to trip when running for my life.

"Hmm, so you," she tapped Ginger's chest with her pointer, "are going to...what? Stand in my way? A few months in this place soften your brain, Farren?"

A low snarl escaped as he moved in the last two inches. "You b–"

"Enough." The sharp command from the Guide caused Nicolette to back down. Farren made an obvious effort to relax, though his fists stayed clenched at his sides. Avery continued, "We're not here to hurt the girl. Please, let me speak with her–privately."

"Not a chance." Farren stayed in front of me.

"If she doesn't talk to me, it won't be a lovesick Protector like Mateusz you'll need to shield her from."

As Farren shook his head ready to deny her again, words came rushing out before I had a chance to pull them back. "What're you trying to say?"

Avery angled her head to meet my eyes. "Believe it or not, but Mateusz is the reason why your energy wasn't annihilated."

I signaled Farren to step aside with a weak nudge. He moved enough for me to stand beside him.

"Um…I think you might… He's the reason why I ended up here, lady."

"A move that unwittingly saved your life."

My curiosity always won over fear. If the woman had information, I wanted it. "You have ten seconds to tell me how."

"Because, Lena, you truly are Tainted."

Lynn Vroman

CHAPTER 6

LENA

REVELATIONS

Farren had to catch me when I fell backward, tripping over the cement blocks. "That doesn't make sense." I spoke to Avery, but my eyes stayed planted on Farren's.

"If you had a true energy reading when Mateusz accused you of treason in your past life, your energy would've still read Tainted—for worse crimes than siphoning good energy to Arcus. But only because the knowledge you kept secret would've threatened those set on genuine treachery. So please, may we speak in private?"

Farren quirked a brow as he held onto my waist, blocking me from view. With a vigorous shake of my head, he answered her. "Again, Guide, not happening."

I tapped his shoulder and gave him a little push. Getting the message, he righted me beside him before folding his arms behind his back, his face an impassive, stoic mask.

"Say what you came to say and go," I said, my voice not nearly as commanding as I wanted it to be.

Strain developed in Avery's eyes when she moved forward, her hands held out, fingers splayed.

Nicolette shadowed every step, as vigilant and tense as Farren.

"Please, if you could–"

I held up my own hand, trying to imitate the Protectors' hardened expressions. "Whatever you tell me he'll find out the second you're gone."

"Very well." She lowered her hands. "You are–"

"So you know, if you give me a 'you're the chosen one' line of shit, we're leaving."

Ginger snorted, his elbow nudging my side.

Nicolette didn't find it so funny. "You will show respect, Tainted. She has risked her life to find you."

"It's okay." Avery placed a hand on her Protector's shoulder. She kept her calm, giving me her attention. "There will be no such revelation." After a glance at Farren, she continued, "If you insist on an audience, I suppose I cannot demand otherwise, yet could we speak where the audience is smaller?"

For the first time since spotting the women, I noticed a scattered congregation acting as if they weren't trying to catch every word we said. Giving a few some irritated glares–which didn't deter their nosiness in the least–I opened the front door and waved everyone in.

Gesturing to the two lone chairs in the barren living room, I peeked in on Dad to find him sitting at the edge of his bed.

"Hey, no worries, okay?" I did a quick surf through the channels he now paid for, thanks to my taking over his money, and set the remote on top of the old TV. "Just some friends from school trying to find me. But stay in here and watch TV for a while."

"You lyin' to me, girl?" He scooted to the middle of the bed, his eyes begging me to say no.

"Is that something you really want to know?"

He stared, cinching a blanket closer to his chest.

Didn't think so.

I put a hand on the knob. "I'll come get you when they leave."

"Yeah, okay." He hesitated. "Hand me the remote?"

When I tossed it to him, he turned the volume up to thirty. I shut the door on the mechanical sounds of canned laughter to find Avery seated in Dad's chair, examining the Indian wall. Nicolette stood behind her like a sentinel, keeping her eyes on Farren. He had no trouble meeting her glare while standing behind the empty chair. My spot, I guess.

Sitting, I cleared my throat a few times to try to get the Guide's attention without resorting to disrespect. Only because her kindness made it hard to be mean. My attempt at being nice had nothing at all to do with her scary Protector's threat earlier. *Yeah, right.* When Nicolette gave Farren a stare that could drop a buck at fifty yards, and hearing the audible swallow coming from behind me, I stopped the throat clearing.

Well, maybe she had a little to do with my newfound respect.

For a few minutes, the single sound in the house was the too loud television's tinny laughter. Being here, feeling the familiar tension, caused anxiety and anger to play tennis in my skull. Not her fault. She didn't realize this place had no cozy, warm feelings reserved by me. But if the bitch didn't talk soon, a lot less Indian pictures would be hanging on the wall due to an unfortunate accident with a wicker chair.

I picked the first picture to aim at when Avery finally spoke. "You seem to have an acute fascination with the native people from this part of the dimension. Proud people, I must say. I've met one who is particularly…noble."

Yeah, that's not what I wanted to talk about. "They're not mine. Look, small talk's great, but maybe we should stick to why you're here." After a glance at her angry Protector's face, I added, "Ah…please."

Avery adjusted her chair so that it faced mine and sat with posture straight and tidy. "You are right." She rubbed her hands together–the only sign of nerves, her face remaining serene. But she didn't start the conversation with me. The Guide looked up to Farren. "What I have to say may cause you some turmoil."

"Don't worry about me. You all already lost my vote in the respect department." If I hadn't known Ginger so well, I'd have sworn he was bored with the conversation by his dull tone.

But I knew him pretty well, and he was ready to snap.

"Watch yourself, Protector." Nicolette's eyes shined, her arms crossing over her chest.

Farren's deep voice trumped her scare-stare, all the dull disappearing. "Next time you open your mouth, I'm going to put my boot in it, got it? Protecting her from words isn't part of the job."

The television in the other room got louder as faint whining accompanied the boxed laughter. These pissing contests were going to give the old man a stroke.

Before a Protector war began in the living room, I stood up. "We're not gonna get anywhere if we have to stop every five seconds to see who's the scariest." I glanced down at Avery. "Talk before these two start busting up my dad's place."

"Nah, I say kill 'em and worry about how to hide the bodies."

If Farren didn't shut it…

I gave him a warning scowl. "Let her talk. If you don't like what she has to say, then you can beat the woman's ass. Deal?"

He rolled his shoulders and cracked his knuckles. "If that's my only choice…"

I ignored the glare from Nicolette and sat down, leaning elbows on knees. "I'm listening."

Avery smiled, softening her features and brightening her blue eyes. She wasn't what I'd call pretty, but her docile face and seemingly inherent kindness had a calming effect. "You haven't changed much in this cycle, Lena. Still the leader, I see."

I squirmed under the weight of her compliment. "Yeah, well, it took a while to get here."

She reached over to squeeze my folded hands before placing hers back on her lap, no longer rubbing them together. "As I told you, what you went through with Mateusz in Exemplar, and here to an extent, has saved your energy from annihilation."

Leaning back, I gripped the armrests. When her placid expression didn't change, and nothing else left her mouth, I said, "Do I even have to ask you to explain?"

Her cheeks pinked and her serene smile faltered. "No, of course not. It's… I practiced saying what I'd tell you so many times." She rubbed her temple, yet composed herself again when Nicolette placed a hand on her thin shoulder. "May I start over?"

I nodded, waving my hand.

"There are things you knew once…things that could have potentially saved lives."

"You're treading awfully close to that 'key to salvation' line, Avery. No disrespect, but I've read too many fairy tales with the same theme." I rubbed the wicker armrests. "None rarely imitate reality."

"I do not speak of children's stories." Her agitation pushed at the passive façade, the color in her cheeks darkening.

Ugh! Fine. Maybe I was being a bitch. But if I still thought it was bullshit, I'd make them leave. Ask them to leave, anyway. Don't think I could make Nicolette do anything. "I'm sorry. Please, continue."

She tucked loosened strands of pale hair behind her ear. "Forgive my temper. Recent events have been most trying." Avery refolded her hands, the bedroom television keeping us company while she collected herself.

The silence gave me time to really look at her. Tension and fear she'd been trying to hide surfaced. Christ, what the hell was I getting into now?

"You see, we have been fed a lie for centuries–more time than even I can comprehend. The first Synod members, from whom many on the Synod elders today descend, found out things about the universe that should've been kept from human knowledge."

"You mean the existence of other dimensions, don't you?"

"Exactly, yes."

The back of my wicker chair began to shred. I turned and my gaze smacked into Farren's white knuckles. When I raised my eyes to his face, it was as colorless as the hands squeezing the chair. He didn't meet my stare, seeing as he was too busy giving the Guide a death glare.

Shaking my head, hoping he'd catch it in his peripherals, I patted his hands before facing Avery. By the grimace on her face, she was completely aware of Farren's boiling temper. But like a pro, she ignored him. "Every Exemplian who is inducted into stations of power in the Synod is told the secret and instructed to perpetuate centuries of falsehoods amongst the population. The system, dispersing energies unto selected dimensions, is preached to be the way the human race will survive and prosper." Sadness etched her face. "But I know different."

"Tell me what you believe." I hoped her answer would ensure Farren didn't go for her throat.

"Because of our evolved brains, giving some the powers to cross dimension lines," she looked up at Farren and pointed behind her to Nicolette, "or the ability to read and guide energies, our tiny world has held humankind's fate without any right. We are called privileged, but in truth we are thieves, stealing life, judging it, for selfish gain."

"Wait. Why're you telling me this?" My eyes widened. "Oh, shit. You're a traitor, like Kendal."

Kendal was Mateusz's woman and the person who I accused of treason in my past life. Because of that, to protect Kendal, Mateusz made sure Old Lena was marked Tainted through a bogus energy reading he fudged. Her energy was then sent to Earth after her execution. All confusing stuff, but it boiled down to this being my life now, Old Lena a memory.

I didn't mean for it to come out as an accusation, but it sounded that way–at least to Nicolette, whose feathers got ruffled again. "Avery is no traitor, Tainted. She's brave...and so, once, were you."

"What the hell's she talking about?" My voice was whispery strands of air, lacing together the words swimming in my brain.

Avery stood, giving her Protector a subtle frown. "During your last cycle, whilst searching for a way for you and Tarek to escape the...privilege of Exemplian life together, you figured out the secret. It was a stroke of good luck that I was the Synod member you confronted."

I watched her pace, letting the information sink in. Not much to say after something like that.

She didn't seem to notice my silence, her story pouring out. "Together we devised a way to change the status quo. You spent years building trust with many Wardens, listening to them, realizing they desired the lines to be closed. I spent the time spreading the truth to those I knew who were unhappy, suspicious. We planned a rebellion, and we were almost ready to act when Mateusz intervened with his false accusations against you." She stopped in front of me, respect glowing in her eyes. "You are the sole person who has accomplished so much with the Wardens–they are the key to ensuring centuries of wrong righted."

"Why tell me all this now?" I wasn't gonna lie–excitement coursed through me. Taking the power away from those who took so much from me sounded enticing.

Avery sat again, her excitement dwindling as concern creased her brow. "We have another problem, one that can't be resolved unless we carry out our past mission."

I knew without her having to tell me. "Cassondra?"

"Yes."

Panic forced me to stand. "Is she going after Tarek?"

She rose, too, Nicolette moving beside her. "She is bent on seeking revenge for her brother's murder."

Farren scooted closer until our shoulders touched. "Wardens are tough to kill. Have to make them pay, though, like Protectors."

If the chair were not there to grasp, I'd have crumbled to the floor. "So, you do think she'll go after Tarek…through me?"

"Yeah, kid."

I swallowed. "Here we go again, huh?"

"Looks like."

Avery jumped in, her voice high. "We can stop her."

"How do we do that?" My mind already left the conversation and worked on a way to prevent getting my family and I killed.

"You are the one the Wardens trust. Believe me, I have tried." She grabbed my forearm, giving a light shake. "You must find a way to speak with them. It is time to finish what we started. We must close the lines between worlds…and bring Exemplar to its knees."

CHAPTER 7

LENA

PLANS

"You have to go to Arcus, tell Wilma and Tarek what's going on." We spent the short car ride home figuring out the next step.

Finish what we started... Pretty much the question we tried to sort out. The risks involved, Farren getting some unwanted company for crossing lines, not to mention having my cycle ending early, were some of many.

"I know." He flicked on the turning signal and pulled in behind Jake's Range Rover. "Let's go over our options one more time." He shifted the car in park and turned to lean against his door, one arm dangling over the steering wheel.

"Well, one, we kill Cassondra."

"Not so easy. She's at least eight-cycled, if not more. Besides, there's no way we could get close to her."

Rolling my neck, I ditched that idea and moved on to number two. "We find a way to threaten her; maybe try to get to the Synod above her."

Farren contemplated that for a minute, tapping the wheel. "That's not so far-fetched." The tapping finger moved to his lip. "I'd need Wilma, of course."

"Yeah, okay, option two sounds promising."

"We'd need to hide you, too, in case shit doesn't go right. She'd come after you, no doubt in my mind."

Electricity I hadn't felt in five months shot through my veins, turning my heart into a pulsating orb ready to break my ribcage. "Ah, well, I know one place she'd never get anywhere near me."

He raised a red brow. "And where would that be?"

My face grew warm, and my pounding heart made my voice too hoarse to sound logical. "She'd never get within a hundred yards of me in Arcus."

Farren chuckled, giving me a light punch in the shoulder. "You're so cute when you get all red."

I pushed his hand away. "Wish I could say the same for you. Anyway…option three."

"Yeah…option three." He rubbed the stubble on his cheeks.

"We close the lines."

He moved to pull the keys from the ignition. "I'd rather deal with one Protector set on revenge than a whole dimension wanting to stay on top of the food chain." I opened my mouth to argue, but he held up a hand. "At least, right now. If we want to start a war, we need more than four people willing to come out of hiding to fight."

Well, he did have a point.

I got out, slamming my door with more force than necessary, Farren following.

"I should talk to Teenesee," I said. "See what she says about everything. I'm sure Avery's name came up in our past conversations."

Farren opened the front door, waving for me to go first. "I like the idea, but let me talk to Wilma and Tarek first."

"Yeah, sure, whatever." Trying to sound nonchalant when excitement bounced off my nervous system and begged my feet to perform a happy dance was tough. I managed, but my cheeks hurt from smiling.

As soon as I opened the door, Mom and Jake jumped off the couch. The pale color dulling their cheeks effectively erased my smile.

Mom hugged me while Jake yelled. Typical. "Is everything okay? Why can't you answer your phone?" His weight bounced from foot to foot. "The whole reason I got you the damn thing is so we can call you."

Untangling myself from Mom's thin arms, I reached in my back pocket for the dead cell. "Forgot to charge it."

"You *forgot* to charge it?" That vein pulsing at his temple probably wasn't supposed to stick out like that.

"What? Farren was with me."

Farren clapped my shoulder. "Thanks for the confidence, kid, but charge your phone."

I held up my hands, nodding. "Okay, okay, I'm sorry, but we're fine. Nothing to worry about."

Mom rubbed my shoulder. "It's fine."

Jake stalked the small living room. "No, it isn't. You had us scared to death." He stopped right in front of me, pointing his finger in my face, and then up at Farren's...and back to me. "Keep the phone charged or I'll lock you in your room, got it?"

Getting mad would make him even more pissed, but the desire to break off his stumpy finger caused me to clench my fists. He took over as father long before Dad got thrown out of the picture, and the protectiveness intensified after he found out the world wasn't as round as Columbus discovered. His love yelled at me, and I had to remember that.

"Got it." I didn't pull out my I'm-eighteen-now speech. Pretty certain that would've exacerbated the situation.

"Good." Jake lowered his finger and turned to Farren. "Who was it?"

Farren and I talked about what we'd say once we got home. Scaring them with the blatant truth was out, we'd agreed, but they were entitled to know the closest information to the truth as possible.

Buying a few seconds to think, I went to the couch while Farren headed toward the tiny kitchen. He came back out with a couple sodas, shaking mine before tossing it to me.

"Thanks, jerk." I tapped on the top, facing the parents. "It was a Synod Guide and her Protector."

Mom gasped, coming over to the couch and giving my hand a death grip. "Did they try to hurt you?"

"No, they wanted to talk." I glanced at Farren, hoping he'd jump in, give a plausible explanation that didn't sound too deceitful.

Ginger took a long pull of his soda, taking a longer time to swallow. "They were curious after everything that went down in the spring. The Guide knew Lena before, wanted to make sure she was all right."

That possessive look Mom had developed after she found out I'd lived a few times before brightened her green eyes and twisted her lips. "Well, next time she comes tell her you belong here with us now. No need for them to go lurking around the trailer park and theater, scaring everyone."

"Will do. Ah...Farren's gonna go talk to Wilma, let her know what's going on, though." When the worry shaded Mom's eyes again and Jake resumed his pacing, scowling at the soda-slurping Protector and me every few seconds, I rushed to put them at ease. "It's no big deal."

"If you say so." Her eyes made contact with Jake's and some secret message traveled between them. "Just...don't hide anything from us this time, Lena."

Shit. She knew exactly where to aim the guilt. With a quick glance at Farren's passive face–he obviously had no qualms about lying–I gave her a bright smile and some truth. "If there is anything we need to worry about, I promise, I'll tell you." I grabbed Jake's hand, forcing him to stop. "Both of you."

"You better, young lady." Jake's color returned to a more normal shade.

Farren gulping down his Dr. Pepper helped make the sudden awkward silence settling in the room not so transparent. Mom and Jake still weren't comfortable with the way Protectors were able to cross dimension lines. But they wouldn't ask him to go somewhere else.

Always the perfect houseguest, Farren's empty soda can hit the recyclable container in the kitchen. He then stood in the middle of the living room, looking a little lost. "You want me to go in the bedroom or…?" His hand waved around the room.

I shrugged as Mom and Jake made an effort to seem inconspicuous as they headed into her room.

"Here's fine, but listen, Tarek's not staying at the castle."

Farren rolled his eyes, groaning. "Ugh." He gave me a droll stare. "Where'd he build his shack?"

I laughed. "How'd you know?"

"If the guy will build a cabin and live like a savage in the most technologically advanced dimension known, why wouldn't he do the same in a place where the castle is the *only* modern amenity?"

"That predictable, huh?"

"That demented. Where?"

As if I could wipe the smile off my face, my busy hands rubbed the corners of my mouth. "Ah, he said by the riverbank."

Farren threw a hand in the air, opening his fingers. As the tear ripped open, he shook his head. "He better hope the squid play nice." When the last word spit out, the tear sucked him upward, closing as soon as his big body disappeared.

∞ ∞ ∞

After Farren left, I knocked on Mom's door, let them know it was okay to come out, and went straight to my room. First thing I did was plug in my cell. After about three minutes, the thing dinged on and at least twenty texts came through. Most were from Mom and Jake, nice at first, but getting angrier with big caps and lots of exclamation marks. A few were from Belva, whose worry was as apparent. Sighing, I texted her a *We're okay* message and started getting ready for bed.

11:45.

Fifteen more minutes until Tarek found his way into my head. It'd take Farren a little while to find the cabin, and so the rich voice I craved would be mine until Tarek and Wilma felt Ginger's energy. He'd have to walk along the fluorescent river until they did. No big deal, unless the dimension decided to mess with him. That place was like the insecure bully on the playground.

Before I could sink into the memory foam, my phone dinged. Belva's frantic message met my irritation. *Thank God! I really screwed up this time, right?:(*

My thumbs got busy appeasing her. *No ur fine. Talk tomorrow. Going to bed.*

Thirty seconds later, her reply screamed through. *I'm freaking out!*

My response was to shut off the cell and crawl between the sheets. Not even my best friend had enough power to keep me from my blond giant. Another glance at the clock–11:59–and I closed my eyes, waiting with my arms tight around Tarek's shirt-pillow.

He didn't make me wait long.

Hey, love.

His voice dripped with honey, melting my bones. He called me that every so often, not that I minded. In a few more days, he'd be able to do more than call me cute names.

Wilma didn't like the sleeping arrangements. I haven't heard the end of it all day. She's coming back to you soon, thankfully. But it's nice having someone to talk to, or someone to bitch at me, rather. Don't tell her. No need to swell her head.

Wilma and Tarek had a love/hate relationship. They loved to act like they hated each other.

Anyway, the cabin is comfortable, makes me remember ours. It's not as nice, but I'm working on it. It took fifty years to get our place right, but it shouldn't take as long here when there's not much else to do. Pause. *Did I ever tell you about the fireplace?*

About fifteen times, but I loved hearing the story—loved to hear anything he had to say. Except when he brought up his love for my former self and how amazingly perfect she was.

The stone had to be right; you took a piece from every dimension we went. Hard to mortar, make it fit, but I managed. You cried when it was finished. That day...you finally showed...something. I'll never forget it.

For the past two months, Tarek had been giving me tidbits of our past. I tried to keep the jealousy locked tight, remembering all the details Tarek gave about his life and trying to ignore...*her.* Wasn't easy, though. I curled deeper into the covers. In a few days, I'd make him think of *me.* We'd make new memories.

You—what the hell? Why don't you two ever listen?

And silence. Damn. It didn't take Farren that long to find the shack, after all.

Lynn Vroman

CHAPTER 8

AVERY

LIES

Nicolette opened the portal on the outskirts of the capital where they left her shuttle. Exemplar was never quiet, not even late in the evening, but most sectors in the dimension weren't boisterous or too loud, either. Noise pollution wasn't tolerated, not that anyone living here would disrupt the tranquility with abhorrent behavior. Their arrival didn't cause any commotion. Portal jumping was as common as walking.

Avery touched the passenger door to let the metal read her print. As soon as the door opened, she folded her body in the tiny vehicle. A few seconds later, Nicolette jumped in, used the receiver on the visor to scan her retina, and adjusted the wheel as the shuttle started.

"Do you think she'll help us?" Nicolette's question snuck out of the dark, the Protector's eyes never leaving the airway as she maneuvered her sleek, silver ride through organized traffic.

"I hope so." Avery folded her hands so tight her knuckles ached. "If she doesn't, we are on our own."

"You can talk to the Wardens again, prove you can be trusted."

"And how should I show that? It took years for Lena to build relationships with them, and only after Teenesee campaigned for her."

"So, we'll go to Empyrean, make the Warden listen."

"We cannot make her do anything. And she would as soon kill every Synod member than listen to us."

"I won't let her touch you."

Avery glanced over at her oldest, truest friend. They'd been Paired for her last three cycles, their Pairing always welcoming and accepted by both. "You could not stop her, my friend."

Silence answered. Both knew the bitter truth. Without Lena's help, Exemplar would never stop its corruption. The lines needed to be closed, and one Synod Guide and her Protector didn't have the key–Wardens' trust and cooperation–to accomplish the feat. If she had to use the false threat of Cassondra to convince Lena, so be it. Cassondra did want revenge; she just hadn't acted upon it– yet. Guilt settled in her stomach, but…so much more was at stake.

"If Lena doesn't agree, we could force her."

"That would make us monsters." Avery squeezed her Protector's shoulder. "However, I believe what we've done already classifies us as such."

"Stop feeling guilty. I'm willing to sacrifice my morals for the entire universe. You should be all right with it too."

Nicolette had a point, yet the idea didn't sit well. "I have faith in Lena. I only hope she will forgive me."

Nicolette set the shuttle on the landing pad situated on the roof of Avery's building. Each building had one, yet the one gracing all Synod members' home quarters were more extravagant, like their apartments. As the shuttle landed, a digital reading of the registration on the undercarriage guided the vehicle to the lift closest to Avery's apartment.

When they got out, Nicolette picked up the conversation where they left off. "She's not the same Lena, not even close. She's a girl." They stepped into the lift.

Avery's hands folded tight while Nicolette crossed her arms, scowling at their reflection on the mirrored doors.

"Yes, but she's been through much, which undoubtedly matured her. And she is brave. Did you not see that?"

The lift gave a lilting ding. Avery put her hand on the door and guided her right eye to the receiver above. In moments, the door swooshed open, closing as soon as the women stepped over the threshold.

"You give humanity too much credit." Nicolette went straight for the stainless steel kitchen, pressing a few buttons on a control panel situated on the counter. A second ticked by before a steaming cup of coffee, raw sugar and soymilk coloring it a caramel brown, popped up.

Avery waved around the sparse room full of biodegradable beauty. "Yes, but, could you imagine what a gift all this would be, how we've managed to live with the environment, if we had not lost *our* humanity somewhere along the way?"

Nicolette smiled, blowing the steam from the top of her mug. "You're such a romantic."

She smiled, her face heating. "One of us must be."

"You're my favorite person, you know."

"And you are mine." Avery winked and went to her computer. "I need to catch up on some correspondence. We have been gone far too long."

"It's been two days, not long enough to be missed." Nicolette set her mug on the counter and headed to her room. "I need to take this suit off, give me five."

Avery nodded without looking up from the thin screen. She decided years ago living with her Protector wasn't only convenient, but helped staunch the monotony that plagued life in a dimension that thrived on maintaining the status quo every day, every year…for centuries. Nicolette managed to spark passion whether in a debate or being in the same room. They were two halves of a whole. Sisters.

More than sisters.

As promised, Nicolette came back into the main room five minutes later, wearing comfortable, loose clothing and looking nothing like the warrior she was. All soft around the edges, she grabbed her mug and shuffled over to the over-stuffed couch, snatching up her hand-held from underneath the dark screens.

Rubbing her neck, Avery scrolled through her notifications regarding new energies and recycling Exemplian energies–her areas of expertise as Creation Lab overseer. Funny how she handled the most reprehensible parts of her world, yet led the fight against it. The irony was never lost on her. At least while she and everyone else had to play by the rules, the new energies and recycled Guides and Protectors were treated with compassion and respect. Well, apart from being lied to.

A document popped up on a lab missive, showing seven new energies added to the population. Her shoulders tensed. Much higher number than normal, seeing as the usual number added up to no more than two new energies per year. The amount was the second largest instance within the last six months. Twenty new energies in less than a year. A problem she'd have to bring up during the next sequester.

Avery massaged her temples, the headache that accompanied the job sneaking in. High new energy percentages weren't the lone problem.

Peculiar...

She squinted, looking closer at the new energy entries. All Protectors–like the batch of thirteen six months ago. Her stomach dropped. If she were being truthful, the oddity of recent events resembled too closely to a recruitment of sorts. A trip to the Creation Lab reached the top of her to-do list, too.

Yawning, she forced her mind to still, a technique that took centuries to perfect. The guilt she carried when dwelling on the atrocity done to innocent energies, especially her participation in it, used to keep her awake for days. Nicolette would go crazy, trying to get her to leave the apartment, eat, and bathe...any function that required her to do more than punish her psyche with images of innocents living as slaves in the guise of privilege.

Then Lena came to her, changing everything. A brilliant Guide with unique empathy and talent for finding truth waltzed into her office on the rare occasion she made it there and gave her an out she'd been unknowingly pining for.

Shaking her head, to clear even Lena from her foremost thoughts, she concentrated on the final task. One quick look into her private messages and she'd retire for the evening. After punching in her password, she skimmed a few messages until one caught her eye. Dread filled her to the core. "Oh, no."

Nicolette jumped up from the couch, her loose clothing no longer hiding the warrior. "What is it?"

Avery's lips grew numb and her hands trembled. On unsteady legs, she walked over to the screens that fed the satellites' images–screens that had been ordered to remain blacked out since Mateusz's death for fear others may use them as he did for selfish gain. Synod elders had demanded a period of Exemplian isolation from other dimensions to allow for what they deemed a strong need for contemplation. In truth, the blackout was simply another form of control.

But someone decided the isolation was over.

She touched a button, and the monitors came to life, showing dimension images at random. "They've turned on the screens."

Lynn Vroman

CHAPTER 9

LENA

WILMA

Dreams were great, especially when they starred blond giants with dimples and gray eyes.

"Wake up!" Wilma didn't agree.

I snuggled deeper. "I'm not done yet. Come back in an hour."

Thwack.

"Ouch!" She probably left a palm print on my ass.

Next went the covers.

"Get out!"

Then went the bed. She yanked my foot and pulled me to the floor.

Still, I crawled over to my comforter, more out of spite than anything. "Give me a minute, for Christ's sake!"

"You got five."

I squinted through eyes not yet ready to open to find my Protector looming over me, arms across chest and tension straining her blue eyes. Her normally frizzy, curly hair was in worse shape than usual. With all the extra color compliments from a stay in Arcus, she looked a little deranged, too. *Somebody didn't like sleeping on the cabin floor.* "Make me breakfast?"

Wilma shook her head, mumbling about ungrateful brats. Before she shut the door behind her, she said, "Five minutes and make your own damn breakfast." As the door slammed, she yelled down the hall. "Farren! Make coffee!"

I smiled.

The boss was back.

∞ ∞ ∞

After I took twenty minutes to shower, change, and make some eggs, we all sat in the living room, including Mom and Jake, to figure out the next step. Farren squeezed in between Mom and me on the couch, his fingers dodging my fork as he snatched food off my plate. Jake took the chair while Wilma held council, standing in the middle of the little room, blocking the television.

I watched her as I chomped on toast, swerved my plate away from Ginger's greedy paws, and tried to fake calm. If she didn't give the okay, I wouldn't be seeing Tarek outside of my dreams any time soon.

With an annoyed huff, her usual MO, she cleared her throat. "Thought we'd have more time before the bastards came creeping round."

I swallowed some eggs. "Avery isn't bad, Wilma. I could tell."

"Oh, could you now? So, what's the plan, Lena? Listen to a Synod member? Send you to other dimensions?" She quit with the questions. "Your punishment is to be here. If you go traipsing around on false information, your energy is in trouble."

"I don't give a shit about my energy. Didn't expect to live more than once, anyway." I handed my half-empty plate to Farren, no longer hungry. "Besides, Avery said I'm in trouble regardless of how good I live this time around. My energy'll read Tainted." Mom reached over Farren and squeezed my leg as my voice got higher. "Do you think we should do nothing? Write her off as a liar?"

As my temper got hotter, Wilma managed to stay calm, albeit irritated. "Now, I didn't say that either, girl."

"Then what're you trying to say, Wilma, 'cause all I hear is nothing."

She narrowed her eyes and came right into my personal space, bending until our faces were level. "What's got you so anxious to start a war?"

Stunned, I sat back. Farren gave me a sympathetic punch on the shoulder the same time Mom felt the need to come to my aid. "That's unfair."

Wilma didn't even look at her. She kept me pinned with her blue daggers, waiting for my reply.

Well…shit. She found me out. Shame warmed my face while I inspected my fingernails. "I'm…having a hard time figuring out the answer to the question." Wilma backed up as I raised my gaze to meet hers. "What do you think we should do?"

After another sigh, she re-crossed her arms, hitting us with her stare. "Well, you're right about one thing. We can't sit around and do nothing. But that means everyone who's close to her," she pointed at me, "will be in danger whether it comes from Avery or Cassondra."

Shame dug in deeper, setting up camp in the pit of my stomach. I'd never even considered Mom, Jake, and… "We need to tell Belva."

Farren stiffened next to me before handing the plate to Mom, already heading to the door. "I'll go get her."

The door slammed on Wilma's command for him to sit back down. "That's just great." She ran a hand through her messy curls. "Another lovelorn Protector to contend with."

I barely registered her dig. But she was right about one thing–my priorities were screwed up. Something I'd worry about later. "What's the plan, then? We can't leave them here alone."

Before Wilma could answer, Jake spoke up. "I won't let anything happen to your mother, Lena. She'll be safe with me."

With a tight smile and a quick look at Wilma, who nodded, I said, "Maybe, if one shows up, but Tarek wasn't the strongest, not by a long shot, and neither is Farren."

Jake's shoulders sagged when he looked to Wilma who again nodded in agreement. No time like when he's down to kick him harder. "You can't protect her, not alone." I stood, wanting to be on level with Wilma when I addressed her. "Avery said Cassondra wants revenge."

"I know what she told you. What do you think? Farren came to Arcus for a vacation?"

"Yeah, so I'll bet if anyone can help us see if Avery is lying, Teenesee would."

She stayed silent, worrying her bottom lip.

I didn't let her in on the little fact that Farren and I had everything figured out already. But Wilma might not see it our way. She needed to be handled delicately, like a thorny flower. Guilt ate at me, though, because my main objective was still Tarek.

"Farren can stay here." I looked to Jake. "With you two, Mom and Belva should be safe. We won't be gone for long, just long enough to see if Avery is lying."

Wilma walked to the window, leaning against the sill. "We definitely need to have a chat with her. And...shit. I guess you need to come, too. Safest place for you is by me."

Wow, that was easy.

"All we have to do is wait for Farren to come back, then." Really, I tried hard not to smile. Cassondra could be on her way right now, but...Tarek.

She didn't say anything while giving me that hard stare she kept for special occasions–like when I really pissed her off.

Squirming a little, I went to stand by Mom. She wrapped an arm around my waist, while Jake snatched my hand. But I couldn't take my eyes off the angry Protector perched on the windowsill. "What?"

She bit her bottom lip, shaking her head.

"*What, goddamn it*?"

"What happens next, Lena? After we talk to Teenesee?"

"Ah, if Avery's telling the truth, Cassondra needs to be stopped."

"Uh-huh, and who's supposed to do that?"

With a shrug, I held out my hands. "Well, you and Farren. Who else?"

Her frown deepened. "I see, and what do you think you're gonna do?"

My own anger crept in. I peeled Mom's arm from my waist, stalking the few feet to the window. "Where're you going with this?"

If I thought for a second me looming over her had any effect, I must've been high. As if enjoying the challenge, she stood, meeting my glare. But we all knew my tall, lean body was no match for her chubby, short one. "Sit. Down."

I thought about refusing her. The look on her face, and the knowledge that she could pretty much make me do anything she wanted, changed my mind. The attitude stayed as I flopped on the couch, my arms crossed. Wasn't gonna admit to pouting, though.

When she hovered over me, the frown still in place, I managed to throw a little more irritation her way. "Well?"

Uh-oh. I trusted the frown more than the smile. "So, the plan is–if the Guide isn't lying–for me and Farren to waltz into Exemplar, kill Cassondra? While you, what? Hide in Arcus with Tarek, maybe?"

The squirming took over again. "Not kill her... I don't know, go above her head? Try to close the lines? Avery said–"

"I know what she said! Close the lines? Going against Exemplar is a death sentence." She bent low, her voice getting lower. "Whatever move we make will start a war, girl. If it's true some Exemplians like Avery are tired of the rules, they'll rebel as soon as an aggressive action is taken against any Synod member. And do you think those self-righteous assholes are gonna sit back and let a bunch of unhappy campers ruin what it took centuries to create?"

"I..." Yeah, hadn't thought that far ahead.

"And what're you gonna do when you get to Empyrean and Zander finds out you're there? Say, 'nice to see ya, but I'm off to be with my boyfriend'?"

Now that question threw me. I hadn't even considered him. "What do you care about Zander?"

Her lip curled and disdain deepened the blue of her eyes. "He hasn't stopped fighting for you, not even for a minute."

I leaned back on the flowered cushions. "He made his choice, and I'm not gonna feel responsible for it."

Her eyes widened and her heavy cheeks burned red. "*He made his choice?*"

Oh, no.

She waved her hand and the plate on the floor crashed against the front door. Another wave brought me off the couch, suspending me in the air. Mom's scream filled the room as she tried to come to my side, but Jake grabbed her arm and shook his head.

"*You* are his choice. He gave up his world...went against his own Protector, for you."

I couldn't even kick my feet, just stayed frozen in the air. Her rage scared me a little. It also forced me to search for the right thing to say to calm her down. "Why're you so mad?"

"That you can't see why pisses me off more." Her hand waved, and I landed in a crumbled heap on the floor. "You don't get how serious this is. If that woman told you the truth, she risked her life–another person you can add to the list of people who gave up everything for you."

Ouch. That hurt. I swallowed. "I understand exactly what people have done for me."

She grabbed the front of my shirt long enough to lift me to my feet, waving at Mom who broke Jake's hold.

"Let me go, Wilma." Mom stood, frozen by Wilma's hand, seething.

"You're done making excuses for her. You all are." Wilma returned her attention to me, and I held my eyes level with hers, refusing to let the tears fall. "After everything, you've learned *nothing*. Yeah, you found a backbone. So what? What good is it when your one goal is to find a way to be with a man? And you wanna know something else? The man you put above everyone understands the problem. He *gets* it."

The tears escaped, and there wasn't a damn thing I could do to stop them. I searched out Mom, whose eyes filled too, but she stood frozen, unable to help.

I willed my lips to stop trembling. "I do get it, Wilma."

Faced with her disappointment–the anger was easier to swallow. "No, you don't. All you see is an opportunity." She wrapped a hand around my wrist and closed her eyes. After a few seconds of reading my thoughts, she said, "And no amount of denying is going to change what's inside." Her pointer finger pierced my heart. "Right here."

She straightened, waving her hand at Mom as she stormed into the kitchen. I tried, really tried, to staunch the tears leaking from my eyes and running down my cheeks. But one look at Mom's tortured face and Jake's resigned one, as though he agreed with Wilma, gave my pity party permission to continue.

Jake stayed where he was, watching, but my mother rushed over, throwing her arms around me, guiding me to the couch. "She's wrong, baby." She stroked my mussed hair.

Her words made me cry harder. "No, she isn't." I buried my face and let her console me anyway. I tried not to get her blue blouse messy, but when I finally dragged myself from her arms, a big wet spot in the middle of her stomach proved my efforts futile. "Sorry."

God, I so did not deserve the compassion swimming in her eyes. "Don't be." I knew she wasn't talking about the wet spot. "It's okay to be in love, Lena–and it's okay to be young and think about nothing else. We've all been there."

Wilma's booming voice, a little raspier than usual, came from the kitchen. "Stop coddling her, Jacie."

Mom's eyes hardened, but she refused to look away from me. "She's my daughter, and I can say and do what I please." She swung around to meet the scowl of probably one of the strongest people not only in Earth, but in a few more dimensions, too. "Her past is yours, her present and future are ours. She's eighteen, for God's sake! What do you expect from her?"

Silence.

That fueled Mom to keep going. "She's always had to sacrifice, and I think it's about time she *does* find some enjoyment in *this* life."

Wilma crossed her arms and gave the front door a glance. "If she doesn't get her head out of her ass, *this* life isn't going to last much longer."

Mom stood, her tiny fists balled and ready to take on my bored-looking Protector leaning against the doorjamb. But as soon as she took a step forward, the door burst open.

Belva came rushing to my side, her face bright red for a change. Farren closed the door, satisfaction lighting his eyes. She opened her mouth undoubtedly to accuse Farren of being an asshole, but then her gaze met mine. "What's wrong?" She threw her arms around my shoulders and crushed my face into her neck, patting my head. "What'd you do to her?"

Even though my face pressed into her rose-smelling skin, I knew exactly whom she trapped with her accusing hazel eyes. After a few more renegade tears, I pulled away. "It's okay, pal." Scrubbing away the remaining moisture on my cheeks, I continued, "Listen, could you stay here for a day or two?"

Belva's glare remained planted on Wilma, answering me with her own question. "Why do you still put up with that bitch? She's a fucking lunch lady."

As Wilma's hand went up, Farren went to stand in front of my friend. "Please, Wilma."

Wilma dropped her hand, giving him a sneer. "Then control her, or I might relieve some stress."

Farren nodded, sitting next to Belva. "We need you to stay here, with me, for a while."

She gave him a scathing look, her lip curling. Whatever happened on the way here had her looking at him with much less enthusiasm than usual. "For what?"

He switched his attention from me to Wilma, a clear help-me message written all over his face. Since Wilma refused, smirking, I took over. Voice still a little unsteady, I said, "There are things I haven't told you, stuff that sounds too crazy to be real."

And how do we proceed from there, self?

She wanted to know, too. "What would those things be?"

"I…well…" As pissed off as I was at her, I looked to Wilma, pleading.

She rolled her eyes and huffed. "Oh, fine!" She stomped over to the couch. "I couldn't care less if you stay or go, but these two—for some reason that's completely beyond me—care enough to want you to live."

My turn to comfort as Belva leaned into me, her body shaking. "What the hell's she talking about?"

"Nice, Wilma." I rubbed Belva's arm. "There's too much to explain, but know there are some dangerous people out there who'd do anything to make my life miserable, including hurting people I love."

Her eyes, a little wild and a lot confused, searched mine. "So call the cops, right? Call the cops, Lena."

"Ah, the people who don't like me much… The cops can't help."

"Well, why not?"

"Because—"

"Enough!" Wilma grabbed my arm, yanking me off the couch and away Belva. With one more fluid move, she heaved my friend into Farren's arms. "You take care of the details." She raised her arm in the air and opened her fist, the tear screaming open.

Farren folded Belva into his arms, more restraining her than looking to comfort, as she screamed, the whites of her eyes taking over her entire face. I struggled against Wilma's hold to show my dislike for her tactics. But it'd take more than me—like at least fifty of me and a few Farrens—to actually force Wilma to do anything.

She yanked me closer to her side as the wind picked us up off the ground. Belva screamed louder. I mouthed *sorry*, but couldn't really feel anything except excitement. It didn't matter that terror paled my best friend's face.

I also didn't consider how pissed Wilma was or how I'd prove to her that I cared about the situation. Because all I could think about was exactly what she accused me of.

CHAPTER 10

LENA

ZANDER

Empyrean was as perfect as the picture I held sacred in my memory since Tarek brought me here, when he kissed *me* for the first time. We landed in an alley in the heart of a floating city. When we hit the main streets, I gawked while people shopped. Vendors called out, giving a good-natured ribbing to those who ignored their wares.

Wilma told me once when I asked about Empyrean's evolution that even though the dimension surpassed Earth there wasn't any visible evidence of modern technology. She stressed *visible*. From my first visit, I remembered running water and working bathrooms, but that was the extent of what I thought modern. Wilma also said Empyrean's evolution was almost as high as Exemplar's. The population here knew about dimensions, including what Exemplian Guides and Protectors were. Exemplar even considered Empyrean their "sister world." I had asked her who would choose to live without convenience, and Wilma's answer was an eye roll, followed by a snotty, "People who know what that shit does to humanity, that's who."

As I watched the way people interacted with each other–no interrupting phones, computers, or the stressed hustle that goes along with being technologically savvy–I finally got what she meant. I wouldn't call the scene

Utopian, especially with the few shoving matches in the middle of the street. Not to mention the two women obviously fighting over a smug guy, grinning like an idiot watching them go at it. I envied their passion, their desire to connect to something that didn't need to be charged every four hours.

The smells coming from the food vendors made my stomach growl. Not the typical fast food, processed crap I ate every day. Don't get me wrong, I liked that stuff, but the fresh fish twirling on spits and bread still steaming from time in the ovens made my mouth water. Clean food.

Wilma didn't seem all that intrigued. She pulled me into the fray, and through it, heading toward a connecting bridge leading to Teenesee's home. I let her drag me by the wrist as I took in the cobblestone roads and bridges with all the enthusiasm of a two-year-old. The floating streets bouncing us around reminded me of my old waterbed without the frigid cold that went with it. The ground felt soft, too, due to the slight give of the cobblestone, yet the rock was as hard as pavement. Walking through the town was a perfect feeling of contrast.

"Do you feel that? When you walk, do you feel it?"

Wilma hadn't said two words after handing my ass to me back home, and to be honest, it was the first time she'd ever given the silent treatment for longer than five minutes. I'd say anything to get her talking again, even if all she wanted to talk about was my bad attitude.

Relief loosened knots in my stomach when she decided to answer. "Yeah, I feel it."

That was all she gave me. No smartass comments, no telling me to stop talking like an idiot, only a simple answer she'd give to anybody she didn't much care about. The knots tightened right back up. "Wilma, you can't stay pissed at me."

She stopped when we made it to the backside of Teenesee's manse, which deceptively looked like a small, quaint cottage from our vantage point. Wilma let go of my wrist and sighed. "I'm not pissed. Scared more like. For you, your family, Tarek, Farren, this place...every place I've ever been to. This is new territory for me. The walls are crumbling down, and I don't have the strength to hold it all up."

I didn't expect that answer, not from the strongest person I'd ever known. Her fear sent the flags up in my brain. For some naïve reason, I thought she could take care of the problem, like she'd been taking care of everything for the past five months. Hell, my entire life–ah, lives.

Deep breath. "Well, you don't need to hold them up alone." I hugged her. Affection she wasn't comfortable with, but indulged me when I needed it. As I squeezed, she swatted my back in an irregular pound-pat pattern. "I won't disappoint you again."

The awkward patting turned into a fierce hug. "You never disappoint me. Ever. You've been through too much, and you deserve to be happy...with Tarek or whatever else you want. I wish it could be that easy."

Okay, I wasn't gonna cry. "I will be happy." Maybe a few tears. "After we fix what's happening."

Did I hear a sniffle?

She pulled away and snorted, turning her face to the door.

Yup, I think I did.

"Well, you're gonna need a few more lessons with Farren before you can help me kick some ass."

Tension gone. At least, the tension between us dissolved, giving way to our normal I-talk-Wilma-bitches relationship. Unfortunately, new tension managed to dance in its place.

The back doors flew open after a quick knock, and the dull fuzz entered my brain before seeing him.

Zander.

His face was the same as I remembered, except shadowed with a patchy beard. He wore the plain, beige clothes most men wore here, but his body filled out, making him look much older than the teenager I went to class with every day for three months.

"Lena!" He gathered me in his arms and swung me around.

I laughed, five months helping to soften the anger. "Put me down before I get sick."

He stopped swirling, setting me on the ground, and looked at Wilma. "What're you guys doing here?" His face darkened. "Is something wrong?"

"You could say there's a problem or two." She nodded at the door. "We need to talk to Teenesee, you too. We could use all the help we can get, I suppose."

"Well, let's go. Teenesee's in the upper sitting room, the one with the big balcony."

I nodded. "Lead the way."

Wilma walked ahead of us. "I'll go find her, talk to her in private first. Why don't you guys get something to eat?"

I knew a brush off when it was being swept at me. Whatever. "Ah, okay, sure."

Zander was all smiles. He hugged me one more time, rubbing my back, making me warm, and maybe even uncomfortable in that good, tingling way. "I missed you so much."

Shit. Maybe I missed him a little, too. I just hoped it was my Zander he decided to be and not the one who tried to get me killed.

∞ ∞ ∞

"It's good to see you again, Teenesee."

The Warden's face lit up, like before, as she drew me close. "You look stronger, my friend."

Her warmth and fresh smell, like a spring breeze, relaxed me. "I've been working on it."

"So your Protector has told me." She pulled away, the adoration causing her face to glow still confusing me. Why someone like her, a Warden, was interested in someone like me was a mystery. "And it seems we've found ourselves in a spot of trouble, no?"

Seriously, this woman and I were close? How much cooler must I have been before to accomplish that? *Another thing to hate about my past self.* "You could say so. We were hoping you might be able to help."

She tilted her head. "You still dress like a vagrant."

I smiled, not at all offended. "Yeah, well, Wilma didn't give me much time to change."

Wilma's answering snort made Teenesee laugh, the lilting sound akin to what I'd bet angels sounded like–if angels actually existed. "I think I may be of assistance, despite how difficult your appearance is to endure."

"We'd appreciate it."

"Come," she said, gesturing for Zander and I to follow. "If I am to share secrets, there must be those I trust willing to listen."

We sat in a circle of cushioned chairs, all in bold red and gold colors. The breeze coming from the large balcony ran through my shaggy hair. The wind plucking at the jagged edges of my outgrown style looked nothing like the romantic sway of Teenesee's long, sleek red hair. I wasn't sure why it made me feel like the ugly step-cousin when it wasn't important.

Teenesee stood in the middle of us. Once she had our attention, she folded her hands in front of her bare midriff, her bright yellow dress highlighting ebony skin almost the same hue as Zander's. "Wilma has told me what Avery revealed to you, Lena. About the lines?"

Zander stiffened beside me and his head whipped from the Warden to me. "She doesn't mean..."

"Yes, boy, that Avery. Now pipe down and try not to interrupt." Wilma's raspy voice sounded too harsh, not fitting in with the tranquil room.

She gestured to Teenesee, who gave a slow nod, and continued. "What she has told you is true–all of it."

My mouth went dry. Reality always hurt when someone yanked off the rose-colored glasses. This problem went from huge to infinite in ten seconds. Teenesee confirming Avery's words...well, it looked like our issue wasn't as easy as stopping Cassondra anymore. Not saying stopping her would've been easy, but...

I leaned up, and Zander's hand found mine. "What are we dealing with, exactly?"

"The lines were never meant to be crossed." Teenesee paused. "Exemplar's Synod has warned for eons the ramifications of bleeding the lines. But you see...the lines are already distorted. Because of Exemplar, energies have been misplaced and manipulated for even longer than I have lived."

Mad scientists. I came to that conclusion after Tarek talked to me in the spring, explaining the way Exemplians are born and reborn. But this...damn, so much worse.

Teenesee flicked a hand Zander's way, and when he didn't budge, she raised a brow, making a scooting motion. Grunting, he moved over. Teenesee took his place beside me, and said, "With their science, Exemplians have advanced the human race in their world, making them capable of taking that which is not theirs to have. Energies from other realms."

Zander piped in. "What are you saying? They–we're– energy thieves? A whole dimension?"

Teenesee kept her attention on me as she answered. "They are indeed thieves, though many are unaware." She grabbed my hands. "But you, Lena, they have unwittingly given another chance to defeat them. Their past punishment is your salvation and a true testament to the beauty that is nature."

A tear dripped from my eye. I had no idea why, but what she said made me ecstatic and mournful at the same time. "How?"

"Because here you are, ready to fight again." Teenesee's eyes dimmed. "Unfortunately, Exemplar holds True Wardens captive with threats."

Fear I hadn't felt in a long time danced its way back, magnifying the fuzz Zander's presence had. "That's it? There's nothing we can do? We just wait around until they come get us?"

Determination squared the Warden's jaw. "I would not wait around for anyone. Would you? We *were* at their mercy. Until you came along, all those years ago, and offered hope."

I swallowed. "What do you have in mind?"

"We close the lines, end their reign."

"And how are we going to pull that off, Warden? There's a handful of us and a whole dimension of them." Leave it to Wilma to shed some shitty reality on the optimism.

"Yes, the odds are unsettling, but not impossible. Quite a few True Wardens have been ready to end the hold Exemplar has had on their worlds. And now that Tarek controls Arcus, we have a chance at success."

"Why do you keep saying that? True Wardens? What the hell does that even mean?" Zander fidgeted, his hand continually scrubbing at the scruff on his chin.

Teenesee's eyes glittered. "Exemplian Synod elders found that by killing natural-born Wardens, they could absorb their energy, the purest energy. If a Warden refused to cooperate, those animals would terminate them, and an Exemplian would gain control of the dimension. A few True Wardens have survived the infiltration." She bowed her head. "And only by adhering to the Exemplian cause."

Zander jumped up, flinching under Teenesee's glare. "How could the whole damn Exemplian population be living a lie?" He turned to Wilma. "Wilma?"

My Protector's face was pale as she kept her focus on Teenesee, ignoring Zander. "Shit, this got heavy."

"You don't believe it?" Zander marched toward her, his control cracking, showing a scared boy. "She's telling us we're monsters–all of us."

"She's telling us we've been lied to. Used. Something your Protector has already proven to you."

His body shook, his splayed fingers showing how much. "What agenda could they possibly have?"

Teenesee answered when Wilma stayed quiet. "It takes resources to create and maintain what Exemplar has built. Worlds with the much-needed materials get the best energies to help cultivate their lands. The others are drained of everything but the weakest, becoming dumping grounds."

He made a sound between a groan and a cry before facing me. "You don't believe it, right?"

"I do, but you aren't monsters, Zander. You're pawns, victims, like everyone else."

"No." Zander stormed from the room, slamming the marble door in his wake.

I jumped up when Wilma went to go after him. "I'll go."

It took a few minutes to catch up, but he could never outrun me. "Zander, wait!"

He kept going until we made it down the flesh-colored drawbridge and into a field where a few people were digging up what look like emeralds and slinging them onto horse-drawn wagons. When he finally turned to confront me, his face was a tortured, tear-stained mess. "You actually believe it?"

I stopped short, almost slamming into his chest. "I... Yeah, Zander, I believe her."

"I used to help track down the traitors, find out where they would've gone by studying their histories. Come to find out, people who were only guilty of not wanting to accept their privileged status." He raked a hand through his hair, searching behind me, watching the emerald farmers. "If what she said is true, I've helped ruin more than your life."

"Zander, you didn't ruin–"

He shook his head and covered his ears. "No, don't. Don't give me some bullshit pep talk." He yelled, kicking at the ground. "I should've known, especially after I found out about you."

Well, this I could help him with. "But I wasn't innocent. Mateusz did me a favor, according to Avery. I knew about all this and tried to start a rebellion."

Disbelief skated across his face for a second before it changed to something brighter, more aggressive. "A rebellion? You mean a rebellion against assholes who knew what they were doing was wrong. Is that the rebellion you're talking about?"

I'd ignore his sarcasm because he was pissed, but it still festered under the skin. "If I had succeeded, a lot of people would've died going up against Exemplar." I put my hands on his chest. "*We* can make sure we do it right this time. Make sure they don't ever hurt another innocent person or manipulate energy again."

Without even realizing it, I had made up my mind. I didn't want to stop Cassondra. I wanted to stop her entire goddamn world. I finally got it. Tarek, as important as he was…damn…some things had to come first.

"Yeah? And how do we do that? Didn't you hear Wilma?"

The odds didn't look good, but hey, it sure as hell beat doing nothing. "We go to the True Wardens first. Start with the ones who want to stop Exemplar."

He covered my hands with his. "And then what?"

Picks hitting the dirt coupled with the farmers' soft chatter in Empyrean tongue filled the space for a few minutes. What next? I had no idea. "We'll figure it out."

He smiled, some misery leaving his face. "Great plan, but I'm glad you're here."

"Me too." I went to punch him in the shoulder. "Hey, nice shirt, by the way. You look like a… Oh, shit. Oh, shit! *Run.*"

In the middle of the field, the sky crackled and the wind picked up as the atmosphere ripped open, plunking at least thirty Protectors on the ground. They all wore those sizzling black suits. As soon as their feet touched the field, weapons were aimed and firing.

The farmers turned into warriors as they flung the emerald rocks at the intruders, the green shards exploding into fireballs as soon as they touched something solid. The explosives didn't slow the troops down much as the flames bounced off their suits, fizzling out.

I grabbed Zander's hand when he refused to budge, his eyes wide and mouth slack. "Run, goddamnit!"

After a tug on his fingers, his eyes found mine and determination hardened them. We both took off for the drawbridge, the heat from Exemplian weapons whizzing past us, getting close enough to burn the tips of my ears. I kept Zander's hand in mine as I picked up speed, ducking and dodging the orange flares hitting the ground, igniting the buried emerald rocks the farmers missed.

When we reached the bridge, my arm yanked from its socket. Pain shot through my legs and up my spine as I fell to the glossy surface. I glanced behind me.

Zander lay motionless, his head sporting a wide gash surrounded by blackened skin.

I scrambled to his side, the pain in my legs forgotten while I put pressure on his wound, the hoard of Protectors closing in.

Panicked, I did the only thing I could. "Wilma!"

Lynn Vroman

CHAPTER 11

LENA

CHOICES

Wilma raced across the bridge, her heavy body as agile as a sprinter's. "Get down, girl!"

Waving her hand, she swept the first round of ten Protectors thirty feet back before propelling Zander's body closer to the door.

I stayed on the ground, holding my hands out to show her Zander's blood. "Is he gonna die?"

She pulled me to my feet. "Get indoors. Lock yourself in a bedroom. Go, now!"

I shook my head, watching some of Teenesee's people drag Zander through the door. When a second wave came in shooting a relentless string of orange light at Wilma, I jumped up to stand behind her. The first few taser shots didn't stop her as she waved away five Protectors and threw a few others. But the barrage didn't let up, the pain becoming clearer on her face.

I set my focus on the one aiming directly at her heart. Using moves Farren taught, I jumped into action, getting a running start before giving him a side kick in the knee. The surprise attack worked. His body dropped as his weapon switched from Wilma to me. Before he had a chance to squeeze off a shot, I struck him under his nose and slammed my hands against his ears. With a little help from Wilma's hand, he flew back with seven more Protectors.

The sky opened up again. An army dropped down, too large to guess the numbers.

"We need to leave." My calm tone betrayed the fear roiling and thrashing in my gut as I stumbled backward to stand by Wilma.

"Sounds like a good idea." She closed her eyes and touched her temple.

"What're you doing?"

She kept her eyes closed for a few seconds more before answering. "Giving Tarek the message." She grimaced. "Looks like you got your wish."

Didn't that make me feel all dirty inside?

Clopping hooves on the bridge's sleek surface had me forgetting my guilt for about a second. Teenesee rode out, her face hard as her beauty heightened to the point *I* had trouble looking at her.

Without acknowledging us, she leapt from her horse and charged to the frontline, meeting the third wave of Protectors head-on. Most stumbled, their mouths slack and eyes admiring when they stopped to look at her–the distraction she needed. Her whole body turned to a mass of reflecting green energy. In an instant, she balled the verdant light with her palms and threw it at the third and fourth waves of charging Protectors.

Their suits didn't protect them. If they managed to survive the blast, they lay on the ground thrashing in pain and blood. I slammed both hands over my nose. The smell of burning flesh forced me to hold onto my stomach's contents with sheer willpower.

In the stunned silence, with the agony of the dying and wounded filling the field, Teenesee turned to us. "You need to leave. Hurry."

I came forward, still mesmerized by her amped up face. "They're here for me. You'll pay if we leave. Maybe we shou—"

"You must leave. Remember, close the lines." She focused on the Protectors behind the casualties, her body creating another massive wave of green light.

Before I could argue, Wilma gathered me up and opened her hand to the sky.

∞ ∞ ∞

She dropped us on the doorstep of Tarek's cabin. Ignoring all the Arcus color, I barged through the door to find it empty. No point in yelling for him, the whole place was as big as my living room. "He's not here."

"Oh, observant, aren't you?" Wilma stayed at the door, not bothering to come in.

"So, what? Do we look for him?"

"Go ahead, but I don't think the squid are gonna like you any better this time around."

Damn, she wanted me to beg–and I had no problem doing that. "Well, you can help, right?"

"Nope. He knows you're coming, and I'm sure he's on his way back from…whatever the hell he does around here." She lifted her arm. "Stay inside."

"Wait! Where–"

She left, the tear sucking her up as the wind slammed the door shut.

"Hey!"

Ripping the door open to yell would've been stupid, but I did it anyway. "Wilma, goddamnit! Come back!"

Squealing and tentacles scaling bark convinced me to lower my voice. "Please…"

Of course, she couldn't hear me. Not like she'd come back if she could.

With one last wary glance at the squid, I shut the door. The cabin didn't offer much in the comfort department, but Tarek had built every inch. That was enough for me. The bed was big enough for one person, but still cozy with a thick quilt and pillow. I lay there, trying hard not to think about our situation moving to the worst side of the spectrum. A Protector army? Jesus, it took one time for me to break the rules, and they sent an army…

Oh, no.

Farren broke the rules, too, which meant everyone in my apartment might have had a visit from the bastards. I sat up, my heart tapping double-time. When Mateusz waltzed in that morning… When he took Tarek away from me…

There wasn't anywhere to go if a few Protectors decided to make Farren pay. Make me pay. Kill my family

I flung open the door to find squid not ten feet from the cabin. They didn't move closer when they saw me, but they screamed. Guess they knew the cabin was off limits, and I knew their territory was as blocked from me.

"*Ugh.*"

I slammed the door. So stinking frustrating to be stuck while… I didn't even want to think about it. I plopped on the bed and grabbed the pillow. At least it was something to cling to as I waited, doing nothing as Exemplians were potentially killing my family.

Nope. Not good enough.

I threw the thing back on the bed, ready to face whatever wanted to take a swipe at me outside. The damn things weren't fast; I could outrun them. I just had to make sure to dodge a few tentacles. Wilma would know if I were in trouble, and so I was gonna get myself in trouble. She'd have to come get me. Well, hopefully she'd come.

As soon as the door swung open, my anxiety dissolved.

There he was, stalking through squid lined on either side of him. His face, that same beautiful face, but glowing with vivid color.

Tarek.

I forgot about the squid and ran. They squealed, but didn't move, understanding who was in charge. As Tarek opened his arms, I jumped, crushing my lips on his.

In a move I remembered well, he bent to lift my legs and wrapped them around his waist. He kept moving toward the cabin, never taking his mouth off mine. When the door shut, he set me down, his dimples almost enough to make me cry. "Miss me, did you?"

"Not at all."

He gave a low growl and kissed me again. When he pulled away this time, neither of us could breathe without heaving. "Liar."

Lynn Vroman

CHAPTER 12

LENA

FINALLY

The five months separating us disappeared with one glimpse of his smile. My heart slammed against my ribcage.

Shit.

Wilma was right. Tarek caused everything else that should've mattered to take a back seat. Using the small reserve of willpower I had, I left his arms and concentrated on what had me opening the door in the first place. "I have to get home. My family…"

His smile stayed in place. "She didn't tell you? As soon as Farren heard the first portal open, he brought everyone here. They're at the castle." He chuckled. "Your friend is a little upset, but otherwise they're fine."

Relieved tears blinded my vision. "Thank God! And, no, Wilma's pretty pissed right now. Guess she wanted to punish me a little."

He gathered me into his arms again and kissed the tip of my nose. "She can hold a grudge."

"Yeah, especially when she's right."

"What happened?"

I gave him another kiss, wishing I could block out everything wrong. "Let's say I missed you. A lot."

"And I you." Another kiss. "As much as I'd like to show you, we need to get to the castle and figure out what to do with everyone. This place isn't exactly set up for human guests."

"You live here," I glided a hand down his muscular arm, "and don't seem to be suffering."

"All right, one, you have to stop that, and two, it's a benefit of being Warden. I'm immune to...dying from the elements."

No, I didn't stop touching him. Couldn't, really. My hand traveled up to his neck and curled into his soft hair. "I'm glad you're immune."

After one more kiss, I went to open the door. The squid were still standing guard, but they didn't make a sound. Tarek came up behind me and pressed a hand at the small of my back. Even that innocent touch had my nerve endings sparking and tingling.

As we walked through the symmetrical forest, every single squid climbed from the tops of their perches. If I didn't know any better, I'd say they bowed as Tarek walked passed. "Now what the hell are they doing?" I pointed to the nearest bowing cephalopod, half tempted to pet its head.

"They know trouble is coming."

"Protectors?"

His face tightened, but those dimples came out to reassure me. "They'd be stupid to try to get at me again."

"Again? They've already tried." Can't believe I forgot how calm my giant could be when death lingered at the edges.

"A couple times. They lost."

I looked into his eyes, surprised to see the coldness in his voice matched the icy set of his jaw.

If he weren't the man I loved, I would've run as far away as possible. "How strong are you?"

He glanced down at me. "Wilma isn't the toughest kid on the playground anymore."

∞ ∞ ∞

Frigid temperatures hit me first. Memories followed soon after. The last time I skidded across the icy path to the castle, Mateusz had me by the neck.

Funny how time didn't help ease all fears.

As soon as the pointed black towers came into view, I faltered. Tarek didn't urge me forward; he stopped with me, pulling me closer to him. Trying to control the terror threatening my rational thought process wasn't easy. Almost impossible.

Tarek's soft voice brushed against my ear. "It's okay, love, breathe."

When he spoke, I managed to suck in air, the scent of rotting fish subtle, but aggravating the memories I didn't care to relive. "Doesn't exactly give me the warm fuzzies."

His chest rumbled, vibrating against my back and having the right effect on my nerves. "We'll make new memories, erase the old. You'll be thinking fuzzy in no time."

I turned to wrap my arms around his waist, nuzzling his chest. "I *did* miss you. So much."

His arms tightened. "If it's even a quarter of how much I missed you, I'm a lucky man."

What sucked about loving someone who was smack dab in the middle of a possible dimensional war were all the interruptions.

"Lena!"

Mom screamed my name from the pudgy white hut attached to the first sleek tower. As she slid toward us, Jake, Belva, and Farren crowded the doorway. Everyone had different expressions. Jake's strained face contrasted the awe in Belva's. Farren's face shined with excitement. Damn, my Protectors liked a battle.

When Mom ran into me, Tarek had to stand as a brace against my back to keep us from face planting the ground.

Her hysterical laughing/crying jag helped ease my fears. At least everyone was safe.

"Let's go inside, Mom. Don't want to make the wildlife anxious."

Her eyes grew wide and her gaze moved around Tarek to find the squid watching the exchange from the tree line. "What is this place?"

From all the conversations we'd had about Arcus, I knew she understood exactly where we were. Seeing all the color and oddities in person, though, was definitely not the same as a two hour, in-depth conversation detailing everything. "Beautiful, isn't it? Ah...in a deadly sort of way."

Her laugh got higher and her smile wider.

Sighing, I glanced at Tarek, who had a smirk coloring his lips, and grabbed Mom's hand.

After I went through the gauntlet of hugs, we all sat in the very room where Tarek became Warden. He got busy building up the fire while I scavenged some trunks lining the walls where the bookshelves used to be. Finding four thick blankets, I shooed everyone to the couch so we could leech each other's body heat until the fire did its job. Farren declined the offer, choosing to help Tarek. He was the only one wearing pants. The rest of us were dressed for summer.

As the two men built the flames, they spoke softly, but their loud voices carried to the couch.

"We managed to stick it in deep this time, brother." Farren's whisper was as inconspicuous as a nose wart.

Tarek snorted, poking the flames. "Yeah, a few broken jaws aren't going to solve this one."

"Too bad. Always liked a good fight, cleans the stress right off my shoulders. What's the next move?"

"We wait for Wilma. Until then, we keep these guys alive until we can find a safer place for them."

Okay, I didn't like where their conversation headed. "Um, excuse me? Fellas? I'm not going anywhere, ah, safe. Got it?" When they both stared, I rolled my eyes. "Look, I get it, we can't stay here, but with some food and water, we can stay a few weeks at least." I pointed to Farren. "You can make a quick food run, jump back before getting caught."

Tarek didn't say no, which was a plus. He'd probably like the company. Farren, on the other hand, had a lot to say. He stole a glimpse at Belva, who didn't seem as upset as Tarek made her out to be. "No way, Lena. There are other places, safer dimensions to stick you guys until this shit gets worked out."

With a pat on Mom's hand and an encouraging look from Jake, I got in Farren's face. "From what Avery and Teenesee said, I'm the one who can help get things straightened out."

When Farren glanced behind him, obviously looking for some support from Tarek he didn't get, he waved his beefy hands in the air. "Guaranteed the screens are programmed to watch our every move here. All it'll take is me leaving one time for them to snatch me up. And then what, huh?"

I tilted my head. "If what you say is true, taking us somewhere else, somewhere they won't have a problem invading like they did in Empyrean, would be stupid."

Tarek finally stood, brushing the bark off his hands. "She's right. One bad guess and you all will be dead." He sighed. "Look, Wilma keeps a stash here, but it'll only last a couple days. The river's safe to drink from, and a few animals are eatable–disgusting, but safe to eat."

"I don't know, brother. I–"

"Farren! Stop. Whatever's going on, I'm not going anywhere else." We all turned in shock to see Belva standing with her hands planted on her hips. "If this giant, ah, guy." She gawked at Tarek. "You're a guy, right? Not some weird manlike monster?" At Tarek's subtle nod, a smile curling his lips, she continued, "If he says we're okay here, and if Lena thinks we're safe, I'm staying."

Farren's face reddened. "Belva, being here...it's not ideal."

"And where is the ideal place?"

"Ah...it's...umm..." Stammering Ginger was a new development.

"Exactly. Here, it is." Belva held her chin high, even though trepidation danced in her pretty eyes. "Are you familiar with the place, Lena?"

I looked to Tarek, who shrugged, that smile still teasing his lips. "I guess a little."

"Good," she said. "Let's find a place to crash." She gestured toward Mom and Jake. "You two coming?"

Jake shook his head as Mom covered a smile. Who would've thought we'd all take this crap without being committed? Had to admit, my bubble was pretty awesome.

"Suit yourselves." She laced her arm through mine. "Let's go have some girl talk." She gave frazzled Farren a wink and Tarek a soft smile.

"Looks like we both have a lot to confess."

CHAPTER 13

LENA

GIRL TALK

"Okay, if you leave any good stuff out, I'll never talk to you again." Belva hopped onto the old, mildewing bed with absolutely no concern for her health. I, on the other hand, stayed away from the thing, worried about all the little exotic insects that might be living there.

The room wasn't much nicer than the one Casimir locked me in during the first trip to the castle. At least this time, I could keep the door open. "And what good stuff are you referring to?"

"Oh, come on! I see the way that guy looks at you. Jesus, he looks like a Greek god." She paused, her eyes shining. "Is he, you know, a god?"

Leave it to Belva to reduce the danger we were in to a Q&A about men. "No, he's not a god, but…"

She flew to her knees, bouncing on that disgusting bed, the smile on her pretty face stretched wide. "But what? Come on, Tulman, spill it."

"Okay, okay, jeez." I sat on the edge of the no doubt infested straw mattress. "Remember how you said I'd understand if I ever found *the* guy?" At her nod, I continued, "Well, I do understand because mine starred in my dreams since I was eight."

Her hand went to her heart as her smile softened and her eyes grew dreamy. "That's so romantic." The dreaminess turned demanding. "Do not leave a single detail out."

We spent the next hour with me rehashing everything that had happened over the spring. How I dreamed of Tarek, how we met in the woods…how he took me to Empyrean…that night we came back. When I got to the part where he sacrificed everything to keep me safe from Casimir and now spoke in my head every night, my friend was a blubbering mess.

"That's so beautiful. He *is* a god, Lena, because you're his goddess."

I laughed, but when her face stayed serious, the words sunk in. "Yeah, I guess. Too bad the entire universe does just about anything to make sure we're always apart."

"Well you guys are together now. It's up to you to keep it that way."

If it were that simple. "Enough about me. What I'd like to know is how are you taking all this so well? Doesn't this place scare you?"

She cocked her head to the side. "Funny thing, I was scared when Wilma took you, but when we got here… This place is so…"

"Terrifying? Dangerous? Smelly?"

"Perfect."

I grabbed her hand and tugged her off the bed. "Nuh-uh, wrong answer."

She struggled to pull her hand from mine as we flew down the stairs. I ignored her and everyone gaping at us when I stormed through the room and through a myriad of doors until we made it outside. As soon as the frigid air hit us, I released her hand and waved for her to follow.

As we slipped down the ice, I said, "Do you smell that? It's death." I pointed at the tree line, not willing to get too close to the squid. "Those are real, Belva. And their screams? I still have nightmares."

Her face didn't shine with fear, but excitement. "They're beautiful. Look at their color, the color of this whole place. It's paradise."

"*Paradise?* Jesus, I think you've cracked."

Her laugh tinkled through the thin air, causing the squid to perk up. The crazy part? They didn't squeal.

"I'm fine, Lena. Amazing, actually." She laced her fingers with mine and ran for the pink monsters. "I want to see the woods!"

She might be the pretty one, but she definitely wasn't the smart one—or the strong one.

With a hard yank, I pulled her back into the castle. "We're not going anywhere near there without Tarek. It might look like a fairyland, but the place will kill you."

"So dramatic, but fine, you win…for now."

∞ ∞ ∞

When we joined everyone else, the fire managed to make the room cozy—too cozy. Mom had all the blankets folded in a stack on the trunks.

I'll bet Farren wished he'd put on shorts now.

He and Tarek both had sweat soaking their shirts.

"Sauna isn't what we should be going for." I pulled my hair into a short ponytail with the band I always had around my wrist. "I can barely breathe."

Tarek's dimples appeared, making me forget to be irritated and uncomfortable. "Sorry. Not used to guests."

I went straight to his arms and tried to avoid the bigger sweat marks on his shirt as I leaned my head against his chest.

He pulled me close, rubbing my lower back. "Jake? Open the door? We can at least get some air in that way."

"Yeah, okay. And after we make sure everyone is comfy, maybe we can all actually talk about what the hell we're doing?" His eyes shined with what I'd classify as glossy, straightjacket crazy, his smile wide, showing off his crooked eyetooth.

Maybe my bubble wasn't taking it so well, after all.

Mom got up to open the door, and then guided Jake back to the couch. She turned to us, not nearly as freaked out as her man. "He's right. We need to know what to do. Sitting around isn't accomplishing anything."

"Well, Teenesee said we need to close the lines, and so that has to be the objective," I said.

"And how do we do that? Ask the Synod nicely to stop being thieving assholes?"

"Funny, Ginger. If that's what you wanna do, have at it. But I was thinking more along the lines of seeking out True Wardens, trying to get them on our team."

Tarek's arms tightened around my waist. "They had a connection with you in your last cycle. They may not want to deal with you...now that you know next to nothing."

He was scared. I'd be lucky if he let me do anything but stand right beside him. I tilted my face up for a kiss and he obliged. After a pat on his cheek, I went to stand by the couch, needing the space to think clearly. "I may not remember, but I *am* the person they trusted. If I explain, tell all the facts, I don't think it'll be hard to convince them that I want the same thing they want."

"These people, the Wardens, they're strong, suspicious. They likely won't give you a chance to explain." Tarek wasn't gonna give me an inch.

"Well, Teenesee didn't kill me when we went to Empyrean the first time. Give them some credit."

"That was different. You and she–"

"We have to take the chance, Tarek."

"Not with you, we don't."

Mom got up, shrugging off Jake's grip. She stood next to me, her chin raised as she looked at Tarek. "Do you have a better plan? How do we stop this...this place from coming after Lena?"

I almost interrupted to let her know there was a ton more at stake than me dying, but she shot me her I'm-talking look. I shook my head, held up my hands, and took a step back.

Tarek's eyes hardened and he adjusted his big body to stand straighter. "My plan *is* to keep her alive. I don't much care about what happens outside of that."

Even Farren threw an incredulous look his way. "You serious? Fucking Exemplians just attacked their strongest ally, brother."

"This whole thing stems from Cassondra being pissed. We take care of her, the threat is over," Tarek said. "Isn't that what Avery warned? Cassondra seeking revenge? We'll deal with that. Only that."

"There's more than a grudge going on. They came to me, too, guns blazing. You know as well as anyone they're usually more covert about that shit!"

"It's not Lena's job to save the fucking universe."

I stood between Farren and Tarek when Ginger's face got all blotchy and the stammering began again. "I get it," I said. "We handle the imminent threat, but we've got a chance to do something. Really *change* something."

Tarek's eyes lost the edge. He pulled me close, and said so only I could hear, "I can't lose you. Not again."

I threaded my fingers through his hair, bringing his ear to my lips. "Wilma's right. We have to think about more than us this time."

"I can't protect you if you leave here." His voice shook as his fingers kneaded the small of my back.

"We'll figure it out." I turned to everyone else. "We'll wait for Wilma. Until then, let's get the supplies and find out where we're all sleeping. I'm beat."

Mom pulled Jake off the couch, and Belva went to stand next to Farren. He didn't waste any time slinging an arm across her shoulders, fitting her to his side. "Ah, where'd Wilma go, anyway?"

"Back to Empyrean." The scary, hard edge no longer deepened Tarek's voice. Always fascinating how fast men could kiss and make up.

"Maybe I should go, too. Help her out," Farren said.

"That'd piss her off. She'd rather have you here to be able to take these guys away fast if things go bad." Tarek poked the fire once more and went to the trunks. "Wilma's there in case the bastards trickle in, trying for sneak attacks."

I followed him to the trunks, helping with the food and water. "You think they'll…ah…trickle in?"

He handed me a box of granola. "Yes."

CHAPTER 14

AVERY

TRAITOR

Avery breathed in slowly, trying to calm her rapid heart while the security scanner read her pupil. The screens being on… The coincidence did not sit well.

Once the doors breezed open, she and Nicolette stepped through the threshold for another security check, a body scanner buzzing around them. The floating balls beeped, their access lights flipping to green. With a waving hand and a bored look that defied the storm within, she sent the annoying apparatuses away.

The Creation Lab hadn't changed in her two-day absence—hadn't really changed in centuries. Of course, the typical rows of computers filled the room, some displaying holograms that Guides scrutinized. Others that computed formulas in bright red numbers above hunched bodies of more Guides trying to crack the few secrets left in the universe. This lab was ever efficient, ready to destroy the potential lives of energies new and old.

She passed the busybodies, who innocently believed they were making the universe better. Some pulled themselves away from their work long enough to acknowledge her. Another eye scan later, with a hand up to stay Nicolette, Avery stood in a second clear-screened room facing humanity's worst mistake.

Numbness–the feeling as familiar as her own skin–settled on her shoulders and worked its way to her toes. Opening emotions would put her back in that dark place, the place she'd lived in before Lena came to her with a way out–an end.

Mechanical arms stripped her clothes and replaced them with the sterile, skin-tight suit and mask. She kept her attention on the bodies. Some without faces or definite shape lay like dolls in huge compression chambers. Piled in haphazard order by shape and gender, the infant chamber gave her numb shield the biggest challenge. This was where new energy ended up when deemed privileged enough, strong enough, to be an Exemplian. No parents, no real childhood. The general population didn't know that. Implanted memories took over as soon as an energy entered a corporeal form.

Then the magic happened.

Artificial DNA thrown into the energy mix, giving these pseudo-humans abilities no one should have. Abilities like her own.

Exemplian life was not completely bleak. They'd give some bodies the ability to procreate, have life made the natural way, the right way. It all sounded beautiful, miraculous, but really it was to keep the population under control, give no one a chance to be suspicious.

Until Lena.

A sigh pushed the guilt away. She stepped from the sterile chamber. Deception never took a holiday.

Reports finalized. Check. Pairing requests authorized. Done. Older energy requesting retirement–not many. Odd. Protector to Guide ratio–completely unbalanced.

Avery leaned back, studying her screen. The new energy influx drove her bloody nuts. Too many were being sent here and all being docked as Protector. As if they were preparing for another war... "Oh, no."

She jumped when the warning emergency light blinked and dinged politely. Before she could gauge the problem, bright, multicolored lights, hundreds of them, rushed into the energy containment tubes. The wall screens came to life with all the recycled lights' MOS codes. All were Protectors, dumping into the chamber faster than the screens could keep up with the tally.

"Oh…*no*," she repeated, as if the loud command could stop the screaming flow of Protectors, squeezed in tubes so tight the energy looked like one large, bulging light, an ancient fluorescent bulb.

She didn't take the time to strip from her sterile gear as she tore from the room, on her way to the one office where she'd find answers.

"Cassondra!" Avery ignored the two admins trying to stop her.

Nicolette made sure the two men didn't follow Avery inside the new authority commander's office.

Cassondra stood in front of her screens, all tuned to Empyrean. The colorless woman, with pale hair and alabaster skin, didn't bother to turn around. "I'm surprised. I would've thought you'd be here sooner, but…" she turned those watery blue eyes to Avery, "you've been unreachable for two days."

Avery stayed silent, though rage made her lips tingle with everything that needed said.

"I was concerned, our Creation Lab overseer not here? Not where she is supposed to be? The Synod elders agreed." Cassondra turned back to the screens. "We concluded now was the perfect time to re-activate the satellites. And guess what we found in our desperate search for one of our most valued members?"

Avery watched the screens, flinching at the carnage. Protectors and Empyreans lay slaughtered as the blue lights of Guides absorbed the flailing globes of Protector energy.

Authority Guides also collected green orbs–the dead Empyreans. "What have you done?"

"We have traitors, Guide. Those who wish to destroy the very foundations on which this universe thrives. Months of inquisition, weeks of information processing, and we finally have answers." The calm in the commander's voice made Avery's skin prickle. "But...you can imagine my surprise when I found our little wayward Guide at the center of the rebellion."

Fear licked stinging paths through her limbs. Avery didn't have to ask; she knew whom Cassondra meant. "Are you certain?" The composed façade had taken centuries of practice. The placid facial expressions consisted of years staring into a mirror, making sure no tells showed. But all that practice, all that time, couldn't hide her thin, reedy voice, which sounded like a hovercraft's vapor engine.

When Cassondra turned to face her this time, those dull eyes were alive–terrifying. "I have never been more certain."

What have I done...?

"Perhaps we could talk to her Protector. Maybe someone has led her astray."

"Enough, Guide. The girl is not stupid, and she has been warned. She refused to stay in her dimension, as ordered. If some...other traitor has given her false information, well I'm sure we will find out whom." Cassondra tucked her hands inside the sleeves of her robe. "We have found this rebellion to run deeper than her present cycle. It seems she has co-conspirators who have not given up their treacherous ways." Those dead eyes chained Avery to the floor. "And we *will* find all who are responsible, Avery. Every. Single. Traitor."

The threat, as subtle as a thin breeze, ricocheted off the walls. Avery swallowed. "That is...troublesome, indeed."

A mirthless smile tugged at Cassondra's thin lips. "I am pleased you agree."

Avery glanced at the screens, trying to grab hold of the calm slipping away at a much faster rate. "What shall we do with the Protector energy? Their documents… Many of those soldiers have chosen retirement after this cycle. We should make sure they are sent somewhere safe, away from the battle."

"Recycle them back to Exemplar–all of them. If they refuse once their bodies go live, terminate their energy, file it as a Tainted."

"But–"

"We are at war. No one gets a choice. Synod elders are in agreement with me that Empyrean and its Warden will be the first to suffer for their treason. They do not wish for our sister dimension to threaten the Exemplian population. Teenesee has harbored this traitor, and now she will pay with her world. Everyone who helps Lena will face retribution. I will take everything from her, as she…" Cassondra cleared her throat, rare emotion flitting over her face. "I will take from her before I kill her."

Fear slithered through her blood. *I did this!*

Lena would pay with more than her life. So much more.

"You may leave now," Cassondra said.

Avery backed toward the door, a plan already forming in her head. She had to get to Lena. "Very well."

"Oh, yes, I almost forgot." Cassondra kept her attention on the screens as more Protectors shot to Empyrean, carrying newer weapons used for one thing: complete annihilation. "The Synod elders have given permission to scan all private documents of Synod members. I trust you will comply?"

Avery's lips grew numb and she had to hide her trembling fingers behind her back. "I–yes, of course."

Cassondra turned to her, excitement shading her face. "Excellent."

She knows...

Avery pushed the door open. "Good afternoon, Commander."

At Cassondra's nod, Avery left, hooking Nicolette's elbow, more to keep from falling, as she rushed from the building.

Nicolette stopped her before leaving the front doors. "What's wrong?"

"Please..." Tears threatened but Avery held them in check until they were as far away from the building as her legs could take her before they gave out. Nicolette held her up, concern in her eyes.

"She...she knows, Nicolette. We must leave. Now."

CHAPTER 15

LENA

SQUID WHISPERER

As soon as the door shut, my face heated and a tidal wave of shyness washed over me. The small cabin I had romanticized turned into a claustrophobic sauna. I had dreamed of this moment for five months. Granted the circumstances were different. There wasn't some big dimensional war brewing. But we were finally alone, with no threat of company, and I couldn't stop shaking.

"What's wrong?" Tarek moved behind me, massaging my shoulders.

"I…well…" My eyes stayed glued to the narrow bed. "This is gonna sound crazy."

"You're scared? Nervous?"

"Bingo."

"Me too."

I turned. His eyes clouded and his mouth parted enough to notice his breath coming out in quick gasps. I raised a brow, covering his heart with a sweaty palm. The rapid pounding had my own anxieties bottoming out. If this man, Arcus's Warden and certified badass, was feeling nervous about spending the night with me, maybe I was a bit of a badass, too.

I stood on my toes and touched my lips to his, smiling. "So…um…"

He grinned, trailing a finger down my cheek. "Kissing? Kissing is good."

Relief filled my legs. I thought I was ready. Guess not. Not yet. "Kissing sounds better than good."

He scooped me up. When he set me down on the bed, Tarek covered my body with his, all his weight supported by his elbows. He kissed me light, and then deeper, not even trying to touch me, no matter how hard I tugged. I groaned and punched him in the shoulder.

A laugh vibrated off his lips and hit mine. "Problem?"

"Kissing requires a little more touching." I bit his bottom lip.

"Ouch! Be nice." His tongue skated across my teeth marks. He then brushed a hand through my hair, his eyes softening and voice no longer playful. "I don't want you to leave."

"We can't ignore it, Tarek. We can't." I pulled his head down until our foreheads touched. "But we can put it on hold."

"That's not good enough."

I wouldn't convince him; he'd never agree to anything. So I kissed him.

He went to break free, and I touched his cheek. We had hours. Hours I refused to spend in reality. "Stay."

He cupped my face, his gray eyes belonging to me. "Always."

∞ ∞ ∞

Hours later, we lay there, the bed too small to be comfortable for two people, but we managed. Well, I was fine on top of Tarek, using his wide chest for a cushion. He'd cramp up after more time like this.

When I pushed on his chest to get up, his arms tightened around me. "No."

I smiled, tracing the muscles etching his stomach. There might've been only kissing, but I insisted we do it without his shirt on. "Hey, if you like me using you as a cushion…"

"I love it."

"Me too."

We had talked about nothing important, mostly me rehashing the last five months.

I missed his smile.

I missed his patience.

I missed everything about him.

But as much as I enjoyed the reprieve, time ran short. To take more would cross the line from selfish to cruel. "We can't let them keep attacking Empyrean."

The finger skimming over my shoulder stilled. "There's nothing we can do to help."

"We need to talk to the other Wardens, cause a stir, pick a fight. Get their focus off Teenesee's world."

"We'd need an army. Otherwise it'd be suicide."

"It's my fault. If I hadn't–"

"No, stop. Stop, okay?"

Silence followed. Guilt wanted to keep arguing the point, but that wouldn't solve any problems

He was right about the army, though. Not a thing I could do to keep an entire dimension from massacring innocent people. Farren and Jake? That's all I had, really, besides Wilma. And she was pretty busy at the moment. Shit. Maybe– "I got it!" I jumped up.

Tarek sat, giving me that wary look a jogger gives a growling dog. "What, exactly, do you got?"

I straightened my wrinkled T-shirt. "The list! The list, the list. That's what we'll do."

"You're going to have to dial down the crazy and explain yourself better."

Dial down the crazy? Not nice.

"Wilma gave me the list. You know. The list with all the names?"

He stared, his whole body tensing as he white-knuckled the edge of the bedframe.

"The list I wrote." I shook my head and paced the tight space. "I mean, the past me...the old me...whatever. The one with the symbol? It has a ton of names on it. All people who obviously had some issues. We find the people on that list, we have an army."

The wooden frame creaked before Tarek let go to fold his arms across his chest. "A couple problems with that plan, love."

Again, silence. *Ugh!* The pauses were not as endearing as I remembered.

I waited thirty seconds more. "Well?"

"First, someone needs to get the thing. Protectors are more than likely waiting at your place for you to show up." He raked a hand through his tangled hair. "And let's say by some miracle you get the list. How are we going to find people who have spent almost twenty years hiding from the Synod? If they can't find them, we don't have a shot."

"We have to try. That list is our one fighting chance."

He stood completely still, pursing his lips. No argument would work. I was right, and we both knew it. "Why do you have to go? We'll send Farren and Jake; tell them where to look."

Tarek putting my safety above everything...made me realize exactly what I had been doing. I put him above everyone, too, even getting excited when the notion of danger popped up, just so I could be with him. Danger, I might add, that landed on Teenesee's doorstep. This would be a perfect opportunity to prove to both Wilma and myself that I wasn't some selfish kid. I wanted to show her how much I did care about what others have done for me by returning the favor. "This isn't Jake's problem, and

Farren…yeah, he'll want to come, anyway. Has to so we can cross the lines. But I'm not a fragile doll, Tarek. I'm going."

His head dropped and his feet received all his attention. "I hate that I can't go with you."

I went to him, lifting his chin. "I love you. More than my own life, I love you. But don't make me resent how much you want me safe."

That did it. His cheeks sagged as he nodded. "Okay…I… Okay."

∞ ∞ ∞

Morning light hit us, and I awoke cramped and sweaty, Tarek's chest was definitely not as comfortable as my bed when shoving in a few hours of sleep. I pushed off his stomach and flopped to the floor like a fish on a boat to the background music of his laughter.

"Not funny." With a stretch, loud joint cracks followed. "Arrangements are gonna have to change if you want me to sleep over."

He adjusted to his side, smiling. "I do enjoy our sleepovers. Perhaps a bigger bed?"

I waved my hand around the room. "Ah, perhaps a bigger place so we can fit a bigger bed? Why build so small, ace?"

"Awful demanding, aren't you?" He threw a pillow, thwacking me on the side of my head. "And had I known I'd be with you again, I'd have built you an entire city."

"I don't need a city. Honestly, I don't need a bigger place. I need you." Smiling, I tucked the pillow under my head, enjoying the extra space on the hard, splintered floor. "But I'm surprised Wilma didn't kick your ass, sleeping in here."

He chuckled. "Surprising, yes. She wasn't so upset after I let her have the bed."

"Well, you're a regular gentleman." I closed my eyes, drumming fingers on my stomach.

Talking about Wilma had my mind wandering to Zander and shame washed over me. Last time I saw him he was unconscious with a nasty gash marring his temple. "Has Wilma talked to you at all? Let you know what's going on over there? Any news on Zander?"

Tarek stood, stretching as he cracked his neck. "Zander will live. And it seems things were quiet as of last night. I haven't heard from her since. I tried a couple times with no answer, typical when she's in a temper. But…the Protectors' energies weren't left, which means the attack was calculated." He paused, looking out the small window. "There had to be a nest of Guides somewhere, ready to take them back to Exemplar. In the past, whenever Exemplar had gone to war with another dimension, they made sure there were Guides, lots of them…"

"A nest?" I stayed on the floor, too comfortable to get up. But a thought niggled at my brain. "You think Exemplar is actually starting a war with Empyrean? Like an all-out…war?"

"Highly unlikely. It'd be a ballsy move. They probably brought a few Guides to make sure Empyrean didn't become any stronger than what it alrea–Oh, right. That's it!"

I pulled myself to my feet, his excitement making me nervous. "What?"

"Like you said, we pick a fight. If we can get those list people to fight with us, we'll use bait in other worlds to get the Synod to notice. They'll send an army if we cause a huge stir. We find the nest and kill the Guides. And then with the Warden's help, any Protectors we kill, their energy will stay in that dimension, make it stronger." His smile brightened. "*This* could be our way to close the lines. For good."

"You think that will work?"

He tugged at his hair, his eyes wild and shining. "If we make other dimensions stronger than Exemplar, they won't be able to do anything but leave everyone alone, starting with Empyrean."

Crazy plan–reaching, really–but it sounded better than the nothing we had at the moment. "Well, let's get the list."

He folded me into his arms, his face bright. "There might be an end to this."

"Tarek…when it's all over, I'm staying here."

His arms tightened. "You can't. Arcus is too–"

"If we can make other dimensions stronger, we can do the same to Arcus."

He kissed the top of my head. "I like the way you think."

The squid disagreed. Their squealing symphony so high it made my eardrums sting.

Tarek shoved past me on his way to the door. "Stay here."

Nope! I ran up right behind him.

"Damn it, Lena." But obviously, whatever riled up the squid was more important than me listening because he kept moving.

The screeching pierced my ears as we raced for the castle, following the squid as they swung with speed I had never witnessed from tree to tree. But when the forest's edge came into view, I ignored the ear pain and moved faster.

"Belva!"

Where the blue ice met the rich soil, my best friend stood, reaching out to one of those gigantic pink abominations. A thick trunk slithered from a tree, meeting her hand with a gentle stroke while squid perched in the closest trees looked as though they bowed their heads–the queen and her court. Tarek and I stopped, with me slamming into his back, when the animal touching Belva's hand let another tentacle escape the tree to nuzzle her cheek.

"What the hell?" I had a hard time closing my gaping jaw. The scene looked innocent, sweet. I almost forgot how deadly the things were.

"I have no idea." Tarek groped for my hand, holding so tight my knuckles clenched together, and moved forward, slow and cautious.

The squid didn't acknowledge us, their focus solely on Belva petting their pink, squishy friend. When we got close enough, I let go of Tarek, ducking underneath the amorous squid's limb, and touched Belva's shoulder. "Hey, pal. Ah, what're you doing?"

Her smile had the animal audience making purring noises as her admirer's tentacle played with her lips. "Making new friends, apparently."

I shot Tarek a raised eyebrow, and he gave me a weak shrug. Clearing my throat, I said, "Why don't we go inside, okay? Let these guys, ah, get back to whatever it is they…do."

When Belva sighed and her smile disappeared, the animals whined like toddlers. Taking a step back, she waved a hand in the air, motioning in the direction of the woods. With muted grumbles, the squid all retreated in unison, scaling their tree trunks and climbing deeper into the verdant, thick leaves.

Tarek stomped a path to the castle, shaking his head while I grabbed Belva's hand, her face flushed and breathtaking.

"How'd you do that?" I pulled her up the icy path, hoping none of those things followed.

"I...I don't know."

Laughing, I bumped her shoulder with mine. "You're the goddamned squid whisperer."

Lynn Vroman

CHAPTER 16

LENA

TROUBLE AT HOME

"No, Lena. Not happening." Jake stomped back and forth by the fire, the blanket he had wrapped around him thrown on the floor.

"It's all we got right now, Jake." I switched attention to Farren, who sat next to Mom and Belva on the couch. After we told him about Belva's little animal show, he couldn't stop gazing at her, his reddened face full of awe. I nudged Farren's shoulder. "You okay with it?"

With what looked like effort, he peeled his eyes away from Belva's face. "Yeah, I'm game. In and out, I'm good at that."

Belva's hand went to his leg and squeezed. She frowned, but kept quiet.

Farren leaned forward, his big palm covering her hand, and pointed his eyes at Jake. "I'll take care of her, old man. She'll be fine."

"I can't… It's not safe." Jake knelt down in front of Mom. "Jacie, we can't let her. She's just a girl."

Tarek came up behind me, putting his hands on my shoulders. "No, she isn't."

That he had my back, even when I knew he was scared, swelled my heart. But Jake ignored him, keeping his attention on Mom. "Jacie?"

Her eyes filled as a shaky hand cupped his cheek. "Lena hasn't been *just a girl* since she was five years old. I believe in her." She lifted her eyes to mine. "You come back, Lena. Come back."

"I will, promise." I turned into Tarek's arms. "Thank you."

He hugged me close, and whispered, "If anything happens, if they hurt you, they'll pay."

∞ ∞ ∞

Farren opened a portal in the theater, bringing us right into the kitchen. The lights were all off and the only sounds keeping us company were the humming coolers. Still, I felt the need to whisper. "The kitchen? Really?"

"Did you have somewhere else in mind? A resort, maybe? Disney World?"

"Shut up." I left his arms to look out the tiny window on the door. "Oh, damn."

"What?" Farren came up behind me, breathing down my neck. "Oh…damn."

The lobby sat bare, nothing off. Nope, except for the yellow police tape glaring at us through the glass doors in the main entrance.

Farren cleared his throat. "We got problems."

"No kidding." I backed away from the door and went for the coolers. "Want a drink?"

With a shrug, he opened the cooler himself, picking up a Coke. We stood there, drinking soda, studying the blinking light inside the cooler.

"Need to get that fixed," he said.

"Yeah, I'll add it to the list."

Farren grunted, throwing his empty bottle into the recyclable bin. After a loud, obnoxious burp, he went back to the door, peering through the window. "Police involved isn't a good sign."

"I would say it's not." I threw my own empty in the can and went to stand beside him. "Time to figure out what's going on."

He nodded. "We need to get the paper."

Really? Man, even in a crisis. "You think now's the time to read the latest headlines."

"Yeah, especially if we're a part of them."

Oh. "Point made." I glanced at the digital clock on the wall–3:00 a.m. Arcus time definitely didn't coincide with Earth's. "There's a Quicky Mart open twenty-four hours down the street."

"Looks like that's where we're headed. But we need to stay off the sidewalks, in case…"

"In case of what?"

He smiled, challenge lighting his dark eyes. "Use your big brain, Lena. Figure it out."

I thought for a second, and then…police, crime… "Right, good idea."

"I'm full of them."

"You're full of something all right."

I grabbed the spare keys to my place from the office before sneaking out the front doors and into the humid night. Farren led the way using side streets and backyards until we made it to the bright beacon that was the Quicky Mart. A brilliant red sign claiming they sold cigarettes at the state minimum graced the window.

One thing I hated about these little places? The damn music piped into the speakers. All the elevator music did was encourage me to leave fast, which was probably the goal. The bright, fluorescent lights put me in a good mood, though. "Ginger, I'm thinking clown, maybe Bozo?" I pointed to a security mirror, and Farren's eyes followed my finger.

The Arcus color wasn't as kind to his red hair and fair skin as it was to me. I looked good after a dose of Arcus– not conceit, a fact. The first time, when my bed had pulled me into the dimension, I came back looking like an amplified cover girl. First time I had unwanted attention, too. Of course, it faded, which I prefer.

Farren had no problem with his new face and laughed at his reflection, his cheeks flaming red on skin so white the blue veins underneath looked like the thin, squiggly lines on a road map. "Now, *I* can make this work." He rubbed his chin.

"Yeah? In what world, Dracula?"

Eyes so dark they were black, he'd definitely pull it off. Well, he could pass for Dracula's redheaded stepbrother. "I'll still have the ladies drooling. Bet?"

I went to the newsstand and grabbed yesterday's *Pocono Record*. "Imma pass, thanks." I held up the front page. "Shit. Besides, I think catching attention for you right now isn't a good idea."

Farren's picture, the one I gave Belva of him in the ring looking dangerous and mean, smeared the front cover with the byline: Wanted for Kidnapping and Possible Homicide.

"Oh…oh, yeah, that's not good." He snatched the paper from my hands, giving the bored cashier a quick glance before skimming the article. "Looks like Belva's parents think I'm some sort of raping kidnapper. And…goddamnit, a body was found at your place."

I grabbed him by the elbow and charged out of the store, the tinkling bell on the door sounding like an angry rattle. "Whose body?"

As we walked, he kept his eyes down. "Don't know. They didn't give a name. But…you and your mom are wanted for questioning." He switched directions. "Jake too."

"Where're we going?"

"Well, we can't go to your house."

"Obviously."

"And so I guess we'll do a B and E into Wilma's, come up with a plan."

"Sounds good."

We cut across backyards, the single alarm to our invasion a few yappy dogs. As we slunk up to the back window of her house, we both scanned the inside, making sure everything looked normal. When Wilma's living room appeared as dull and quiet as usual, Farren took off his shirt and wrapped it around his fist. "Back up a sec."

I moved behind him as he jabbed the old window, the sound partially muffled by his T-shirt. With a grunt and a wave, he gestured me forward. It didn't take much for him to heave me into the shattered window. I landed on my ass and rolled in time to miss his boots on my face. "Damn, easy, Ginger."

"Gotta be quicker." He stomped by me and headed to the television. For the short stint Farren lived with Wilma, he managed to get the cable turned on. She hated it, but never got around to shutting it off.

Thank God, she didn't because as soon as he turned to a local channel, our faces smeared the screen.

∞ ∞ ∞

From an earlier recording, we watched Belva's mom cry into her husband's shoulder in front of their multimillion-dollar Tudor. Her dad's face was pale with deep, saggy bags under his eyes, which added to his scary words about the big, mean-looking redhead who spent too much time sniffing around his innocent daughter. Oh, and he mentioned the low-life trailer scum she began hanging around. All us trash were in on some terrible kidnapping murder spree with Belva being taken hostage. In seconds, the story shifted to an unknown man's body stripped naked and cuffed to the old radiator underneath my living room window.

Belva's parents didn't surprise me at all. They had made sure I understood Belva's association with me wasn't acceptable. On more than one occasion, I made sure they knew I didn't give a shit. But the guy... "Well, who the fuck is that?"

Farren shook his bright red head as he sat on the edge of the couch. His black eyes grew so hard and cold, I'd definitely mistake him for a vampire if I ran into him on the street. "A decoy."

"Ah...what?"

He lowered his head before turning to face me again. "Deee-Coooy."

Nuh-uh. Nope. "Don't." I punched him in the shoulder.

He brushed it off like a mosquito bite and stood. "Remember how I said the authority found ways to make Protectors pay? Well, I just got paid." He dragged a hand through his hair and shut off the television. "My face all over the news, that's what they want. If I ever came back here–which, ha, I did–I'd be on the Most Wanted. Guarantee my DNA is all over that guy. I get busted, sent to jail, and well, I can't exactly open a hole around people, right? I'm stuck in prison. Spend my life there if I'm lucky. Or maybe one night, I have a visitor who finds it necessary to gut me and have my energy destroyed."

I laughed. Couldn't help it. Talk about conspiracy theory. His serious face caused my laughter to dry up, though.

"Not funny, Lena. Not funny at all."

I tilted my head, keeping my butt planted on the couch. "Oh, come on! You really believe that? Besides, who the hell would think of doing something that...that psychotic?"

"Me. It was my MO. My specialty, you might say. Varies with each dimension, but the concept stays the same."

My insides grew cold.

He made eye contact for a second before staring at his booted feet. "Not so funny, huh? When I told you about all those faces that haunt me? There was a time I had no trouble sleeping. Targets, that's all they were. And the innocent casualties? Part of the job."

Farren. Funny, sensitive, awesome-friend Farren, a cold-blooded killer. I swallowed. "So, who do you think that guy was?"

A deep sigh wracked his body. "Some poor dumb bastard in the wrong place at the wrong time."

I swallowed again, or at least tried to. My throat felt like I had an active beehive lodged in it. No, I wouldn't admit a strong pull of fear tightened the knot in my stomach. So, Farren was a sociopath... No, no he wasn't– not anymore. God, I hoped not anymore. "Well, um, I guess we need to be careful."

He looked up, and the hurt tightening his cheeks made my heart lurch. Definitely not anymore.

"You're afraid of me," he said.

I went to him and wrapped my arms around his waist. No, he was my brother. Because we didn't share the same blood meant nothing. "I'm not afraid of you. Afraid for you is more like it."

His body shuttered as his arms slipped across my shoulders, holding me tight. "Glad I have you, kid."

"Not a kid, but right back at you."

Farren rubbed my upper arms with a loud half-yell, half-groan. "Ah, okay, enough with the sappy. I'm not good at it." He headed to the bathroom. "Where's the list, anyway? And don't say–"

"In my bedroom, under my mattress."

"Yeah, don't say that." He turned the knob and shut the door behind him.

I stalked up to the door and banged on it.

"*What?*"

"Why can't you open a hole in my room?"

His groan was louder than the pee hitting the toilet bowl.

"What? I mean that's the easiest way, right?"

After the toilet flushed and the water stopped tinkling from the sink, he opened the door a crack and peeked through. "How many times do I have to tell you? We can't open a portal to jump into a portal in the same dimension. It's physics."

If he didn't stop talking to me as if I were slow, I'd have to rearrange his handsome face. "Okay, you've never explained it and why didn't you take us to my room in the first place?"

He stalked to his old room where he still kept a lot of his stuff. "Because I didn't want to chance a Protector waiting for us there."

"Did you ever think they might be waiting at the theater or here?"

"They'd be dumb to wait here. No one wants to go against Wilma in a one-on-one, and… I guess I didn't think it through all that great."

I crossed my arms, the sweat and grime from the stay in Arcus mixing with the summer heat of the mountain. The feeling crawled under my skin. A shower was a must, even if I had to change back into these clothes. At least I could wear one of Wilma's shirts.

When I didn't say anything, he shrugged. "Hey, I'm not used to being on the other side. Give me some credit."

"We don't have room for mistakes, agreed? Think things through from now on, Ging–damn! What're you doing?"

He unbuttoned his jeans and pushed them down his hips. "If you don't get out, you're getting a show."

I covered my eyes and pulled the door shut. "You're a pig."

His laugh echoed through the door. "And you're annoying."

Touché.

∞ ∞ ∞

As far as plans went, ours sucked. All we needed were five minutes to get in and out. Unfortunately, Farren spotted the two unmarked police cruisers sitting near my driveway. I highly doubted they'd be nice enough to let us attempt to save the universe by giving a blind eye.

Okay, maybe that sounded dramatic. A little. Their lives wouldn't be too affected. This life, anyway. They'd thank us if they knew there was a solid chance they could spend the next few lives as a squid in Arcus or worse in another place.

Whatever. That didn't matter now. The list did.

The plan involved diversion. A small fire–actually, a big one was the first option. Farren wanted to torch the theater, said Jake would understand. I disagreed. The place had more memories in it than the Smithsonian. At least it did for Jake. If all went right, Wilma could persuade local law enforcement and Belva's parents to forget the dead body and kidnapping thing. Didn't give justice to the poor guy chained to the radiator, but we'd take care of revenge for him. I wished we had his name. The first casualty in the attack on Earth and no one even knew it.

"Hey, dream girl. You want to get out of your head and join me for a second?" Farren's terse whisper was as gentle as his jab to my shoulder.

I squatted lower next to the neighbor's porch across the street from mine. "Sorry."

"All right, listen. I'm going to backtrack, get closer to the car." A red sedan parked a block from my doorstep was our unfortunate target. "As soon as the thing goes poof and those bastards take off, you get in, get the list, and get the hell out, understand?"

"Yeah, yeah, I got it. Make sure you disappear before they make it to the car."

His amped-up face scrunched into a wounded stare. "Where's the faith, kid?"

"Calling me a kid when you look exactly the same age sounds stupid, Ginger. Can you even grow a beard, yet?" Mostly because I hated to swell his head, I grudgingly added, "I do have faith in you."

"Hey, no need to get salty because I age better." He squeezed my knee. "And thanks."

"Whatever." I snuck a glance at the closest unmarked. One cop poured something from a thermos while the other read the paper. The guy in the driver's seat had to be about fifty and that many pounds overweight, but the one in the passenger seat sipping his drink looked to be about twenty-five and completely in love with being a cop. All muscle and buzz cut, like he spent his free time watching *Cops* reruns and *NCIS*. I hoped the two in the car farther down the street resembled frumpy cop. It'd be easier to get away if the blow-up routine didn't work. "Do you feel any Protectors?"

"Not from here." He scrubbed his hair, tension tightening the skin around his eyes. "Shit. Okay, new plan. I'll backtrack farther, take a trip behind your place, and if I feel anything, I'll let you know."

"How?"

He laughed, shaking his head. "If somebody's there, you'll know. Trust me."

When he went to leave, I grabbed his forearm. "Wait a second."

Concern etched his brow. "What?"

His face, the Arcus color making him look deceptively deadly, twisted my heart. If anything happened to him… "Don't get killed, okay?"

He squeezed my hand with a grunt, his eyes going to my house. "You can't get rid of me that easy, kid."

"Promise?"

Farren didn't answer, his jaw developing a tic.

"Farren, you promise? Promise me, right now."

His eyes found mine, emotion swimming in his dark eyes. "I will if you will."

My arms snaked around his neck, the weight of what we were doing finally sinking in. "Deal."

"Get in, get out. Easy peasy." He pulled away and scanned the street one more time. "If anything does happen, you need to stay strong. We have to end this shit, with or without me."

"I get it, really." Maybe I did, but if anything did happen, I didn't know if… It was a lot to ask, giving up the guy who slid so easily into the role of my brother. Not to mention it'd kill Belva. "Remember: I have faith in you."

Farren tapped his temple with a grin. "Got it right here." He rubbed his hands together. His face shined with excitement, like that same enthusiasm most guys have on football Sunday.

So not right in the head, but whatever. I'd rather him be excited about possible chaos. Shaky knees and skittish nerves would get us killed.

After a wink, he faded into the shadows, careful to avoid the streetlights. The sidewalks had a few stragglers, most looking a bit wobbly as they tumbled from a house a few yards down. I guess the cops didn't give a shit that a raging party with a few people I recognized from my graduating class was in full motion. Under-agers and public intoxication wasn't as important as a dead body and kidnapped girl.

I kept my focus on Farren as he waited for the few people to trundle off, talking way too loudly into their phones. For a big guy, he moved stealthily. If I weren't paying attention to his every move, I would've missed him. A glance in the direction of Frumpy and Robocop allayed any worries. Neither one perked up with a glance in Farren's direction.

When he disappeared behind my house, tension tightened my shoulders. The longest five minutes ever ticked by. Finally, I spotted Farren's red hair in the first hints of dawn's sky. He sided up against the house next to mine, giving a quick thumbs-up in my direction. His white smile flashed in the shadows, causing me to roll my eyes even as I relaxed with a long exhale. I understood courage. What I had a problem with was the crazy.

Farren pulled the hose from his back pocket and took off for the car. He swore our archaic crap could blow up fine with a hose and a match. Something about the stupidity of gas in combination with machinery. Solar power, he always said, gave enough energy to run everything without a flammable liquid.

As long as I saw a street-side bonfire, he could light the damn thing any way he wanted.

When he disappeared, I got ready to run. Track helped my speed–it also helped me take off at a moment's notice. Wilma's shirt ballooned around me, and so I tucked in the edges until the ends peeked through the leg holes of my dirty jean shorts. No need to have a parachute slowing me down. My concentration stayed on the car parked by my doorstep, house key held pointed and ready in my right hand. Frumpy and Robo looked to be in a heated conversation with the younger cop's hands waving while the older shook his head and kept his eyes on the paper. Mount Pocono's finest at its best.

The blast came quick, as if Farren had pre-soaked the car before siphoning out the tank and lighting the match. The cops jumped, Robo's flailing hands smacking Frump in the face while his paper smashed against the window. In seconds, sirens blared and the car skidded, making a U-turn with expertise. A quick glance at the second unmarked showed them doing the same thing.

I was off. Though I pumped my legs as fast as I could, dreamy slow motion plagued me the thirty yards to my house and around the back to the stairs leading to my kitchen door. I skipped steps, leaping more than climbing, and stuck the key in the lock. A twist and a push and I was in, heading straight for my bedroom. I refused to look at the chalk outline on the floor by the living room radiator. Acknowledging the dead guy made his sacrifice too real.

The house looked like a rave party took place. Furniture lay busted and scattered all over, the door to my mom's room dangled from its hinges, and my room wasn't any better.

Trying to remember the place wasn't important, even though it represented the freedom Mom and I fought for, I pushed through the rubble to get into my room. A snort escaped when my eyes fell on the tipped mattress. Did I say the list hid under my mattress? Correction. It hid *inside*, sewn in to be exact. Home Ec taught me a little.

Whoever decided to give our place the hurricane treatment didn't get what I needed, thankfully. I ran into the kitchen and grabbed a steak knife off the floor. Wasting no time, I stabbed the memory foam, digging in the blade until papers crinkled. The knife dropped to the carpet as I felt for the thick, folded notes. I tugged the yellowing stack free before finding my bag and shoving it in. I then went to my closet and searched my little hidey-hole, covered by some loose drywall the same blue as my walls.

"Yes!"

All the money I had saved for college and my ID were still there. At least I had that. My phone was nowhere in sight. I threw what I had in my bag, along with some clothes, and went to the living room window, forcing myself to stand in the dead guy's outline. Still no sign of any cops near my place, but a few were racing toward the show, along with a couple fire trucks. Turning on my heel, I went to the back door, flew down the stairs to our designated meeting spot, and waited.

And waited.

Waited some more.

Night disappeared completely and dawn snuck in to spoil our cover. If Farren didn't show in the next few minutes, the sun he swore by would give us away. As all the bad ideas crept into my brain, from him blowing up with the car to getting arrested by Frump, his red head bounced in my view. Relief brought me to my knees, my only cover the bush beside the local bank's ATM. When he caught my eye, his smile stretched wide and his gait turned into a cocky saunter. Shaking my head, I stood to meet him.

Before I could take a step, Farren stopped, a hand going to his head.

Shit. *Shit!*

The unmarked that wasn't by my house, squealed to a stop, not three feet away from Farren. Impressive, seeing as how Farren stood in a backyard, complete with an herb garden and swing set.

Over the din of the sirens, Farren waved his hand, and mouthed, *Go to Wilma's.*

I threw my bag into the bush and went to stand by his side.

He wasn't having it, shoving me hard toward the bank. "Don't be fucking stupid."

"I'm not leaving you."

Two men left the car, doors staying wide open, and approached us, interrupting our argument. Both had smirks on their plastic-looking faces. Before I had a chance to get into the fight, Farren charged both with one of those war cries heard in movies involving angry Highlanders.

The noise surprised the two Protectors for seconds. But seconds were all Farren needed. Holding his arms wide, he clotheslined both in their necks. They dropped, but jumped right back up, double-teaming him.

I raced to one, kicking him behind the knee before smashing my elbow in his back. He screeched, rolling off Farren, who got busy bashing the face of the other one he managed to hold under his weight.

My guy wasn't done, either. He stumbled to his feet and charged me. Before he could tackle my ass to the ground, Farren grabbed the guy's ankles, which unfortunately helped free his target. "Run!"

I still didn't want to listen, especially when both guys pounced on him, giving Farren a proper beating. Feeling desperate, though, I ran. Ran until I made it to the fire–and to all the cops standing around said fire. I had to hold the edge of my T-shirt against my face, the smoke invading my lungs and stinging my eyes. "Help! That guy from TV's beating up two cops!"

At least five cops turned in my direction, including Frumpy and Robo. When they didn't move, I repeated, "The guy. From TV. Is. Beating up. Two cops."

They finally sprang into action, following me as I took them to Farren. Right as we got there, one Protector had his arm raised about to open his fist, while his other arm curled around Farren's neck.

"No!" I ran, prepared to tackle the bastard, when hands cinched my waist.

Five of the four cops approached Farren, their guns raised. One said something like "freeze," while the two faux cops fumbled for the cuffs hooked to their belts, shifting into their roles. "We have him subdued. Lower your weapons."

Obviously, the Protectors didn't have persuasion talents because Robo moved forward, gun still drawn. He jumped on Farren's back, now three guys "subduing" him, as Ginger's surprised face found mine. He didn't struggle, though, just put his hands behind his back, doing everything the cop told him to do. The chaos continued, the cop holding me letting go to help.

Once they all had him on his feet, Farren, my brother, looked my way with a subtle nod aimed at the alley by the bank. I snuck away walking backward into the shadows, grabbing my bag before taking off to Wilma's.

Now all I had to do was figure out how to bust Farren out of jail.

Easy peasy. Yeah, right.

CHAPTER 17

LENA

WINSTON

Once I crawled through Wilma's window, I threw my pack on the couch and...paced for a while. My nails received a rough manicure, thanks to all the chewing, while I became an expert at convincing myself we were all fucked.

What other choice did I have? Farren getting arrested was a lot better than those assholes taking him to Exemplar for... I couldn't even think about it. Some time in a jail here would have a more positive outcome than an energy annihilation there. But how the hell would I get him out? I wasn't James Bond, for Christ's sakes.

If Wilma would pop in this minute... I looked up.

Come on down, you're the next contestant...

Crap, I was pretty damn close to losing it.

By the time six rolled around, I flicked on the television to scout the morning news. The fire was the main story, and so was Farren's arrest. The footage they had of him walking from the station and getting into the back of a police car made him look like a deranged killer. Arcus color highlighting his face and being five or six inches taller than everybody around him had a lot to do with it.

Farren didn't give them his real name, either. Even though my nerves were raw, or maybe because of it, when the anchor lady said, "A man claiming to be, 'Magically Delicious,' had no identification. Authorities are trying to find his true identity, though no fingerprints are on record..." I laughed until the tears rolled.

Silly Ginger.

Now what...now what...now what...?

I wished a *Break out of Jail for Dummies* book existed. It'd make things so much–

Lena.

Tarek. I concentrated on his voice, letting it calm me.

Things are worse than we thought.

That didn't calm me at all.

Avery sent Nicolette with a message. Pause. *Exemplar is definitely starting a war, beginning with Empyrean. Cassondra won't stop until Teenesee is dead and the dimension is under Exemplian control. We need those people. Now.*

Oh. My. God. Guess Exemplar was pretty fucking ballsy.

*Avery said...*Silence. *She said to look for Winston Candell. He's there in Earth.* Another pause. *Living in the same area as you.*

"Okay...and...?" I yelled at Tarek's voice. Inside my head. His stupid pauses...

Contact him by text. He gave the number. *She said to tell him the favor is due.*

Well, now all I had to do was get my hands on a goddamn cell. Shit. Walmart, here I come.

Have Farren approach him. Winston...he's... A heavy sigh. *He's dangerous, strong. A notorious Protector known for his...dislike of anything Exemplian. But he owes Avery. She said he might know where some of those people are. Be careful. I love you.*

I hopped off the couch and exchanged Wilma's shirt for my own, changing my shorts too. It took five minutes to leave the house, ball cap low over my face to avoid any chance of recognition. As I headed to the bus stop, a plan formed.

Winston Candell might be dangerous, but he'd help free Farren. Whether he wanted to or not.

∞ ∞ ∞

I set up the phone and punched in the minute card numbers during the bus trip back into town. Once the bus stopped at the drop-off, I rushed to the doors, annoyed by some lady taking her sweet-ass time, giving the driver a lecture on how to avoid potholes with each step downward. When I finally made it out into the hot, sweaty morning, my temper was ready to explode. The woman's lecture was futile. Trying to avoid potholes in PA was like trying to avoid breathing. And she cost me another five minutes.

Despite the heat and hunger nagging me, I didn't stop until I hit Wilma's front door. After pulling Winston's number from memory, I texted him the message and set the cell next to a bowl of fake apples in the kitchen. The guy would probably take forever. I'd text him again after I got something to eat. Hopefully, Wilma had some real food and not that nasty–

The phone vibrated on the beige laminate counter.

Holy shit.

All the anxiousness built up waiting for the reply turned to hesitation. What if the guy was a dick? Worse, what if he decided to kill me for my guilt-by-association status with Exemplar?

Then I thought of Farren and nothing else mattered.

I reached for the phone, not really sure what to expect, but a quick, *Martin's Convenience 15 min,* wasn't it.

No, *who is this?* Or, *how'd you get my number?*

Whatever.

I grabbed my stuff, along with a snack cake, and went to meet him.

It took about ten minutes to walk to Martin's. The parking lot teamed with activity, being the closest convenience store to the biggest water park in the northeast. People in all stages of dress pushed in and out the doors, some wearing skimpy swimming suits and flip-flops. And *some* people should've really considered throwing on a couple more layers of clothes, especially a particularly hairy guy in too-tight trunks.

A few people hung out in front, an older couple making out, some kids asking a few people to buy them cigarettes, and a guy with dreadlocks slouching against the brick wall, earbuds planted in his ears. Not knowing what else to do, I leaned on the wall about six feet from Dreads and waited. I wasn't sure what to look for, but from what Tarek fed my brain this morning, I pictured someone as big as him. Easy to spot. Next overly muscled guy who came through, I'd give him a nod…or something. A thumbs-up? I pulled out the phone. Maybe asking the guy what he looked like would help.

I texted him the question and slumped to my butt, keeping an eye open for any Protector-like people. Finally, a big guy with an Abercrombie body sauntered toward the door. That had to be him. I had no clue why he'd come wearing swimming trunks, but maybe he thought it wise to blend.

I stood, stretched my back, trying to act casual, and walked over. After a deep breath, I held out my hand. "I think you're here for me."

His mouth formed a lopsided grin. "Am I?"

Cocky, annoying, too hot for his own good…yeah, I found my guy. "Look, let's skip the whole horse and pony, okay? Come on. I have a place."

His smile widened. "Damn, I do love the Poconos." He moved into my personal space and traced a finger down my shoulder until he held my hand in his. "All I got is a fifty. You okay with that?"

I backed up, yanking my hand from his grasp. "Wait. What?"

"All right, seventy-five, but I'm talking full access to–"

"Save it, asshole." Okay, so I picked the wrong guy. "I was mistaken."

He came closer. "A hundred, that's all I can offer, baby." This time when he went to touch me, I grabbed his hand, bending his fingers until I heard a crack, and kicked out his knee. After fighting Farren for months, this guy was like beating up my grandmother.

He lay on the ground, moaning and whining about how expensive whores were here. I knelt beside him, making sure to keep my voice at a whisper. "This is what you're gonna do, tough guy. Get up, stop acting like a pussy, and be on your way." When he stayed put, I bunched his silky, sun-bleached hair in my fist to assist him.

"Ouch! Stop, you're hurting me!" He pulled away, his voice shrill as spit gathered at the corners of his mouth.

I swear the guy had tears pooling in his eyes. Definitely not Protector material.

"Go on now, Ken, get back in that fancy car. We don't want no trouble, you heard?" Dreads came up behind me, his voice like a melody. Almost hypnotizing.

The wuss-bag must've found it hypnotizing, too, because he limped back to his Mustang. Just like that. No argument. Stumbled away like he hadn't been beaten up by a girl.

I turned to face Dreads, my want to tell him to butt out and the inherent need to be polite warring with each other. "Ah, thanks, man. Appreciate it."

He nodded, a small smile lighting his dark face. I gave a half-hearted wave and steered around him into the store, needing a drink. The smell of chlorine mingling with body odor polluted every air particle in the place. I'd always hated how people thought swimming in chemically treated pools gave them permission to skip the showers.

I grabbed a water from the cooler, pissed off. Seriously, fuming. Not only did some dick mistake me for a hooker, but also Winston didn't bother showing up. A thought hit me: *If you don't come back, I'll make them pay*...

The bastard better show because I wasn't going back without Farren. Hell, I couldn't.

I went to stand in the checkout line. Dreads walked in and headed to the coolers, grabbing a soda.

Damn, his arms...more than his arms. Tattoos painted every part of exposed skin. They were beautiful, like a masterpiece on flesh. He came up to stand in line and caught me staring. I swung around, heat creeping up my neck.

He stood so close the beats from his earbuds vibrated off my back. I should've been annoyed, but he smelled so good, unlike the sweaty chlorine people from the park. No, he smelled like ocean and coconuts. Yet when he took another step, making it impossible to move without touching him, I'd had enough. His cool tattoos and pretty smell no longer gave him a pass.

I turned. "Hey, I said thanks. That's all you're getting from me."

He still had that closed-mouth grin on his face as he bobbed his head in time with the music streaming in his ears. I doubted he could hear, and so I whipped back around, muttering creative names under my breath. Language I mastered thanks to listening to Wilma's sharp tongue.

Four people still waited ahead of me in line. *Damn it.* For every step I took forward, Dreads was right behind me, saying nothing, while listening to his music.

I had faced giant squid, angry Protectors, a fucking Warden. This guy... He wasn't gonna get away with...whatever the hell he was trying to do.

I circled around on him again. "Backup, asshole."

He tilted his head, staring at me with dark eyes so ancient they defied his young face.

"Do we have a problem?"

With pursed lips, he shook his head. Even over the blaring music, he could hear me, which meant he probably heard every nasty thing I muttered. Good.

I tightened my hold on my bag strap. If the guy wanted money, he wasn't getting it from me. Nope, I'd be keeping my stuff today. He was a lot smaller than Abercrombie and my height. I could take him.

But in that moment, that second, I learned the size-doesn't-matter lesson.

"Even with all the shit you been through, you still gravitate toward stereotypes." He *tsked*, wagging a finger. "Shame."

My face went numb. "Huh?"

I think you're here for me.

His lips never moved, but his smooth voice blared in my brain, repeating the same thing I had said to muscle boy.

Oh, crap. I swallowed. "Winston?"

He nodded, never bothering to take out the earbuds.

My mouth opened and closed like a guppy's, trying to spit out an apology, something confident to say, but Tarek's warning, *let Farren approach him*, rang in my ears. I didn't give a shit about that warning when I thought Abercrombie was the Protector, but this guy. This guy...

"Next!"

The cashier's loud voice drummed into my head, not really registering.

"Um, kid? You're next."

I switched my attention to the counter, my legs like rubber. "I'm not a kid."

"Whatever. That it?" He pointed to the water bottle clutched in my hands.

"Ah, yes?"

"It's not a trick question. A buck five." He held out his fleshy palm.

One hand released the bottle long enough to dig out two dollars. When he went to hand over the change, I shook my head, not willing to let go of that damn bottle again. It was the only thing keeping my hands from shaking. "Keep it."

He threw the change in the red plastic penny container by the register. "Ain't you generous? Next."

When Winston began to leave, the cashier tried to reach over the counter. Good thing his fat belly prevented him from actually grabbing Winston's arm. "Hey, you paying for that?"

Ignoring him, Winston crooked his finger at me until I followed him to the door.

"Hey, buddy, you pay or I'm calling the cops." The poor guy's face blossomed into a bright tomato as he rounded the counter, the other customers staring on in surprise.

Winston sighed and aimed a hand at the struggling, heaving cashier. "Stop."

The guy froze.

"Now, I'd pay for this, but I'm a little short this week. Let's agree to an IOU."

The guy's eyes glazed over and his jaw slackened. It was the same look my dad and mom had when Mateusz used persuasion on them. "Yeah, sure, okay."

Winston turned his focus on all the other people, his blond-tipped dreads slipping over his shoulder. "Y'all go on about your business, all right?" When they gave him a glassy-eyed nod, he added, "And for the love of... Take a damn bath."

Holding my elbow, he guided me out the door.

I forgot all about nerves as soon as we left the store. The guy washed a few brains for a goddamn Mountain Dew. Not cool. I yanked my arm from his hand. "Why the hell didn't you pay for that? Christ, you turned a whole store into zombies for a soda."

He smiled as if he didn't give two shits–which he probably didn't. "Like I said, a bit short."

"A bit short?" Even though I yelled, annoyed by his apathetic attitude, I followed him when he sauntered across the parking lot, sipping on his pilfered soda. What other choice did I have? My moral compass wouldn't get Farren out of jail. "I'd have spotted you the cash."

He pulled out his buds and kept on walking until we reached a bright red crotch rocket. "Don't need your charity, Tainted."

My eyes grew so wide, I swear they were gonna roll onto the cement. The Tainted remark didn't bother me. I'd heard it enough in the past five months. But...my charity? Brainwashing a bunch a people was better than asking for a five-spot? I flailed my hand at the house of zombies. "But...those people...you...can't..."

"Yeah, I can."

I dug my fists into my hips, the water bottle cold against my skin. "You're... That's..."

He threw the half-full bottle into a trashcan lining the lot and unstrapped a helmet from the back of the bike.

Well that was a big slap in the face. "You didn't even finish it? You brainwashed people for a half bottle of soda."

That smile–no, it was a goddamn smirk–returned to his lips. I sputtered on for a few seconds longer while he watched, nodding his head...patronizing me. *Ass*. When I finally shut up, he handed over the helmet. "Put that on."

The black helmet might as well have had snakes slithering from the tinted visor. No way was I getting on that bike. I backed up a few steps, shaking my head. "Nope. Not a chance."

He jammed it on his head. "Suit yourself." He climbed on the bike and started the engine. "Get on."

"Ah, maybe you didn't understand me. I'm not getting on that thing."

His shoulders slumped as he shut down the engine. Leaning back, his feet braced on the ground to support the bike, he flipped up the visor. "If you don't get on the bike, I'm leaving you here."

The way he looked at me, as if he could see right inside. "I'm... I don't like motorcycles."

He kept staring, and if I didn't know better, I'd swear he actually succeeded in persuading me. As the seconds ticked by, my fear of the crotch-hugging rocket dwindled. In a slow, almost enchanting gesture, he slipped the helmet off his head and handed it to me.

When I still didn't accept it, too busy locked onto his ancient eyes, he said, "Been watching your latest activity on the news. Good job, by the way, going public this time." The helmet moved closer to my hands. "You need my help getting that Protector out of the clink, but if you don't come with me now, my offer's off the table, you heard?"

Really, I wanted to talk, but...*how the hell did he know me?*

The helmet somehow managed to find its way into my hands after I put the water in my bag and strapped it on my back.

"Good girl. I guarantee you got eyes on you everywhere. We need to ditch the tails, and we can't do that taking the bus."

The man had a point.

I put on the helmet and he kicked on the engine again. When the eye contact broke, I found my voice. "Don't kill me."

His chest vibrated with a laugh as I clenched his waist and held on for dear life. "I'll do my best."

We zipped through town, and indeed, a car followed our every turn. Winston didn't rush through traffic, though. He took his time, obeying all the traffic laws–until we hit the interstate ramp. As soon as we merged with traffic, my stomach dropped and I screamed. Or at least I tried to scream. The pressure from going a bazillion miles an hour gave me enough oxygen to squeak. I squeezed his waist so hard I had to wonder if Winston was still able to breathe. But he didn't slow down, especially when a silver Mercedes kept pace with us. He looked behind him before kicking the rocket into a higher gear.

Then we were flying. He ripped in and out of lanes with sharp, quick movements, his dreads hitting my helmet. I concentrated on that tapping sound so I wouldn't give in to the panic and do something crazy, like jump off. We passed a few police cruisers, but none zoomed out behind us. I'm sure Winston did some freaky mojo on them. Christ, he did it for a half-bottle of Mountain Dew. I don't know how long we were racing at that speed, but when we slowed down to hit an off-ramp, I almost cried with relief. My life flashed before me on I-80. Something I'd never forget. At least no Mercedes joined us.

When he drove into a restaurant and parked, I had trouble peeling myself from his back. To his credit, Winston didn't throw me off. He just pried my fingers from his waist and gestured to the side. "Go on, now."

I slid from the bike, stumbling as my tingling feet touched asphalt. Fried food smells coming from the diner didn't sit well in my stomach, which was somewhere near my tonsils. The helmet made my head too heavy, propelling me to the ground. I palmed the lot, trying to regain control of my breathing while on all fours. For the record, I didn't give a shit about how stupid I looked.

Not even when Winston laughed.

Okay, maybe a little when he laughed.

A little.

He squatted in front of me and unhooked the helmet's strap. Soon as the head coffin pulled free, gushes of air inflated my lungs. Even the sticky humidity felt cool and refreshing.

I stayed on the ground a minute longer, taking in greedy gulps of oxygen. No way did I look in Winston's direction. The smirk he probably had plastered on his face would've made my position more humiliating. Not until he moved to lean against his bike did I think to get up to find my self-respect.

Playing like the last five minutes never happened, I shrugged off my backpack and with unsteady hands, pulled out my water. After downing half, I screwed on the cap and looked around. "You plan on stealing lunch, too?"

He didn't answer, his attention glued on the diner's front doors.

Whatever. He could hate me all he wanted. As long as he helped me.

I sat in a patch of brown grass at the edge of the parking lot, the dead fauna scratching my thighs, and finished my water. If he got off hanging out in restaurant parking lots, so be it. The guy had the ability to persuade an entire store, and so persuading a few rent-a-guards who might accuse us of loitering shouldn't be a problem.

But our little parking lot powwow ended when a pretty Latina woman walked from the restaurant. She obviously worked there, seeing as most people who were smoking hot didn't walk around wearing black aprons and sensible shoes.

Winston stood, meeting her halfway. Her smile made her prettier when he picked her up in a hug while her arms captured his neck. After he kissed her, he leaned down to whisper in her ear. I watched the whole scene like it was Shakespeare in the park.

Freak, much? I felt like a peeping Tom. But how Winston, a hard ass from Exemplar who had no problem brainwashing for a soda, could make any woman smile confused the shit out of me.

Unfortunately, her smile disappeared when her eyes gravitated toward me the longer Winston whispered in her ear. She pulled back from his hold, her body movements telling me how unhappy my presence made her. When the woman stalked over, I hopped up on my feet. Whoever she turned out to be, I wasn't gonna let her take a swing at me. I set my bag on the ground and waited.

She was a few feet in front of me when the accusations flew. "Who are you?"

I wanted to sound like a bitch, at least a little intimidating, but her dark eyes were a lot more intense than Winston's. "Lena?"

She held her hands out, her whole body moving, reminding me of Jake when he got pissed. "What? You asking me who you are?"

I looked to Winston for some help. He stood behind her, arms crossed over his chest, saying nothing.

"Um…no?"

When she went on a tangent in Spanish, pointing her finger from me to Winston, I'd had enough. There were bigger things to worry about than a jealous girlfriend. I looked over her head–not hard, because she was five-foot-nothing–to glare at Winston. "Seriously? Can't you scr–"

"Take a lap, Tainted."

What? When I didn't move–my ears assaulted with what were probably not very nice Spanish words–he nodded toward the back of the restaurant, near the dumpsters.

"You want me to...what?"

"Gone on, now. Don't come back until I give you the signal."

"The signal?"

This signal. Now leave.

Damn. His voice sounded a little more aggressive inside my head. I didn't want to stick around, anyway. "Fine. Whatever."

I snatched up my bag and made sure to swing wide, away from the now quiet, seething girlfriend.

The loud vent fans from the restaurant didn't mask the yelling near the crotch rocket, no matter how far I walked behind the building. The woman was pissed. Christ, jealousy annoyed me. *If she could see my giant, she'd–*

Damn, even my thoughts made me sound thirteen.

All for you, Farren. And I'm gonna kick your ginger ass as soon as we get you out.

I endured the rotting smell of food and dirty dumpsters for fifteen long-ass minutes while I, and everyone else within a fifty-foot radius, heard Winston get his balls handed to him. When squealing tire sounds ricocheted off the rusted, metal garbage bins and the yelling died down, I figured I'd get my signal. Another twenty minutes passed before *come on back* echoed through my head. No aggression laced his voice, only defeat.

That didn't stop me from taking my time. I circled around, going the long way until his bike revved. Then I ran, afraid he might leave me. Maybe save that payback for a better time.

I made it to his side, and he handed over the helmet, not bothering to look up. Before I pushed the thing back on for another terror-filled ride through the mountains, I had to ask the burning question. "Why don't you scrub her mind?"

He glanced up, the hard edges of his face softening. "Because I love her."

Oh...oh, wow.

Respect blossomed in my chest. Every crap thing he'd done up to that point forgiven. I hopped on behind him. "Try going for just eighty this time. I don't like having my stomach in my throat."

Winston's shoulders relaxed some as he started the engine. "I'll think about it."

Lynn Vroman

CHAPTER 18

LENA

JAIL BREAK

We raced over more back roads than I knew existed, twisty roads with steep hills that dropped off in an instant.

On a red crotch rocket doing at least sixty.

By the time we turned into a driveway belonging to a gothic house under obvious construction, I didn't give a shit if Uncle Fester came out or bats flew from the windows. Whatever waited in the old place would be ten times better than taking another suicide trip on the back of a motorcycle.

We didn't stop in the driveway. That would've been too rational. When we were two feet from the front door, Winston held out a hand and wiggled his fingers. The padlock near the knob unlocked, and the heavy oak door swooshed open as we rolled through to a huge living room with no furniture except for a mattress and a mini-fridge.

As soon as the engine died, I got off and wobbled to the mattress, plopping down on a few blankets. Actually, even though my body still hummed, the mattress was comfortable and the blankets were soft.

Winston didn't say a word while he pushed the bike under a little alcove. He then went to the fridge, which sat on the bottom step of a wide staircase that led to…well, the obvious answer would've been upstairs. What met the top step was scaffolding that held paint cans, spray paint, and brushes strewn all over platforms. Curious, I lay back and found the ceiling half-painted with scenes so beautiful, so rich and deep, they took my eyes hostage. When I noticed the floating city in the far right corner, tears threatened.

Empyrean.

Wilma and Teenesee.

They were in trouble while I...damn. I needed to get to them.

The slamming fridge door distracted me from the tears, thank God. I brushed away a few on my cheeks and rolled to my side as Winston walked over holding two Styrofoam takeout containers. I sat up when he offered a box to me. The wings inside smelled amazing, and cold wings, especially BBQ cold wings, were almost a delicacy in my neighborhood.

We ate in silence, with me staring up at what I assumed was his masterpiece and him looking straight ahead, seemingly not loving the wings as much as I did. He ate mechanically, as if it were just for sustenance. Which, obviously, was the reason why we all ate, but most of us when given wings ate with some pleasure.

My nerves couldn't take the silence anymore. I had questions–also a big request. I licked some sauce off my fingers before pointing up. "This all you, Michelangelo?"

Again with the nods. A simple yes would've been nice.

"They're, um, pretty."

He reached into his pocket, stuck an earbud in his right ear, and kept eating.

Nope. It'd take more than that to shut me up. "So, you wanna talk about it?"

He took another bite before answering. "No."

I scooted closer. "Listen, I get it. I understand. When me a–"

"Don't care, Tainted."

158

"I'm trying to say that I get how difficult loving someone is when you're…different. You don't have to be an ass."

He sighed. "What do you want me to say, huh?" A pause. "Shaina…she's everything, okay? That's all you need to know."

Farren's voice echoed in my head. *Protectors aren't so easy to kill. Still had to pay, though…*

I wouldn't push. I didn't really want to know, anyway. It'd make what I needed to ask harder. "Yeah, sure. Okay."

He finished his lunch and took my empty container before getting up to throw them into a trash bag by the door. "All right, here's the plan. We go tonight, around midnight. I get your guy, and then you two get gone. Understood?"

I stood, wanting to be fine with that, really. But, no. "That's not exactly all I need from you."

He laughed a little, shaking his head. "Well, that's all you're gonna get."

I pulled the list from my bag and handed it to him. "Um…Avery doesn't know Farren is in jail. She thought you might be able to help find those people. I-I need your help getting Farren. *We* need your help finding an army."

The small laugh turned into a huge one. "An army? You dumbasses planning on taking out Exemplar?" If his voice weren't so musical, I would've been more pissed.

But I still fumed. I had to bite my tongue. Literally bite it to keep from going off. "No, not yet, anyway. We need the army to stop Exemplar from taking out Empyrean."

The laughing stopped, replaced with paper crinkling, his hold tightening on the list. "What're you talking about?"

I told him the story.

"Goddamn, you can't ever stay out of trouble, can you? Whatever life you live." He unfolded the list and skimmed through it. "You're never going to find these people."

"I know. That's why we need you."

Paint cans rattled and the scaffolding shook as Winston stared at the papers, his fists curling around them. I backed up, ready to throw the mattress over my head if cans and metal started dropping on us.

When he finally spoke, the urge to hide grew stronger. "I don't know where the fuck they are." His eyes pointed to the ceiling. "I've spent twenty years making sure you people didn't find me. Stayed off the radar, stayed hidden…now this."

"Hey, I love Empyrean, too. I don't want to–"

"You don't get it." His voice stayed soft, his eyes glued to his paintings. "It's not about Empyrean. Not really."

"Well, then I don't get why you're so pissed."

He finally looked down. The dread in his eyes made him young, vulnerable. "Where do you think Exemplar gets their power?"

I shrugged. "Farren said the sun."

He shook his head. "That's a lie they tell everybody. You ever see those green orbs during your illegal trips to Empyrean? The ones buried in the ground?"

"How do you know I've been–?"

"I know everything about you, Tainted. From this life and the last. Answer the question."

Well, that was disturbing. But the picture of those farmers hurling the orbs at the Protectors entered my head, erasing the weird stalker comment and causing my throat to dry up. Those green balls I thought looked like emeralds exploded into fire as soon as they touched something solid. *What the hell…?* "Yes. They were like bombs or something."

"They ain't bombs. That's power. Those orbs, they *are* energy, some sort of magic Empyrean shit." He handed the list back to me. "They're the reason why people like you and me exist. Why our energy is so fucking strong."

Fear tickled the back of my neck and left goose bumps on my arms. "I don't understand."

"You, me, all Exemplians, we're science experiments. Science experiments created with help from those magic balls...Empyrean power."

∞ ∞ ∞

He wouldn't elaborate, even when I begged, demanded, and begged again. All he'd say was it didn't matter. That part he got right. What mattered was making sure Exemplar didn't succeed–something Winston still refused to help us with.

I didn't stop nagging about responsibility and concern for others–Wilma taught me well.

Until he froze my mouth.

When I decided to use my feet and fists to get my point across, he lifted a hand, sending me flying onto the mattress, freezing my entire body. "Get some sleep."

Fighting against his hold made my lips ache. I managed a few closed-mouth screams, but with my head unable to move and my arms at my sides, all I accomplished was screaming at the unfinished painting on the ceiling. Oh, and giving myself the mother of all headaches. The shitty part about the whole thing was how Winston managed to ignore me. He slept, called who I assumed was Shaina, and showered. What I would have given to take a piss, maybe wash the layers of sweat from my body. Drown the bastard in the toilet.

At some point, I fell asleep, the exhaustion from the past two days too much to fight. I lay curled on my side when I woke up, once again in control of my body. My sore lips felt like I'd spent hours holding my mouth wide open.

Jackass.

I sat up, my bladder ready to explode, and scrambled to the room I'd watched Winston go in to take a shower. When I came back out, feeling ten pounds lighter, Winston stood by the front door. Under his T-shirt, a sizzling undercurrent zipped light from his neck to his stomach. A taser rested in the lip of his sweats.

"You think the fairy suit's a bit much? I doubt brainwashing guards will require Exemplian protection."

He shot me that stupid smirk. "Ain't the guards I'm worried about."

"You really think Protectors are staking out the place, waiting for me to break him out?"

"Of course they are."

I snorted. "Yeah, because they think I'm that crafty."

"No, because they think you're that stupid." I opened my mouth to give him a verbal ass kicking, but he held up a hand. That worked. No way would I give him a reason to freeze my mouth again. "They don't have high opinions of people who are not Exemplian. It's their flaw and our advantage."

"And how are we gonna use that?"

He crossed his arms and shook his head. "Imma give you a minute to think of the answer on your own."

What a cocky sonofa–oh. Oh, yeah. "Use me as bait."

He tapped his temple. "See, you ain't all stupid."

I stretched, annoyed. So what if the asshole wouldn't help find the list people. As soon as he freed Farren, we'd head to Arcus–where decent people were ready to help. Screw this guy. "What time is it?"

He opened the door, his bike already in the driveway. "Don't worry about it. Let's go."

Dick.

∞ ∞ ∞

Since Farren still sat in county, we'd have to go right into the heart of Mount Pocono. The jail connected to the courthouse, something I found stupid. But, hey, I'm no criminal expert or anything.

As we drove down Main Street, the bar scene was in full swing. Drunks staggered too close to the curb, their driving counterparts too close to the sidewalk. Police patrolled, but they never bothered anyone much unless a fight broke out or the driving got too erratic. The perks of living close to East Stroudsburg University. College students on a mission to be complete idiots got some leeway from Pocono's finest.

The courthouse hid two streets behind Main, which made it a virtual ghost town, with the whispers of Main's party curling into the shadows. Winston kept the bike at a crawl, going about three blocks past the courthouse before parking. He even put a couple quarters in the meter.

"You don't have to feed those after six." The guy would steal a soda, but needlessly pay for parking? Whatever.

He shrugged and headed toward the back of the jail. I followed, though not liking the whole trailing-like-a-puppy feeling. The way he walked, as if he owned the damn sidewalk. Man, I really didn't want to be impressed. I had to cling to the hours he kept me frozen. Okay, maybe it was fifteen minutes or so, but still. The fucker froze my mouth.

Yeah, Winston was pretty badass. The epitome of cool. *Asshole.*

But when he turned away from the courthouse and toward the party, I had to question his intelligence, at the very least, his sense of direction. "Um…wrong way."

I mumbled that little directive under my breath. No one ever accused me of repeating mistakes. The guy didn't like questions–proof being my sore mouth.

He heard me anyway. We stopped and he pointed at the loudest crowd, drinking on the patio of an old bar. "Imma hang out here for a minute. You go on and take a lap around the courthouse."

Okay, that command was getting old, fast. "And what do you think should I do after? Maybe get a cone at Dairy Queen?"

"If you want."

"Hey, I–"

He put up a hand, freezing my goddamn mouth again. "If I get too close, they'll feel me. You go, weed them out, lead them to the party, and then I'll go in and do my thing."

When his hold on my mouth broke, I shoved him. As average as he was in height and weight, trying to move him was like trying to topple a megalith with my hands. "Don't. Freeze. My. Mouth." With every word, I gave another useless push.

All he did was lift his hand, turning me into a water fountain statue. You know, like cupid, with one foot in the air and an arm held out. Embarrassing. "Play nice, Tainted, and I'll let you go."

My ego couldn't take another beating. At least he kept my mouth free. "Fine. Stop it."

He waved, and I fell to my knees. I so didn't want to face his smirk, but my current position left me at a complete disadvantage when trying to maintain a little pride. I stood, straightened my tank, and smoothed back my sweaty hair.

He watched with boredom written all over his dark face. "You done?"

Deep breath in, slow breath out. "Yes."

"Okay, take a lap."

"You know what? I hate that. Hate. It. Say it one more time, and I'll…I'll…" Damn, I'll take another lap.

He smiled a genuine smile this time. "You got guts. I'll give you that." He hung an arm across my shoulder and squeezed. If I thought he had any redeeming qualities, I'd have sworn he tried to comfort me. "Fighting Protectors won't get your friend out of jail. It'll just get us noticed."

Ugh! Full of all the right answers, wasn't he? "How will you know it's clear?"

He guided my attention toward the patio party. "Because you're going to get lost in the crowd, make 'em find you. The chaos will distract them enough not to pay attention to the extra static my body'll create. As soon as you're inside the bar, I'll get your friend. Wait fifteen minutes and find your way back out on the street. I'll pick you up."

"You only need fifteen minutes?"

He took his arm off my shoulder. "I need five, but I can't fit you both on my bike."

Impressed, really, I tried not to ooh and ahhh. "I'm not twenty-one. They won't let me in."

"Already took care of it."

Of course, you did.

"All right." I backtracked down the cracked sidewalk until the noise level quieted. Before crossing the street, I glanced behind me. Winston disappeared, taking a huge chunk of my courage with him.

The closer I got near the jail, the more my nerves acted up. The tangy sewer smell coming from the storm drains elbowed its way into my nose. Cats fought a few blocks away and a thumping base came from a house I couldn't see. Once I made it to the courthouse, I closed my eyes and tried to shut out everything, searching for the sound of footsteps.

None came.

I walked farther down, until I stood by the brick wall of our small county jail. Barbed wire topped the wall, but that was the only clue it housed criminals–or drunks spending the night in detox. My dad paid a visit on more than one occasion.

Sneaking glances around me, I rattled the metal gate once or twice and made sure to act as though I avoided the cameras, anything to make it seem like a serious breakout attempt.

I listened for any stalking-like noises, while the distant base and mewling cats kept me company. If the bastards didn't start crawling from the shadows soon…

Lena.

Tarek's voice floated through my brain. It didn't help me relax, though. Strain colored all his words.

*Come back. Now. Things are…*pause*…things are bad.*

Anxiety went into overdrive. I wanted to scream, yell for the fuckers to come get me. Didn't happen, though, regardless of how hot the panic bubble in my throat burned.

Then the shadows moved.

Swallowing the terror proved tough, but I managed. They came in slow, at first. I kept my direct attention pointed at the parking garage straight ahead, while catching four shadows coming closer in my peripheral. I didn't want to alert them, but I didn't want to stick around and get caught, either. All it'd take would be one zap with a taser, and I'd be in the next portal to Exemplar.

I rattled the gate one more time before moving toward Main. The dumbasses thought they were stealthy, darting in and out of the shadows, hiding behind streetlamps, or acting like locals when I turned around every so often. Christ, who were the stupid humans now?

I counted three guys and one woman. They all looked ridiculous, with their contego suits so obviously on and under their summer clothes. Unfortunately, their tasers were probably in their hands waiting for a clean shot, too.

Lost Energy

After rounding the corner to the world of drinking and college co-eds, I picked up my speed, heading straight for the patio with Christmas lights decorating the four small trees surrounding it. The foursome followed, crowding the door a few feet behind me.

A big, bald guy with tattoos from his skull to fingertips demanded ID from everyone in front of us. Waiting set me on edge. The one thing keeping the Protectors' tasers from shocking my back were some half-dressed girls, who spent time ogling the people set on killing me. Granted, they were okay looking, but their eyes were dead. Why couldn't the bubbleheads see that?

The bouncer's face turned all slack-jawed as soon as I hit the head of the line. He moved to the side, his milky brown eyes glazing over. "Go ahead."

"Thanks, buddy." I rushed inside; the heat from all the bodies packed in stealing my breath. It didn't take much effort to blend in with the crowd.

Didn't take much for the Protectors to find me, either. I stood in the middle of the dance floor, swaying a bit as the four of them flanked me from every angle. They all nodded to each other before moving forward. Nothing better than feeling like the fox in a foxhunt.

I made eye contact with one of the guys and smiled, wagging my finger. The action stopped him, exactly what I'd hoped for. He searched the crowd to find his buddies. If they thought I'd trapped them, maybe they'd take their time trying to get me.

That worked for a while. They stood stalk still, other people bumping and grinding against them as they danced. The woman looked ready to yank my head off, and I'd bet she was more than capable of doing it. They all kept a vigil on the room, checking the exits, the bar. I swayed to the music, trying to act as if I knew exactly what I was doing. Smiling hurt my face, but I forced it to stay there. Even with the body odor masked with flowery perfume stinking up the place, I managed to put on a decent I-got-you show.

When they realized nothing was happening, they moved in like a machine, my shaking head and wagging finger not working in the least. We played this game for about ten minutes, five minutes short of Winston's proposed time for me to get back outside. I snuck deeper into the crowded floor, but they kept coming, heaving people out of their way, elbowing those who gave them shit about it. They had me, all four blocking every direction. The single option left was to start a fight.

I had no problem with that.

Before Girl Protector reached me, I knocked some drunken chick to the floor, causing her friends to come to her defense. As soon as the first idiot got in my face, I punched her, bloodying her lip. Her scream reached over the loud music and her flailing hands managed to smack Girl Protector against her ear hard enough for the woman to lose focus on me.

There was my out. I had to jab a few more girls who felt the need to defend the crying drunk on the floor, her short skirt now showing her dislike for undergarments. By the time I made it near the exit, an all-out brawl broke out. All four Protectors were stuck navigating fists and ducking flying glasses.

Once out, air rushed into my lungs. Why anyone thought drinking in a crowded room with strangers was a good time, I'll never know.

"Hey!"

I whipped around to find two of the guys storming my way. Thankfully, the revving sound of an obnoxious crotch rocket filled the background. Smiling, I flipped them off before turning for the street. Winston barreled down the middle, running every traffic light. I had no fear hopping on the back when he stopped long enough to let me swing my leg over the other side. I waved at the assholes, smile in place, but when one smiled back, the hairs on my neck stood at attention. He pointed at Winston and nodded before heading back in the bar for his friends.

I leaned in close to Winston's ear. "What the hell?"

He sped away, not bothering to answer, dodging drunks, both driving and walking, until we zoomed into the parking garage across the street from the courthouse.

Seriously.

Right across the street.

As soon as the bike stopped, I jumped off, searching all the dark corners. "Are you crazy?"

"Maybe a little." Winston cupped his mouth and spoke in the direction of the elevator. "It's safe. Come on out."

In seconds, Farren's bright red hair glowed in the dim light as he stalked over. He scooped me up and twirled me around. "Thank God."

I smiled. "There's no such thing."

He squeezed me tighter. "An expression, kid, shut up."

"Don't call me kid."

Farren set me down, keeping an arm secured on my shoulders. He nodded at Winston, but the cool act didn't hide the awe flooding his face. "Hey, ah, thanks, man."

Winston returned the nod, having no trouble with the cool factor. "You all go on, tell your people I'm done."

I stepped forward, not ready to give up yet. "I hate to admit it, but we need you. Christ, the things you can do..."

Anger brewed below his cool surface, shooting from his eyes. "That Protector? The one who pointed? He knows who I am, and now Exemplar's going to have all their satellites pointed here until they find me." He dragged a hand through his dreads. "Remember how I told you Shaina is everything?"

I nodded.

"Yeah, well, those bastards aren't going to stop until they take my everything. If that happens... For y'all's sake it better not happen." He started the engine, the sound ricocheting off the cement walls, piercing my ears.

I held onto his arm and yelled over the engine, his threat loud and clear. "Bring her to Arcus. We can keep her safe."

"'Bye, Tainted." He zoomed from the garage, never looking back.

"Well, shit, there goes our biggest help." I turned to Farren. "We need to—what's all this?" I pointed at his crazy smile and wide eyes.

"You know who that is?" He jumped—literally jumped up and down like a girl at a boy band concert. "I feel like a goddamned princess right now. He walked in, opened the cell...while all the guards stood there doing nothing. One even held the door open for us on the way out."

"You're a nut, and all I know about that guy is he's rude and froze my mouth for hours." *Okay, fifteen minutes, but...*

"That guy...*that guy* is Winston fucking Candell."

"Yeah?"

"*Yeah*? That's it? He's the most... He makes Wilma... He's been the Protector for half the top Synod heads. I heard they executed him for treason, marked him Tainted. And he's been living here? Right beside us? Our goddamn neighbor?"

Holy hell. But he was gone, off to save Shaina from...damn. I hated that Winston made me like him, even if he just promised he'd kill us if Shaina were hurt. "Well, we can't depend on him." I hesitated. "Tarek said there's trouble."

Farren dropped the fangirl act and returned to Protector mode. "Let's go."

I strapped my bag tighter to my back and wrapped an arm around his waist. Farren held me with one hand and reached the other to the ceiling. The wind carried us through the silent hole, the pressure something I'd gotten used to. We landed on the front step of the castle.

Before I let go, the door ripped open and Tarek snatched me from Farren's arms, holding me tight as his mouth crashed down on mine.

This. And like Winston, I'd fight until my last breath.

Lynn Vroman

CHAPTER 19

LENA

ANCIENT

Everyone charged out after Tarek.

They went unnoticed.

I stayed lost in my giant, memorizing the way he felt...tasted. He didn't seem to mind my rudeness because he carried me almost to the edge of the tree line, away from the million-question inquisition. Farren could fill everyone in.

Squid in the nearby trees whined like our presence disturbed them. Screw them. If we had to endure their fishy smell, they could deal with us making out.

Tarek kissed me one more time, slow and soft, until my legs tingled. When he pulled away, his palms cupped my cheeks, his gray eyes never leaving mine. "I missed you."

I'd been gone for about a day or so, but...yeah, too long. "Missed you, too."

He smiled, his dimples making my swollen heart hurt. "Good."

Before we could forget the world, the world barged into our space.

"Lena!" Mom wrapped her arms around my back, which forced Tarek to release my face. I had to clamp my mouth shut to avoid letting a disappointed moan escape.

I turned into her arms to find Jake behind her, his face pale with worry. "Hey, Jake."

He squeezed the arm I had draped around Mom's shoulder. "A lot's happened in the last couple hours," he said.

I looked around him and noticed Avery and Nicolette. *This can't be good.* "Ladies."

Avery didn't have the same calm demeanor as when she ambushed us at Dad's house. Lines on her face were deeper and if she had rung her hands any tighter, her fingers might've fallen off. Nicolette had the same bitchy face as before, but this time an undercurrent of fear softened her features.

After a hesitation, giving her Protector a quick glance, Avery came forward, the tears hovering in her eyes now noticeable. "We are in exile, Lena. Cassondra…she knows I came to you. We barely escaped…"

Nicolette pulled her Guide into her arms. "They reviewed the satellite feed. Seems the cameras are always shining on you."

Oh, no.

"Which means what? They see everything I do." I swallowed. "And who I do it with."

She nodded. "If you're doing it in locations they know you frequent."

Shit. Winston.

Tarek broke the silence building around us. "Let's get inside, go over some options." He nodded toward Belva, who stayed glued to Farren. Ginger didn't seem to mind, his arm tight on her waist. "Show Lena some good news first."

Belva left Farren and walked to the forest's edge. As soon as she raised her hands, a chorus of squeals greeted us. When she closed her fists, the squealing stopped abruptly. And after she pushed her fists forward, rustling trees created gusting winds as the giant animals rushed deeper into the woods.

Only after my friend turned to me beaming did I realize my mouth hung open.

She rested her hands on her hips. "Neat, huh?"

"Neat?" I snuck a glance at Farren, who was as slacked-jawed as me. "How the hell'd you do that?"

She shrugged and pointed to Avery, who let out a shaky breath before saying, "She is an ancient."

∞ ∞ ∞

"Is that all I'm gonna get?" I forgot about Avery's unfortunate predicament and drilled her for answers when we all filed into what was now our main room. The fire roared, but it felt nice. Being outside for even a few minutes in shorts and a T-shirt didn't exactly scream pleasant.

"It's complicated, Lena. Not something I've ever witnessed. Honestly, I thought it a myth."

Still not answering the question. I went to stand by the fire, Tarek right beside me. "What's complicated? That those things listen to her or that they understand her little hand motions?"

"Well…both, I guess." Avery sat on the couch, motioning for Belva to sit next to her. It took a few tugs on Belva's part for Farren to release her arm. When she sat, Avery took her hands and turned them to show her wrists. "Come, look."

I had to squeeze in by Farren, who crowded Belva by squatting in front of her. "What are we looking at?"

Avery leaned forward and pointed to the tiny identical birthmarks on each of Belva's wrists. "She's marked. You see?" At our nods, she continued, "This is where Arcus's people had gills. They could breathe underwater, as well.

When I noticed how the animals reacted to her, I asked to see her wrists. I never thought it true, but there you have it."

I rolled my eyes, so ready for her to get to the point. "Have what?"

Avery patted Belva's hands and stood. "It has been whispered for centuries that Arcus used to be highly evolved, the people who belonged here able to communicate with the wildlife. But there was a mutiny, which resulted in Exemplar depleting the dimension of its human energy."

What a nice way to put it. "You mean, they came in and annihilated an entire population."

"Y-yes. But that was before my time. I had nothing to do with it."

Tarek piped in. "She's telling the truth. There are villages not far from here in ruin, long past the point of decay."

Well, shit.

What she said sank in, creating enough fear to make my lips numb. "That's what they're planning on doing to Empyrean, aren't they?"

She swallowed, her eyes filling with tears. "I believe so. Cassondra has declared war. Empyrean is the first target. Earth is rumored to be the next."

All I could think about was Wilma and Teenesee.

No, that wasn't true.

I thought about all the people in danger because of the power-hungry greed of a few. "Why Earth?"

Avery went to Nicolette and curled herself in the Protector's arms. Nicolette held her close and encouraged her to continue. "Cassondra has infiltrated my personal files. She…she has discovered that I've been sending Exemplians accused of treason there to hide."

Oh. My. God. "So the people on the list…?"

"Many can be found there. The Warden, Cheveyo, has promised to keep them safe, hidden, until...until..."

I moved to get right in her face, causing Nicolette to go on the offense–which caused Tarek, Farren, and Jake to circle me.

"Careful, Protector." Tarek's voice remained as soft as usual, his calm in place. He didn't need to yell.

I ignored everyone and pinned the Guide with a glare. "Until when?"

Avery's hands shook as she placed them on Nicolette's arm. When her Protector stepped aside, she faced me head-on. "Until we were ready for the rebellion."

Panic. "Is Winston in your files? Does she know he's there? If they're watching me, they probably saw him, and if he's in your files..."

She nodded. "I-I would imagine they now know about him, yes."

My palm itched, and when my hand curled into a fist, I had to fight to keep it off her face. "Do you realize what you've done?"

"I–"

"You put Winston's girlfriend in danger! *He threatened us*. Why would you have me reach out to him?" Farren's warning hit my frontal lobe again: *Protectors are hard to kill, still had to pay, though.* "If they kill her, he'll come for us. I know it. And...and all those people... I thought you cared!"

She flinched as though I managed to hit her. "I do care." Her voice grew weaker as she went on. "Winston knew what I was doing when I sent him there–saved him! I-I assumed he'd seek out others, build an army. Help the cause."

I shot all my hate through my eyes and stepped closer until our noses almost touched. "Well, you assumed wrong."

177

Tarek reached for me, gently pulling me away, and spoke to everyone in the room. "We need to calm down, think things through. If Lena's right, Winston will be here if Protectors come knocking on his door. Soon." He nodded to Farren. "You make sure everyone stays in this room. I'll go to the woods. I'll feel him as soon as he opens a portal. Maybe I can hold him off long enough for you to get everyone somewhere safe."

Wait, what? Tarek worried about Winston? Like he *really worried* about him? So, so bad. "I'm going with you. Maybe I can talk to him, try to reason."

Tarek shook his head. "You have no idea what he's capable of."

"Where would Farren take them that was completely safe?"

His silence answered the question loud and clear.

"Exactly."

He sighed and closed his eyes, bowing his head. "Fine. Come with me, but if he–"

"I know, I know." I tilted his chin until he met my eyes. "We'll be fine." No, we probably wouldn't be.

He clasped my hand in his before talking to everyone one more time. "*We're* leaving. Farren, if you hear the doors flying off the hinges, go. Take them to Earth, somewhere remote. Find Cheveyo, ask for his help."

Farren stood, pulling Belva up with him. "If he won't help?"

Tarek sighed. "Damn, I don't know."

∞ ∞ ∞

Tarek refused to let go of my hand as we barged through the woods to the cabin. He refused to speak, too. I tried to reassure him a couple times, but a few grunts and under-the-breath cursing were all he gave in return. The river, which had been calm this entire trip, now raged, white foamy water sloshing over the banks. The sky darkened to a deep purple, and the animals stayed hidden. Not even the squid tried to make their appearance known, Tarek's emotions creating too much chaos.

Tarek didn't need to say anything. His world spoke for him.

Once we reached the cabin, he threw the door open, not bothering to shut it behind us. He finally released my hand and paced the small room, running his fingers through his hair, causing it to tangle.

I had no idea what to say. Seeing him like this, losing it. Definitely new.

Words lodged in my throat and swallowing a few times didn't loosen them up. Saying everything would be okay wasn't a lie I wished to keep repeating. We both knew nothing would ever be okay again.

I stood helpless for a minute longer and went to block his path. He almost rammed into me, putting his hands on my shoulders to stop his momentum. His arms folded me close. No words passed between us.

No words were needed.

The river grew quieter.

He scooped me up and carried me to the bed. With gentle hands, he caressed my hair, his mouth finding mine.

I could allow us to drown out the world and all the danger we faced because we needed to remember what it was we were fighting for.

This.

Always this.

As we lay there, our fused mouths performed all the communicating necessary.

Purple light from the brightening sky flooded the room and the river quieted.

∞ ∞ ∞

Tarek curled against my back, stroking my arm, his fingers trembling. After hours of silent calm, his shaking fingers were all that remained from his earlier rage. I turned into him, nuzzling his chest, hating we had to stop hiding soon. Always too soon.

I planted a kiss on his heart before breaking the magic. "Have you heard from Wilma since the last time?"

His big body tensed. "No." He groaned before rolling over me to get up. "It's not like her...the radio silence for this long, even when she's upset. I've tried contacting her, but..."

"...no answer. She hasn't contacted me, either." My mouth turned dry. "Do you think she's...?"

He knelt in front of the bed and gathered my hands in his. "No, of course not." He kissed my fingertips. "Anyway, you'd feel it. The bond you two have, it breaks when one person dies unless..."

"...Exemplian science is around to make sure the Pairing holds during the next life." Funny how we were able to complete each other's sentences, but again, we've had these discussions for a while. Well, they were one-sided discussions with him telling me stories in my head at night, but same thing as far as I was concerned.

I leaned in for a kiss and he obliged, taking his time. After pulling away, he grazed a thumb across my bottom lip. "You need to eat."

His big palm cupped my cheek and I turned into it. "What do you got?"

Tarek's smile, like catching miracles in a bottle, and if it were the last thing I'd ever see, I'd die content. "This and that. I think there's a stale granola bar in the trunk. Not great, but tastes better than the eatables.

"The eatables?"

"That's what I've been calling the animals here that seem safe enough to eat. I don't know what they are, to be honest."

I laughed, pulling him back on the narrow bed. "Stale granola sounds delicious."

His nose touched mine, that perfect smile creating peace deep in my heart. At that moment, love felt strong enough to fix everything. "If it makes you feel better, it has chocolate in it."

I ran my fingers through his tangled hair, giving it a small tug. "Oh, I feel fine at the moment. Though, a little chocolate wouldn't hurt."

Tarek gave me a loud, smacking kiss and hopped from the bed to find my outdated feast. I stood and stretched my muscles before combing through my own knotty hair with my fingers. As soon as we made it back to the castle, I'd change out of the dirty-ass clothes and into the jeans and sweatshirt I snagged before leaving my apartment. Then we'd all get busy figuring out how to find some of those list people. Most living on Earth would be easy enough, thanks to the internet. Yeah, probably not. I had doubts they'd use their real names. Shit, I had no ideas after that.

"Tarek?"

He launched the bar. "Yeah?"

I caught it, barely. He had a throw like a Yankee pitcher. "What're we gonna do?"

His smile disappeared, replaced with a look I'd seen once–the one he gave right before he killed Casimir. "I don't know."

The only sound filling the room was the crackling of the granola wrapper clutched in my hand. We stared at each other, both desperate to be the first to come up with a solution.

He beat me to it.

"Screw this." He stormed over and gathered me up in his arms. "Whatever happens, I'm not giving up. We'll win this time, I swear to you. Those bastards will lose."

I believed him. Believed him with my entire being.

I ate while he sent Wilma another message, telling her I'd be coming there to fight.

Wilma never ignored a dumbass comment.

Seconds after he gave me the thumbs-up, he pressed a hand to his forehead and grimaced. But he smiled through it all.

I leapt off the bed. "What? Did she say something?"

Wilma's raspy voice blared so loud in my head it vibrated my brain. *You keep your fucking ass away from here, missy! I catch you stepping one foot out of a portal, I'll kick your scrawny butt back to Arcus myself. That's not a threat.*

Tears flooded my eyes and relief loosened my knees. I laughed as I cried. "She seems okay."

His dimples flashed. "I'd say so." In an instant, though, his smile vanished. "Oh, no." He rushed outside.

Fear attacked my legs, slowing them down as I ran to follow. "What's wrong?"

As soon as the question left my mouth, a high-pitched scream echoed through the woods, terror laced all through it.

"He's here."

CHAPTER 20

LENA

FLYING SQUID

One person could outrun me.

Tarek.

My lungs protested trying to keep up while we raced to the source of the scream. The trees' symmetry helped with speed, and we were able to go full-bore without dodging branches or tripping over underbrush.

Screams pierced the air again. Tarek's pace went from fast to breakneck.

As we drew closer, the agitated squid shaking tree limbs, we spotted Winston holding Shaina behind him. He threw the more daring pink beasts into the river with a waving hand. Animals trapped in the water squealed until their heads fell below the surface. The squid never reappeared and silence took over.

Tarek reached Winston as another squid flew over our heads and into the water. My giant tackled him, but not before giving some unseen command to the animals. All who survived the Protector climbed high in the trees and kept quiet.

Tarek didn't hold Winston on the ground for long. His big body flew through the air and slammed into the closest thick tree trunk.

Shit!

"Stop!" I ran to Tarek, but he didn't need me.

He jumped to his feet and ran at Winston for more. I grabbed his arm, tugging. I might as well have been trying to move a boulder, but he halted. His body remained rigid and ready to fight.

"Hold on, goddamnit!" My voice cracked. Panic had a way of doing that.

Winston had the calm act perfected, something I thought only Tarek had mastered. Instead, he looked like he could rip off arms and feed them to the squid. I squeezed Tarek's forearm before going to Shaina, whose glassy eyes and pale face said shock had already set up shop.

I swung an arm around her shoulders and tried to reassure her. "It's okay. Everything's fine." Telling that lie annoyed me.

Her wide eyes met mine. Recognition gave her face back some of its color. "You're Lena, the girl from the restaurant?"

I nodded. "The very same."

"What the hell is going on?"

Where to start? "We'll explain soon, promise." I glanced at Winston. "But we need to make sure your guy doesn't try to kill us."

"Kill you? He's not–He's the gentlest man I've ever met." Tarek's snort sent Shaina into a rage. "*You* attacked *him. Dios mío*, are you some kind of giant? You're twice his–"

"Size ain't everything, baby." Winston pulled Shaina from my arms. "I'm not going to hurt any of you as long as I like your answers."

"Well, why don't we all go have a chat with Avery?" Tarek found my hand and stormed toward the castle. "If you don't like the answers, kill her. She's the one who involved you in the first place."

Lost Energy

∞ ∞ ∞

Winston stood by the fire, Shaina still in shock by his side. When we barged through the door with him behind us, Nicolette went into Protector mode, though shaking made her lighted suit look like it vibrated. Farren turned into total fangirl again after realizing Winston wasn't going on a killing spree. Belva, Mom, and Jake sat on the couch, nervous.

By the time Avery finished telling the whole story, we were all pissed off again. Except for Shaina, who stood as dumbfounded as ever.

"So, long story short, we're pretty much fucked. Ah, sorry, ladies." Farren rocked on his heels and folded his arms across his chest.

Winston turned toward the flame, staying silent. No one interrupted, none of us that stupid.

Shaina rubbed his back and whispered in his ear. I had to give her credit. Crazy as all this was for her, she still managed to make sure Winston didn't go apeshit on any of us. I gave up a silent thanks to whoever might be listening that Exemplians hadn't gotten to her before Winston.

When Winston finally faced the crowd, he kept Shaina close. "This isn't as bad as it seems," he said.

A glimmer of hope, faint but blossoming, chipped the heavy stone in my gut. "How do you figure?"

He gave a small smile. "For one, y'all got me."

Yes! But...arrogant, much?

Tarek wasn't convinced. "Okay, great. Just great. Perfect. And what, might I ask, can you do for us?"

Winston bobbed his head as though his earbuds were in and pursed his lips. He then waved a hand at nothing in particular. "I can feel the energy you've collected. You got the ability to bleed the lines, yes?"

Tarek leaned forward, his eyes lighting. "Where're you going with this?"

Winston scanned the room, clearly not impressed. "We do need a few more people, but…"

"But what?" Tarek grabbed my hand. He might act calm for everyone else, but I knew he needed me as much as I needed him.

"I got a plan, Warden." Winston pinned Avery with a glare. "But you're going on a trip first."

Before she could answer, Nicolette shook her head. "Not without me."

"I got no problem with that." He looked at me. "You're coming, too."

Tarek's hand tightened on mine, but he kept silent. I, on the other hand, didn't feel the need to. "And where are we going?"

"To Cheveyo. If what she says is true," he pointed to Avery, "we should be able to convince a few Exemplians hiding out on Earth who have a big enough grudge to volunteer."

"Why does Lena have to go?" Tarek's deep voice shook a little.

Winston shrugged. "He's a True Warden. If she had a relationship with him, we need her to convince him to give up some of those rogues' locations."

"And what if she doesn't convince him?"

"Then I guess I'll have to get her back here before the guy kills her."

"No." The fire jumped from the hearth, flames licking the rug in front of it. Shaina was the only one who bothered to stomp them out before the old fabric disintegrated.

Before another fight broke out, I stepped forward. "When do we leave?"

Actual respect shined in Winston's dark eyes. *Weird.* "Soon."

Tarek gripped my elbow, tight. "Lena–"

"We don't have a choice." I reached up on my toes and whispered in his ear. "Please, don't."

"I won't let anything happen to her, Warden, because you'll have my lady here. I'm trusting you, so trust me."

That seemed to calm my giant some, his shoulders not as tense. He spoke to Winston, never taking his eyes off mine. "You'll have a day."

"That works."

Tarek nodded. "Farren, you go with them."

Farren cracked his knuckles. "Absolutely."

"Now," Winston clasped Shaina's hand and headed toward the staircase, "we're going upstairs for a while. Don't bother us."

Tarek yelled after them as they climbed the stairs. "What if you can't convince anyone to help?"

Winston's soft chuckle sounded like music and soothed like a balm. His confidence made that glimmer of hope shine, no matter how cocky he sounded. "Like I said, you got me."

∞ ∞ ∞

While Tarek, Jake, and Farren argued, trying to figure out exactly what Winston had planned, I went outside with Belva and Mom. They could argue over the details. I wanted to get a better look at what Belva could do with her newfound ability.

We walked through the woods, gossiping as if we weren't hanging out in Arcus. Our main conversation topic focused on guys, with Mom smiling every time we complained about this annoying habit or that awesome way they did everything else. When I prodded her about Jake, her smile deepened, and she said, "Sometimes you get it right."

She sure did, and so did Belva and I, though Farren had yet to admit Belva had already caught him. The entire time we had an interested audience, not only the complete attention from the squid, but the other wildlife, too. Even the tree limbs seemed to bend toward Belva.

Once we made it closer to the cabin, I turned to my friend. "All right, pal, show me your magic."

Mom scooted closer to the cabin's door. "I'll wait over here, if you don't mind."

Belva smiled, tying her hair up in a messy bun with an elastic band. "No problem, Jacie. But don't worry; I'll keep them in check."

The new confidence Belva exhibited made me proud. Not that I wasn't proud of her before, but the way she held herself, like she could take on the world. *Hmm.* I guess she did take on *this* world…and won.

Still, I didn't much trust the animals. They might like her, but they didn't have the same affection for me. I stood back a couple feet, though not as far away as Mom.

She laughed, pointing up. "You've dealt with worse than these guys, seriously."

"Actually, your new pets are pretty high up on my list of dangerous encounters."

"I won't let them hurt you."

I kept an eye on the rustling branches as the things descended when Belva held up her hands and pulled down. "Ah, yeah, thanks."

After two or three crawled close enough, they reached out and brushed Belva with their thick arms, almost how elephants caressed their handlers with their trunks on those Discovery Channel shows. Some that had to wait in line whined, trying to knock the attention-receivers out of the way. No violence marred the actions, more like children vying for attention. They weren't the terrifying monsters in the trees anymore, just sweet, innocent beings wanting love.

I couldn't look away, even though standing this close to them made me more than a little anxious. My friend succeeded in taming the untamable, and I was in awe. Completely and utterly.

After a few minutes, Belva's sweet smile turned down with worry. "Something's wrong."

"What is it?" I searched the sky for opening portals and attacking Protectors.

"They're sad." She soothed them and kissed their tentacles.

Relief relaxed my shoulders, and I concentrated on Belva. An Exemplian attack was the only problem I worried about. "How do you know?"

She kept nuzzling them, consoling their soft cries. "Don't know. I just do."

Oh, right.

Winston threw at least four in the river that I witnessed. Who knew how many more before Tarek tackled him. Maybe these things were a family. I mean, why not? Anything was possible. No way would I tell Belva. Her love for the squishy things was apparent, and if she got pissed enough, she might have her new friends attack Winston. That wouldn't be good for any of us.

Her attention helped their somber mood. Even smaller animals came out to curl around her legs and jump up for a pat on the head. Whatever mojo she had, it helped turn Arcus into a fairy-tale land where everything was nice and pleasant.

That all ended when Tarek came crashing through the woods leading everyone to us, including Winston.

The squid began to hiss, not willing to keep what he did a secret.

Lynn Vroman

Belva waved a hand in the air and clicked her tongue.

Ah, what? Now she could talk to them?

Whatever she did, she managed to calm the animals down, though one curled her into its grasp, protecting her. Farren moved forward but stopped when Belva held up a hand. Her eyes widened, but to her credit, she didn't freak out.

Winston didn't show an ounce of guilt. He watched the scene with the same awe I felt moments ago. "You controlling those things?" He didn't bother to look at Belva; he was too busy smiling.

Belva rolled her eyes. "No, I don't control them. They're not my slaves."

"But they listen to you, right?" Winston moved closer to the one holding Belva, causing it to squeal so loud we all had to cover our ears.

She rubbed the tentacle, doing that clicking thing again. "Yeah, I guess so." She clicked a few more times and motioned toward the top of the tree it held onto. After a hesitation, the thing crawled upward, growling. "Question is why do they hate you?"

Winston didn't bother answering. Instead, he hooted so loud his voice echoed.

"Um, Winston? You all right?" I took a step away from him with each word. If he snapped, I didn't want to be close.

Winston high-fived Farren, who reciprocated with that same dumb look he'd sported since Winston rescued him. Shaina got a huge kiss, which she didn't seem to mind at all. When Winston held his hand up for Tarek, who ignored it with a scowl on his face, he shook his head and came over to fling an arm across my shoulders. "You know what I think, people?"

When we all shook our heads, he hooted again.

190

I smacked his shoulder. "Hey, crazy pants. What the hell?"

He looked up and saluted the hissing squid. "I think we're going to be fine."

Lynn Vroman

CHAPTER 21

LENA

CHEVEYO

Winston didn't bother explaining anything. Honestly, his tight-lipped routine didn't piss me off this time. The confidence he had was enough to convince me. If the guy thought we'd be fine, I'd listen to him. Who cared if he didn't want to share?

Yeah, everyone else.

Winston smiled while people threw questions at him. He said, "Be patient."

That was like telling the Pope to stop praying. Tarek ranted, threatened, and even pleaded a little, hiding the more desperate pleas under insults. Nothing changed Winston's mind. He took Shaina's hand and headed back to the castle.

"You all need to get ready." He nodded toward me, crinkling his nose. "You should bathe or something."

I stopped, Mom bumping into my back. "That's just rude."

He shrugged. But I did take him up on his advice and switched directions to the riverbank. Tarek followed, as did Mom and Jake. The rest went with Winston.

"I think I could wash off some dirt, too," Mom said, rubbing her upper arms.

Jake's face brightened. "Ah, yeah, that sounds like a plan. I'm in."

I sighed. A private moment with Tarek dashed. Thankfully, Jake steered Mom farther down the bank. A straight line of bushes now gave us all some privacy.

I stripped down to my underclothes and headed into the warm water, a soft moan escaping. I waded out to the middle, focusing on the opposite bank. Though dangerous, Arcus really was beautiful. The forest's bright colors and tropical climate had a soothing quality when not all riled up. And damn, it felt good to immerse in the fluorescent blue water and have the tension melt from my shoulders.

Tarek's soft splash rippled into the water. I smiled. *Even better.*

I sunk into the depths, hoping the sweat and grit would loosen from my hair.

By some miracle, the water was clear even with the fluorescent color. The little elephants I hadn't seen since my first trip swam around, jolting me, their trunks giving a tingly zap instead of the bee sting I remembered. I reached out to pet one, but it swam away–and came back to inspect me some more. If oxygen weren't so important, staying down there all day would've been nice.

Strong arms yanked me to the surface. Familiar arms. My giant's. Tarek pulled my legs around his waist and turned in a languid circle. His smile melted my heart. "Hi."

I kissed his nose. "Hi, back."

We moved in that circle a minute longer, his eyes doing all the talking. After a soft kiss, he said, "It scares me, the way you're risking your life."

"Do I have a choice? Because if I do, I choose to forget about everything and be here with you."

He brushed hair away from my face, and then traced a finger down my cheek. "I suppose that's not an option."

"No, it's not." I left Tarek's arms after one more kiss to float on my back. The skyline's shift from purple to gray started maybe a half-mile away. A reminder that everyone waited for us at the castle so we could move forward, try to convince someone else to fight against Exemplar.

Wonder if this Cheveyo guy would be as accepting if we led Exemplians to his doorstep as we did Winston's? Like I did Empyrean's? Guilt festered under my skin. If I had stayed away, Teenesee and her people wouldn't be fighting for their lives.

I'd do everything I could to right that wrong, even risking another Warden's temper.

One more dunk in the water and I swam back to Tarek, tangling myself around him again. He was happy to oblige, his muscled arms holding me close.

I ran my fingers through his wet hair. "What do you think Winston has planned?"

Tarek's face grew tense, all the softness disappearing. "He wants me to bleed the lines between here and Empyrean." He didn't say it like an assumption. He knew it, and he didn't like it.

"Would that be such a bad thing?"

He looked beyond my shoulder, toward the castle. "For the plan to be effective, the lines will have to be severed."

"So?"

His eyes found mine. "Severed lines mean anyone can get through, no need for Protector ability."

Oh. Oh, right, that wouldn't be good. "Are you–I mean maybe that's not what he has in mind?"

"What else would it be?" He didn't wait for an answer and carried me to bank.

Good. I didn't have one to give.

As we dressed, Mom and Jake walked around the bushes, secretive smiles on both their faces. Resolve hit me. Tarek might not like Winston's idea, but if it saved my family–saved Teenesee's world–how could I say no?

Simple, because saving them put Tarek and his world in danger.

Shit.

If an easier solution would drop from the sky...

Actually, I didn't want a goddamned thing to fall from the sky.

∞ ∞ ∞

We ended up in Arizona. Of all the places in Earth to hang out, the dimension's Warden chose the hottest, driest dust heap imaginable. Okay, maybe a slight exaggeration, but the sweatshirt and jeans I had changed into definitely weren't conducive to an Arizona summer. Not even the setting sun helped with the heat.

The sweat factor doubled since our portal opened in a stuffy pole barn big enough for the five of us. The place was empty except for a lawn mower and some shovels. Funny, because when Winston pushed the door open, easily breaking the padlock with a little finger magic, not a blade of grass existed.

"You could've let me in on where we were going. And a tool shed? Nice one." I frowned at Winston, placing the blame directly on his shoulders. The suffocating heat didn't get any better. It hitched a ride with us as we hiked to the center of town.

"Hey, blame little Miss Guide over there. She's the one who gave coordinates."

Avery didn't look comfortable, either, with her long smock plastered to her perspiring body. Small stains showed under her arms every time she raised them. "I am sorry, Lena. Cheveyo designates the landing spot so no one sees our portals. To open anywhere else would show disrespect."

I snorted.

"Again, my apologies."

"Whatever." I cinched my bag higher. "I'll grab a T-shirt from a gift shop or something." I took in the small town–er, I guess it was a small town? "What is this place?"

Winston walked ahead with Farren, obviously neither up for a game of twenty questions. Avery was nice enough to fill me in. "It's what is called a reservation."

I tried hard not to give her a "duh" frown. I knew what a reservation was; I did take history class. Instead, I kept listening even as I pushed open the door to a small shop with T-shirts hanging in the window.

"Cheveyo has lived on this very spot of land for centuries. He has never left, even when the land was stolen."

Okay, time to stop the history lesson. I already had enough to feel shitty about. "Yeah, my ancestors, along with every other person of European descent, were assholes. Got it. I'm already onboard. Question is, why? I mean, the keeper of all Earth's energy chooses to live here?"

She held up her chin, her eyes turning to stone. "He stays because these are his people, regardless of his burden."

Uh-oh. Think I touched a soft spot.

I went into the tiny dressing room to swap my Penn State sweatshirt with my brand new *I Love Arizona* T-shirt. I raised my voice so she could hear me over the cheap partition. "Sorry. My bad."

I came out to her serene smile, the same one she gave during our first meeting. Freaked me out, really. "Forgive me, Lena. This has been quite stressful. I do not mean to be short with you."

"No worries." I walked to the register after grabbing five waters from the front cooler. I pointed to my shirt and the waters, the woman cashing me out barely acknowledging me. "So, do you think he'll help us?"

197

"He respected you before, and I hope he respects you still."

Something hit me. "Hey, you knew where Winston was. Why not everyone else?"

She looked down. "It was part of our bargain…for him to always let me know where he dwelled. I-I sent you close to him…after your execution, hoping he'd find you, maybe help you."

"Looks like that didn't work out for you, either." We filed out of the small store, and I handed a water to the guys. "Don't say I never did anything for you."

"Thanks, kid." Farren cracked open the bottle and took a huge swig.

"Don't call–whatever. You're welcome."

Winston stuffed his in the back pocket of his baggy pants with a nod and again took the lead. Farren shrugged and went with him.

Avery didn't move. She waited until they were half a block down the road and cupped her mouth with her tiny hands. "Gentlemen, you are going the wrong way, I'm afraid. Please, follow me."

Winston and Farren turned. Nicolette smiled as Avery veered toward the open land beyond the settlement. Just like that, we all followed the Guide, her Protector staring on with pride.

We trudged through the sand and stone for what felt like hours. As the three of us walked behind Avery and her guard dog, Winston kept his voice low. "I need to let y'all in on something. The Warden, he does some shit to your mind with his voice. Hell, with any sound he makes. His way of controlling the situation."

I smiled. "You mean like Teenesee's beauty? Don't worry. I can be around her without drooling too much."

The side of Winston's mouth curved up. "Don't get cocky, Tainted. He's like venom on the brain. You'll be smiling right up until he breaks your neck. You might even ask him to do it."

Farren tensed up beside me. "How're we supposed to handle that, man? Plug our ears? Won't that piss him off?"

Winston pulled his earbuds from his front pocket and scrolled through his phone. "Do what you gotta do, but try not to get dead, you heard?"

Well, that didn't sound comforting.

At least the desert was beautiful. It shined at night, the plants and muted color like an ocean bed. Dry air smelled clean, as if the moon brushed away the dust. We stopped at a ridge hiding a small opening wide enough for two people. Avery didn't attempt to walk in, but stood in front with hands fidgeting at her sides. Taking her example, we all waited, no one saying a word.

Nerves snuck through my body, making my hands tremble. This was it. If the guy didn't want to help us–worse, if he wanted to kill us–we were alone. Screwed, really. Yeah, we'd go to Empyrean, but our help wouldn't amount to shit. Unless you asked Winston.

Shadows coming from the opening brought me out of my head. Faint footsteps echoed off the stone and calm washed over me. A person floated toward us, his gait graceful. Winston and Farren flanked me, not helping the nerves at all, regardless of the peace juice flowing through my blood.

All of us had faces painted with that ridiculous Arcus color. Hopefully the guy wouldn't kill us for looking stupid. When the person, who hummed low, ended up being a slight man who I assumed was Cheveyo, the calm intensified, suffocating the fear. I wanted to curl up in a ball and sleep, not caring if poisonous reptiles snuggled with me.

My eyes drooped, and I would've fallen to my knees if it weren't for Winston, who grabbed my elbow and held me up. I searched his face, a drunk smile hanging out on mine. "Thanks."

Winston shook his head, not even close to relaxed. "He's using his crazy shit. Snap out of it."

I tugged on his blond-tipped dreads. "Lighten up, chief."

He held me tighter with one hand and elbowed Farren. "You too. Pay attention or he'll kill you. Both of you."

Farren heeded the warning better, looking away from Cheveyo. As the Warden's footsteps grew louder, Farren slammed his palms over his ears and hummed. I tried. Really. But this feeling, this Zen, why waste it on trying to stay alive?

When Cheveyo spoke, my insides turned to liquid. "I've been expecting some company."

All right, you win. Where do you want me to stand? Or would it be easier to kill me if I lay down.

Farren wasn't so eager to die. He stormed off into the desert about fifty feet, his palms still over his ears and pacing. And Winston? Guess only one of us had the ability to be cool in any situation. I patted his cheek and noticed the earbuds firmly set in his ears. *Oh, right!* Ah, so maybe not so cool after all, huh? Even Super Winston had his kryptonite.

Nicolette sat on a boulder, heaving. Her desire to stay by Avery obvious, but she'd be worthless if things got sticky. Moans leaking through her tight lips said that loud and clear.

Avery didn't seem fazed all that much, though she wobbled when stepping forward with her hand outstretched. "Cheveyo, it is so nice to see you again."

He took her hand. *Hmm...a polite murderer.* "I wish I could say the same, Guide."

"Please, give us a moment to explain." She gestured toward me, and I waved. He didn't wave back. "We've brought Lena with us."

He glanced my way with a slight smile. "She is supposed to be carrying out punishment, not organizing a rebellion." He turned back to Avery. "Is that not what you all are doing?"

Exactly! Thank you. Wait, do I get to keep Tarek? No, not thank you. I pushed Winston's hand off my arm and stumbled forward. "Hey, fu–"

Before I told the guy exactly what he could do, Winston locked me in a hold that would impress any cage fighter and drug me to the side. Once he stopped, his hand clamped over my mouth and his lips butted against my ear. "Shut. Up."

I struggled a little, but like with Wilma, to show I didn't appreciate the censorship. His hand and hold didn't budge.

"Exemplar has come to her, not the other way around." Wow, Avery could talk fast when she wanted to. She gave me a disappointed grimace before turning back to plead our case. "Teenesee is under attack, Warden. And if Exemplar wins the battle…"

Cheveyo held up a hand. "Come."

This time when he spoke, my mind and body bounced back from the brink of Stupidville. I shrugged from Winston's loosened hold, my cheeks burning. Farren joined us, the bright red patches on his cheeks matching the ones flaming hot on mine. As we all plodded into the cave, Ginger bent close to my ear. "You almost told a Warden to fuck off."

Like I needed to be reminded? "Yeah, well…well…you look like a clown."

He laughed. "Maybe, but I still didn't almost tell a Warden to fuck off."

"*Almost*, Ginger. *Almost* is the key word here."

∞ ∞ ∞

In the deep center of the cave, enough room existed for at least twenty people to stand upright. A small fire crackled in the middle, and when we sat, the comfort of soft leather hides and cushioned blankets protected our butts from hard stone. Everything about the Warden and his area screamed calm, even without the hypnotist act he used on us outside. The smell of wet stone created an earthy invisible shell around us. Water trickled from the rock ceiling in the far corner. No clue how there could be so much water in the middle of a desert, but I'm sure it had a lot to do with who lived here.

Cheveyo sat cross-legged on the opposite side of the fire. His slight body didn't hide the sinewy muscles in his arms and chest. His face…boy, his face…all young and dark with smooth skin, full lips, and straight nose. *Damn.*

No one said a word while Cheveyo took his time to scan all our faces. His eyes stopped on Winston the longest, that smile he wore deepening. "You surprise me the most, Protector. I haven't heard from you since your arrival here. Why the change of heart?"

Winston pulled out his earbuds, the music coming from them soft, like Mozart or something. "Sorry?"

I was the disrespectful one?

Cheveyo didn't seem pissed and repeated what he'd asked.

"I returned a favor that ended up turning into a lot of favors." Winston shot Avery, who had the decency to blush, an irritated smirk.

Cheveyo nodded. "Yes, that seems to be the norm when dealing with Exemplians."

He grew quiet again, watching us. Silence didn't bother me, though. The place was too damn cozy to feel self-conscious. After a few minutes, Cheveyo reached into a pouch to his right and pulled out a small pipe. He took a hit and offered it to me. I shook my head, never a fan of the habit, the smell familiar. The trailer parked reeked of weed more nights than not. He shrugged and offered to Winston, who had no trouble lighting the pipe and sucking deep. Farren and Nicolette took it after Winston. Avery declined.

Finally, when everyone was good and high, I pulled the papers from my pack. "Ah, sir, um, we did come for a reason." I handed him the list. "We need help finding these people."

He read the names, smoking his bowl, before giving his attention to Avery and ignoring my request. "Your people are setting up nests here, clusters around my world." It wasn't a question.

Avery fidgeted with her robe's sleeves. "Y-yes. I believe Earth is an imminent target. After Empyrean."

Cheveyo didn't show any anger or fear, though he took a few more hits off his bowl before tucking it back in his pouch. A little weed must do the temper wonders.

"I expected as much, though I did not realize your people were declaring an all-out war."

"I-I have been accused of treason, Warden. Those people are no longer mine."

He nodded, interest lighting his deep-set eyes. "Indeed?"

Her gaze landed on her busy hands. "They found out I have been hiding rogues here." A sob escaped her throat, and Nicolette pulled her close. "They are annihilating Empyrean as we speak. I'm…this…it all falls directly on my shoulders."

The anguish in her voice made my heart ache. "No, this isn't your fault. Cassondra is to blame. Her revenge started this."

She bowed her head, tears falling on her lap. "That is where you are wrong, old friend. I–"

Nicolette shushed her, squeezing Avery's thigh

Weird. But I'd ignore it for now. "Look at me, Avery."

Her shoulders shook, but she held a fist to her mouth, took in a few deep breaths, and faced me.

"She's not gonna win." I meant it, every word.

I nodded to Nicolette, who smiled over her Guide's head, and turned to Cheveyo. "You trusted me before, believed in the chance to right what Exemplar ruined. I'm telling you, if you help us find these people–our army–we can end this. All of this. For good. No more visits from other dimensions, all energy staying exactly where it's supposed to, we can make it happen."

I drilled Cheveyo with what I hoped passed for confidence. We *could* do this. A little help would be nice, but without it, my group wouldn't stop until Exemplar did.

Farren brushed my shoulder and whispered in my ear. "You got this, kid."

I kept my attention on the man with the answers.

Cheveyo smiled, tilting his head. "Now, there is the Lena I remember. I believe you, and I will give you the locations of many, though I cannot force them to help."

"That will be enough. We'll handle the rest."

He held up the list, pointing at the first three names. "Let's start with them."

CHAPTER 22

LENA

EYES WIDE OPEN

"I don't get why I can't come with you." I stomped my feet and rubbed my arms to fight against the chill, the desert night not anywhere near as hot as the desert day.

We all huddled outside the cave, ready to find the twenty or so people Cheveyo gave us locations for. He said some had no desire to be found, and he'd respect those wishes. Others had died, a few suicides…a few more overdoses. He recycled their energy as quickly as it came to him before Guides could get to it. They deserved some peace, he said. A chance to love life instead of regretting it.

It'd take a while to find those twenty, though, seeing as they were scattered around the world. Winston refused to let me come, opting to take only Avery and Nicolette. Farren didn't seem to mind, one arm already in the air and the other snaking around my waist.

I pushed him away. "Easy, Ginger." I went to plead with Winston again. "Come on, let me come. I can help."

Winston shook his head and launched me back into Farren's hold. "Imma let you in on something, Tainted, and you ain't gonna like it."

"What? What could you possibly say that would–?"

"These people probably hate you."

Yup, that got my attention. "Why the hell would they hate me? They don't even know me."

He shrugged. "For starters, I hate you. The you before, ah, you, anyway. And if you come, those people are going to see a familiar face they've spent years wanting to forget. They might try to kill you before we can get a word out."

The tears came so fast, I had trouble holding them back. I couldn't hide the shaky voice, unfortunately. "Why do you hate me?"

"I don't hate *you*. I hated who you were. And I'd bet everything I had these people aren't your biggest fans, either."

See! I knew it. Past me was an asshole.

When he didn't volunteer any more information and began to follow our earlier path back to town, I went after him. "Hey! You can't say something that shitty and not explain."

He stopped without turning to face me. No problem. I circled to his front. When he still didn't offer up an explanation, I pushed him.

"You better watch yourself, Tainted."

I pushed him again. "No, screw that. Talk. Now."

"Or what?"

"Or…or I swear I'll…" I pushed him a third time.

He caught my wrists, his cool never leaving. "You really want to know?"

I had a hard time seeing his face, tears now flowing without restraint. *No* would've been the best answer to his question. "Yes."

He stuffed his hands in his back pockets as his eyes hardened and his mouth thinned.

"Tell me already. I'm a big girl." *Let's disregard the tears and my snot-swiping hand...*

"Kendal was an amazing woman. Kind, gentle, still able to love, even though she lived in that hell for so long."

Oh, shit.

Once the first sentence spilled out, he wouldn't stop talking. "And Mateusz? Good guy, your man's best friend, actually. That is, until your threats against his woman made him fucking crazy." He pulled a hand from his pocket and pointed at me. "You, on the other hand, were a heartless bitch. We were all the enemies. Every last Exemplian was guilty of ruining the universe's natural flow. Didn't matter to you most were in the dark when it came to the truth, or those who weren't wanted to leave the place as bad as you with people they loved."

"I… Avery said I fought for…" What the hell did I fight for?

"You fought against everyone who didn't see as black and white as you." His cool disappeared, replaced by anger that rolled off him in waves. "That list? Those people? You dug, blackmailed those you thought might ruin you and Avery's grand scheme. Save the True Wardens, take away Exemplian power. Right the fucking universe!" He moved closer until our noses almost touched. "Even if that meant destroying every single person who desired freedom as much as you."

I stood my ground, but realized why everyone was so leery of Winston. His anger radiated like an atom bomb. "*I* didn't do it, Winston." I wanted to show courage, but my voice came out airy, betraying me.

His eyes closed and his hands shook as he put them on my shoulders. "Kendal was my friend. What you did to her killed her on the inside. Those people on that list, they left after your execution to try to start new lives, afraid another vigilante would pick up your cause. Avery felt guilty enough to help hide them, show they were recycled in their files or rogues who were unfindable. Like she did for me. My name might not be on that list, but I was on your radar."

Oh, my God. I'm a monster…

His fingers dug a little too hard into my upper arms before letting go. "Finally, I had what I wanted. And now, under different circumstances, you're again threatening everything. These people will feel the same."

The tears came harder. Remorse, guilt, hatred toward myself, all of it brought me to my knees. "I didn't know."

Winston knelt beside me. "Now you do."

I looked past him into the black desert, wishing it'd swallow me whole. "I'm doing it again, aren't I? Putting people's lives at risk? For the same thing."

He cupped my cheek. "It's different now. You aren't the cause for all the fear this time; you're the solution to end it. This life–*your* life–is different. *You're* different, and I'm with you."

"But what if that's not enough?"

His cool dug its way back to the surface. "Didn't you hear me, Tainted? I'm with you, and every pissed off rogue we find will know it."

Okay, okay, I'd admit it. I liked the guy. I mean, really, really liked the guy. "You're pretty full of yourself." I hiccupped a couple times, the spasms from my crying jag not ready to cut my pride a break yet.

"Nah, I'm a facts guy, and them's the facts." Winston stood, helping me up. "Go on now. Get yourself back to your dude before he gets antsy. Tell him to expect these people floating through his lines in a day or so."

My heart split and tore. Tarek. His love for the past, the stories he told about this courageous, perfect woman I could never live up to, all of it was a lie, a lie that burdened me with the consequences.

A lie he'd have to explain.

Later.

"Winston? This plan you have, wanna share a little?"

I didn't expect him to tell me anything, and so when he moved to sit on a boulder and motioned for me to follow, I hesitated. He sighed. "You want to know or not? I suppose I should spill it, seeing as how you gotta leave Arcus sooner than the rest of us."

"No, yeah, it's…"

He nodded at all our spectators still waiting by the cave entrance and held up a hand. "One minute, people." Grinning, he patted the spot next to him. "Sit. I'm about to give you a glimpse of genius."

Too tired and drained to argue that last point, I sat, propping my elbows on my knees. After he spoke for fifteen minutes, using creative hand gestures to emphasize certain parts of the plan, even quashing the initial fears Tarek had, the hope shined hot enough to protect me from the desert chill. When he finished, I stared at him in complete awe.

He raised a brow. "Well, what do you think?"

I had to use all my willpower to not get girlie and fling my arms around his neck. Farren's fangirl face found its way onto mine. "You're brilliant."

He winked and hopped off the boulder, holding his hand out to me. "Told you."

I'd forgive the arrogance because, well, he *was* effing brilliant. "You think Wilma will go for it?"

He tapped his temple. "We've been talking."

Couldn't help but feel a little jealous. "Huh, that's nice, 'cause she hasn't bothered much with me the past few days."

He laughed on his way back to the group. "That's because you're not brilliant."

I snorted. "Whatever."

"And you're not to leave Arcus until she gives you the okay and a location to open the portal."

I shrugged and jumped off the rock. How long I stayed in Arcus depended on what Tarek had to tell me after I dumped all this shit into his lap. I had to go to Empyrean before all my haters made it to Arcus, and it was all my past self's fault. Wilma would understand if I got there early. Hopefully.

Winston grabbed my elbow. "I mean it. Be a good girl and do as you're told."

∞ ∞ ∞

Farren opened the portal nowhere near the castle so we could have a chance to talk alone. When I explained what he and I would be doing in a little while, Farren didn't like it, but went along. There was no denying how perfect Winston had everything mapped out. All Farren would have to do was open a portal. I had the hard part. Confronting Tarek, telling him I'd be leaving.

We walked in silence after hashing out all the details. The squid didn't bother with us. Maybe they were used to our presence, or maybe Belva let them know not to touch us. Whatever the reason, I was grateful.

Before we reached the icy border leading to the castle, I stopped Farren. Concern lighted his eyes, probably because of the tears hovering in mine. He grabbed my shoulders, bending until we were eye to eye. "What's wrong?"

I swallowed, trying to tamp down the desire to sob. Stopped and started a sentence a few time times, too. How to ask someone who felt more like a brother than a friend the tough questions? "Did you hate me? Before?"

Coming right out and asking was one way.

His eyes widened and his mouth formed an O. He cleared his throat, took a breath to speak, and cleared his throat again.

I had my answer.

"So, yes, then?"

He smiled, though his eyes grew sad, and gave me a soft jab to the arm. "Come on, kid. Does it matter? I love ya now."

Tears rolled. "Yes, it matters! Of course! You've all done so much for me, and I don't deserve it. Any of it. You've risked your life, Wilma and Tarek, too. For what? For a…a…bitch who didn't give a shit about anyone?"

"No, we did it–we *do* it–for *you*."

I looked down at my hands, tears now soaking them. Truth always hurt. "Not all of you." *Not Tarek…*

Farren gathered me up in his big arms and stroked my hair while I cried. Just sobbed. I sucked. Big time.

He bent to whisper in my ear. "I couldn't hate you because I didn't know you, not really. You only ever let Tarek and Wilma in."

She didn't even let them in, but I said nothing.

"You were known to work hard, *for* the people. You were loved because of it."

The crying went into overdrive. "But that's the problem, I didn't think about the people. At least, not Exemplians. I lived a lie."

"What? That's not true. You helped–"

"Winston told me. Everything. The list? I used blackmail, Farren. I threatened those people. Bullied them, like I did Kendal."

Farren still weaved fingers through my hair, though now his hand shook a little. "Lena…"

"Was Kendal a terrible person? Bent on some grand plan to destroy the world?"

"No." His voice was soft.

I left the safety of his arms. "Not loving me so much now, are you?"

He gave a quiet smile. This time it reached his eyes. "That, kid, will never change. Even if you decided to go on a mass-murdering spree with pitchforks and a bible." He shrugged. "I'd kick your ass, but I'd stick around to help clean up the mess."

Laughter bubbled from my throat, spilling out. Through tears, I laughed. Laughed until my insides ached. He joined me. We folded over holding our guts, making the squid fidget in the trees.

Nothing felt better than the unconditional, and Farren gave that in spades.

I'd follow him to the end of forever if his big ginger ass asked me to.

CHAPTER 23

LENA

PAIN

Confronting Tarek. A part of me relished blasting him for lying. At least holding back the truth, which was still lying in my book. Another part dreaded it.

I loved him.

With every breath, I loved him.

But how could he have loved the cold-hearted version of me? The version who didn't care who she hurt in order to achieve what she thought the greater good. When he met us at the door, the urge to slap him in the face surprised me so much I had to dig my nails into my thighs.

His relieved smile turned into a frown. "What happened?"

My face *felt* swollen from all the damn crying, and so I'm sure it looked ten times worse. My heart wanted to rip into tiny pieces, but I wouldn't let the tears fall. "We need to talk."

He tried to pull me into his arms, and I stepped to avoid him. "Lena?"

Farren cleared his throat. "I…ah…I'm going in, explain things to everyone."

Neither one of us bothered to watch him disappear into the castle. As soon as Farren left, though, Tarek took a step forward. He didn't try to touch me this time. "What's changed, love?"

213

The cold ate through my clothes and attacked my skin. "Let's go inside first, somewhere private."

"The cabin's private." He stalked by me and headed down the icy path.

"No. Here." I didn't yell. I didn't have to.

He turned to face me, and the sky darkened to a deep gray, almost black as the air turned frigid. "Okay?" He stepped closer. "You're killing me here."

"Tell me about Kendal."

At least the despair left his face, replaced with surprise, which made not touching him easier. "What?"

I wrapped my arms around my middle to hold in the heat and agony. "She an evil plotter? Some kind of sociopath?"

He laughed a little and took another step forward. "Well…no, but…what are you trying to say?"

"Her energy. Does it feel bad, or…or…I dunno marred in some way? Hard to keep inside?"

Please say yes, please say yes….

He stopped and bowed his head. "She… No, her energy is pure."

The ice needed to break, suck me in, and take me away from the pain splitting my chest. "And Mateusz?"

"Lena–"

"Answer me."

"This is crazy." He looked up as the sky turned black and the temperature made the tip of my nose numb.

"Answer the question, Tarek."

"Whatever you heard, don't be–"

"Answer!"

He straightened his back. The black sky opened and hail punched the ground. "No."

I couldn't look at him anymore, the desire to smack him in the face too strong. I muscled the door open and stormed through the rooms, including the one with all the people. My people. The ones who knew me now, loved me.

Me.

I didn't confront Tarek there. With everything going on, the last thing my family needed was to doubt our success. Mom yelled for me, but I threw up a hand and shook my head, going for the stairs. Tarek followed, the only indication of his rage the angry fire leaping from the hearth and the ice storm ricocheting off the castle walls, the sound traveling all the way into the room.

I didn't stop until the third landing, going left until spotting the first open door. The room's smell made my roiling stomach twist and flip like mad, the stench of molded straw and stagnant water making me gag. Who knew how old these beds were. Centuries? Rotting fabrics covering them indicated as much. Ancients, the ones who lived here, thrived here, until Exemplar snuffed out their entire existence.

Anguish and decay doubled me over, dry heaves tightening my already fucked up insides. Tarek stormed in after me, bending to hold my contorted body.

"Don't." I stumbled away, tripping over my feet in the rush to the window. Windows here sucked, so small and too high, leaving no way to escape.

"Lena, please, I'm begging you. Tell me."

The stone, cold and slimy with moisture, held me up. My fingertips ached as they dug in, my nails bending backward. "Everything's a lie."

He kept silent, the ice storm loud enough.

The tears won, racing down my cheeks faster than I could brush them away. My voice skipped and jumped, but I didn't give a shit anymore. "Did you know she was a monster?"

"Who?" His rich voice, quiet and strained, floated into my ears.

I gripped the moldy stone tighter. "You know who."

Silence filled the room, so dark without the light from the gray sky. Only the reflection from the violet forest, now deep purple, gave enough light to keep the room from total blackness. Those pauses, the ones I missed and hated all at the same time, would end up crushing me.

"She...she was...hardened. You would've been too."

"You're defending her. Still."

"In her heart, she wanted to right the wrongs. I...have to believe that. Kendal's actions threatened everybody."

"Stop defending her." The rage creeping from my twisted gut, traveling up my throat, caused my voice to shake.

"She was in so much pain, so much anguish. What she did...I understand–"

"No!" Rage turned apocalyptic, threatening to eat me whole, exploding from my lips. I turned to him. His face, the one that haunted my dreams, became my reality, was now foreign. "Stop it! Stop. Stop. Stop. No more! Don't defend her!"

"Please." His plea stabbed my soul.

"She was selfish, cruel! No one, nothing, was more important to her than accomplishing an impossible mission. Not even you. But, you put her on this pedestal."

His eyes narrowed, and even in the darkness, they glinted silver. Like steel, cold and unyielding. "She loved me."

"Yeah?" *Oh, jealousy, I hate you.* "Loved you so much she neglected to tell you about anything she was doing?"

He pulled his hands behind his back, the action triggering the hail. It began to push through the window. The way his eyes turned to stone...never had he looked at me with such...hate.

His hate fueled the agony, jealousy, and rage already exploding inside my heart. "I'm right, aren't I? She didn't trust you with the cosmic secret. No, she trusted Avery–a Synod member of all people. You meant nothing."

"You need to stop. Now."

"Or what? You gonna kill me? Make me pay for her apathy." I rushed to him, pounding on his chest. "*I* love you. *I* trust you. But still, you think of her as some saint who deserves to be put above everyone? Does she go above me, Tarek?"

He grabbed my wrists, his hold gentle despite the torment on his face and maelstrom outside. "You two...she is inside of you. *You* are *her*. Your love, passion, strength...they aren't new. She didn't start as cold–they made her that way."

He might as well have stabbed me in the heart. "I'm not her, and I never will be." I pulled my wrists from his grip. "I thought you loved *me*. Looks like I thought wrong."

He didn't say a word.

"I can't even... Nothing, Tarek? You got nothing to say?"

Yup, nothing.

A moan escaped my lips, the sound of dying. I rushed to the door, the darkness filling me, suffocating me. Before escaping down the stairs, I turned to face his back. "I'm leaving."

"It's not safe." He didn't argue, though, or try to make me stay. He didn't turn around either.

I hated how I needed him to try to make me stay.

"The others will be coming soon, and my being here might upset them. You can thank your wife, or whatever the hell she is to you, for that." I waited for a reply, anything from him to show I was wrong about how he felt.

He said nothing.

I wasn't wrong.

∞ ∞ ∞

The stairs were an endless, dark path leading me away from my heart. It lay on the stone floor of that bedroom, broken and bloodied with Tarek's boot print.

When I managed to make it into the bright room, the fire now tame, I fell. Just crumbled in the entrance. No more tears came. Numbness attacking from my lips to toes prevented them.

He didn't follow.

Why didn't he follow?

Arms folded me in and the familiar scent of roses filled my nose. Belva. I curled into her, holding on as though letting go would suck me into an abyss. I couldn't hear what she said, my ears refusing to work.

He didn't follow...

Mom's voice penetrated the numb shell protecting me, her soothing words ripping and tearing. "I'm right here, baby."

I looked up, meeting her eyes. Tears hovered there, making them shine like jewels.

With her and Belva's help, I stood. Jake rushed over, not bothering to wipe away the few tears leaking from his eyes. He led me to the couch, shoving a water and granola bar in my hands.

"Thanks." I opened the bottle and took a few sips. I even managed to have a couple bites of granola before my stomach refused to take in anymore.

As I chewed, I found Farren standing close, his face tortured. He said, "Call it. What next?"

I swallowed, the rough grains scratching my throat. *What next?* Dying wasn't an option, leaving one solution.

Fight.

"We leave. Now." I looked to Jake. "Expect visitors, but don't approach any without Tarek. He'll know who the enemy is and who isn't. I-I can't be around when they come. Winston…he'll fill you all in." I nodded to Belva. "Be ready."

She nodded in return and said nothing.

Jake's fists whitened and his lips thinned. "What happened up there, Lena? What's wrong?"

"I can't… Just, please..."

"But–"

"Please." My voice didn't sound like mine. Too hollow, to soft.

Jake breathed in, closed his eyes, and nodded. "Okay, but...fine."

I found Farren again. "Take me out of here."

"But Wilma hasn't–"

"I need to leave." Tears blurred his face, and my numb coating cracked.

He nodded, his eyes sad, but he'd never pity me. God, I loved him for that. "You got this, kid. You *got this*."

I finished off the bottle and handed it to Belva. She accepted with a smile, and whispered, "Farren told me. He'll come around, Lena. Remember, you're his goddess."

No, he'd never see Old Lena as anything else but a saint. In his eyes, at that moment, I was the enemy. In my eyes, so was he. "Whether he does or doesn't isn't what we need to worry about now." I stood, going to Farren. "Please, let's go."

Mom came over and hugged me, Belva and Jake right behind her. "Be careful, baby."

I held her tight before turning to hug the others. Jake had a hard time letting go. "I'll be okay."

He tucked my head under his chin, next to his heart. "Don't get hurt." His voice always so strong, sounded as delicate as paper.

"I'll do my best."

"Do better than that."

"Deal." I went to Farren. "Ready?"

"One second." To everyone's surprise, he stalked toward Belva. Without saying anything, he cupped her face and kissed her. She laced her hands through his hair with a sob. When he pulled away, he said, "When this is over..."

Belva smiled, her eyes shining. "I'll be right here."

"Good." He turned back to me. "Let's do this."

His red face and Belva's surprised joy made my hurt a little easier to bear. But when Farren held my waist, I glanced at the stairs. The pain reignited.

He wasn't there.

CHAPTER 24

LENA

WARZONE

We landed in chaos.

Crying echoed behind closed doors. Screaming followed, so loud it imbedded itself into my soul, and then silence. Death cries.

The streets were strewn with ash and rotting garbage, the smell of corruption enough to make our eyes water. So different from the Empyrean that once resembled heaven and smelled like fresh bread.

The bounce and sway of the town mixed with the stench now caused motion sickness. Stale granola torpedoed from my stomach to my throat, leaving my mouth and landing on a heap of bloody sheets. My foot slipped on the edge of the sodden fabric, and the sheets pulled back to reveal bodies. At least three people, with only parts from others, were stacked on top of each other. The body partially hidden underneath all the others belonged to a kid, no more than five or six.

The hell grew worse farther down the street. Beyond that heap were at least thirty more stacks of blood-covered sheets. Heaves attacked my stomach, no longer able to release anything else. "My God."

Farren picked me up, the knees of my jeans now wet with the blood from innocent people. "Be strong, kid. Don't look at them. Look at me."

His face, pale and drawn, became my focus. I kept my eyes glued to his while he carried me into an alleyway. Seconds later, voices penetrated the muffled cries, the cobblestone streets echoing with loud boots stomping in uniform. Part of me wanted to leave Farren's arms and confront the murdering bastards. A very small part. Fear, a feeling so foreign in the last few months, tore at my insides. A scream formed in my throat, and I had to slap a palm over my mouth and bite down to keep it inside. Metallic blood drenched my tongue.

Farren set me down, careful not to make any noise, after the boots faded down the next street. We stayed there, not moving. Barely breathing. Those boots implanted in my memory, promising nightmares. Only when they disappeared completely did I take my bloody palm away from my mouth. I swiped my lips with the edge of my T-shirt, hand throbbing. Adrenaline rushing through my shaky body made the blood coming from my bite pump out faster.

Farren gasped and took off his shirt, wrapping it around my hand. "Keep pressure on it."

My eyes traveled nowhere but his face, afraid of what else I might discover. "Wh-what's going on?"

Farren held the shirt to my hand himself when I refused to, his grip so tight my fingers felt like they would pop off. "Exemplian martial law. Anyone on the streets will be shot dead. No tasers. Straight-up mercury bullets, right to the head, chest...wherever. Traps the energy. Guides come around and collect the bullets, take them back to Exemplar. "

"Th-there's children…"

"Anyone, Lena. They'll kill anyone."

I pulled my hand from his grasp and held it close to my chest. This beautiful place, turned to ruin. "What will they do next?"

I didn't expect an answer, but Farren gave one. "They'll start going into the houses, killing until Teenesee sacrifices herself."

"No." All these lives… I would gladly take their place. "What if she gives herself up?"

Farren stuck his head out before taking the hand I didn't mangle. "They'll kill them all anyway. This–*this* is an extermination."

A woman's scream, the same scream that blasted the air minutes before, ripped through the vacant street, followed by an infant's cry. I slipped away from Farren and raced to the source.

"Lena! Wait!"

His yelled whisper fueled my legs, pushing them forward. I had to know. I had to make sure. When I reached the house, I peered in the window to find a mother bundling her child. The woman was all alone and had given birth on a dirty floor, the baby's umbilical cord still connecting the two.

There was no choice. None.

Farren came up beside me, his face now white as glue.

"We need to help her."

He shook his head, urging me away from the window. "We can't do anything. All we can do is stick to the plan. If we win…" He looked into the window. "Only if we win can we help her."

I shoved by him and pushed on the door. "Bullshit." Damn thing wouldn't budge. A rattling door was all my shoulder checking accomplished.

The woman screamed, though softly, as if she hadn't the energy left to even do that.

I tried again. Nothing. "Help me."

"Lena…"

"Help me, goddamnit!" All that mattered was the woman and her newborn child. "That baby isn't going to end up under a bloody sheet. Not while I'm alive."

He grabbed my elbow with one hand and covered my mouth with the other. "Which won't be long if you don't shut the hell up."

The woman's terrified whimpering created a whirlwind of anxiety, the beginning of a panic attack. Convincing Farren to help her wouldn't work if hysteria took over my better judgment. Even when footsteps approached, triggering fight or flight, flight really wanting to win, I closed my eyes and breathed in deep. On the exhale, I opened them and took his hand from my mouth. "Please, Farren. Don't let them die."

He tore his gaze from mine to inspect the footsteps coming closer. Shaking his head, he pushed me aside, and with little effort, jarred the door open. The woman's cries grew more persistent as I raced to her, her baby clutched tighter in her weak arms. Blood covered the floor around her.

"Shh...I'm here to help." I reached for the baby, and she cringed holding her bundle closer.

Rapid sentences flew from her lips, mostly coming out as warbled, incoherent yelps.

"I'm sorry... I don't speak Empyrean. Um...Desis? Do you understand?

Her words, still undecipherable, sounded like pleas.

I turned to Farren, who stood by the door, holding it shut. "You speak Empyrean?"

He nodded without looking at me, concentrating on the window.

"Tell her we're here to help."

His attention left the window long enough to give her the message, the language as beautiful as the world used to be. When he finished speaking, the woman, not much older than me, let go of her child with one hand and grabbed the front of my T-shirt. She said something else, sounding more hopeful, relieved.

"Yes, please," I held a finger to my lips, "shhh…"

She smiled, though it did nothing to help put color in her face, her lips white. Footsteps grew louder until we could hear voices mixed in. They were close, right outside the door. Farren, tense and still as stone, stayed hidden in the shadows by the door, his attention never leaving the men and women outside, who laughed and joked. Slowly, I reached for a blanket lying on the other side of the woman and covered myself, leaving an opening large enough to keep an eye on the window. When the mother gave me a confused glare, I held a finger to my lips again and shook my head.

Static filled my head, like white noise. The invasion grew thick, clouding everything but the desire to leave the blanket and run outside. I knew better. Attraction wasn't always healthy. I learned that after Zander. No, there were Guides outside. A lot of them. I clenched my jaw, concentrating on keeping my butt planted on the wooden floor. Magnetism sucked.

As the Protectors and their Guides moved away from the window, the baby let out a high-pitched mewling cry. I scooted farther into the corner, trying to blend with the furniture right before two of the bastards peered through the window. The doorknob creaked, Farren's grip tightening, though his face remained stoic, ready to fight. One Protector, a woman, grinned when she spotted the baby, crying and fussing in the mother's arms. She lifted her gun and tapped it on the windowpane, acting as if she pulled the trigger. The mother cried. No tears came, only the sounds. Her body had no more fluid left, dehydration already having a firm grip.

Fear no longer sat in my gut. Hatred, black and heavy, made my fingertips tingle. I'd only ever wanted to kill another human being once in my life, and what I felt for Casimir didn't even compare to the desire I had to gouge the Protector's eyes out before crushing her windpipe. Hatred overwhelmed all my senses. I could smell it, acidic and rotten.

The Protector laughed when the mother passed out and signaled her partner to move on. Farren and I stayed still for a while longer, even though there was a good possibility the mother lay dead with a crying infant in her hands. When the static disappeared, I shot Farren a questioning look. "They didn't feel us."

He came over. "With all their static, ours would've gone unnoticed."

Good enough answer for me. I rushed to the woman's side, checking for a pulse. "She's alive, barely."

Finding a pulse ran the extent of my medical knowledge. Farren kneeled down beside her, thankfully knowing more. "Check the kitchen for water, a medical kit, clean blankets…"

He rattled off other things, and I sped around the small one-floor home finding everything he asked for. As soon as I found the medical kit hiding under the bathroom sink, I rushed over to him, two carafes of water bunched in my sore hand.

Farren ripped open the metal box and pulled out foreign supplies, most glowing the same color green as those rocks the farmers threw at the Protectors during the initial attack. He unsheathed a large syringe and tapped on the inside of the woman's elbow before plunging the bright liquid into her vein. Her eyes burst open, panic making the whites bright. Farren reassured her with lyrical words I wished I understood.

As she calmed, he held a hand out. "Water."

I jammed a carafe in his palm, my concern switching to the quiet infant. Farren must've been reading my mind because as the woman drank, amazingly having enough strength to hold the water herself, he motioned for me to squat down beside him. "We have to cut the cord."

"What do I need to do?"

He said something else to the woman who released her hold on the child, misery coloring her still pale cheeks. The baby, blue and not breathing, landed in my outstretched hands. I ground my teeth in an effort to keep the horror from my face and a moan from my lips.

After a quick examination of the baby, Farren went to work clamping the cord before using a tiny laser to cut through it. Taking another syringe filled with the same green liquid, and after spending a little more time finding a delicate vein in the child's leg, he pushed the plunger in. In no time, the baby's complexion turned pink and a lusty cry followed. Music. The sound was music, plain and simple.

I pulled the blankets back a little more and smiled through tears before handing the child to her mother. "It's a girl."

When Farren repeated my words in Empyrean, the woman smiled, her deep brown eyes glistening. She wasted no more time and unbuttoned her blouse to give her daughter access to food. In seconds, the baby quieted all but for the suckling while she ate her first meal.

I wiped the tears off my cheeks, the pain in my hand now letting me know it was there, making me wince. "A miracle."

Farren sat back, a deep sigh escaping his lips, sweat shining on his forehead. "Yeah, kid. The best kind of them."

I sat beside him, trying not to gawk at the woman as she cooed and sang to her child. "What was that stuff?"

"Don't really know. Empyrean magic?" He brushed the hair away from his eyes. "Same shit that keeps Exemplian bodies young and healthy. Main ingredient, at least."

"Serious?"

He snorted. "Why do you think this dimension is–damn–*was* so perfect? Exemplar needed to keep it fertile."

Winston's revelation came back to me; he called it Empyrean magic too. "This is where they get the power to help generate people like…like us, too, right?"

Farren gave a sidelong glance and shrugged. "It'd make sense."

"So…why haven't they tried to take it over before?"

"Teenesee's energy is what makes the land so powerful. That'd be my only theory." He slouched against the edge of a small sofa after pulling a picture off the end table sitting next to it.

"Then why would they attack her now?"

He handed me the picture, a frown marring his handsome face. "I guess they're willing to risk taking the strong energy from her people and ship it back to Exemplar. Those Guides you felt? They were in energy form, collecting the dead from inside the bullets."

Shock swirled inside my head. I glanced down at the picture of the woman still pregnant standing beside a man who had an arm securing her waist and a hand on her swollen stomach. Both wore matching bands on their left ring fingers, the same band the woman wore still. Exemplar was willing to risk it because I broke the rules. This…massacre was my fault. I swallowed. "What do you think happened to him?"

He closed his eyes. "She said he's under the blanket out front. Tried to find some food. They shot as soon as the door closed behind him."

My fingers tightened on the picture, the pressure reopening my wound. Tremors attacked my limbs. That hate in my gut churning like hot tar. "I'm gonna kill them all."

Farren shook his head, his eyes still closed, as he crossed his arms over his chest. "Isn't that what you decided to hate about the old you? Black and white, kid, isn't the best way of seeing things."

I wanted to argue, punch him in the head. Cry and sob. Damn. He was right–I wasn't any different from the woman I accused Tarek of...of...double damn.

A lot to make up for–if I lived long enough.

I set the picture on the couch and moved to curl up beside Farren. "I'll fix things."

His big chest heaved with a sigh. "You're not the only one who fucked up, Lena. He needs to explain some shit, too."

That helped the guilt.

It didn't cure the desire to kill each and every one of those murdering bastards, though. Chalk that up on the something-to-work-on list. "I need to talk to Wilma."

"Soon, kid."

Man, I missed her at that moment, missed her with every breath in my body. Tough love always made me feel ten times better. Who knew being called a dumbass would have such positive results? I waved a hand at the mother and child. "We have to take them with us."

He stayed silent.

"Farren?"

He squeezed my shoulder. "I know. We'll give her a day or two to gain some more strength, and then find a way to get to Teenesee."

I closed my eyes, exhaustion promising sweet oblivion. "Farren?"

"What now?"

"You think we have a shot? I mean, do you really think we can take the dimension back?"

"Absolutely." There wasn't any hesitation.

His confidence was liquid gold, melting away all my fear and hardening my courage. "Me too." I glanced over his chest to find our new wards sleeping peacefully, though still covered in the sticky blood. "We need to clean them up."

"Later. Sleep now."

"But–"

"Later."

"No, not later. Now." I shrugged from his arm, and went to find some towels in the back bedroom. Without disturbing the duo, I sopped up the blood with the thick towels and went to fill the carafes with more water. The result wasn't exactly sanitary, but better. Taking some blankets from the couch, I covered them, tucking the edges around the woman's thin body.

After snuggling up to Farren again, I pulled another blanket over us. He smiled, his eyes closed. "You're all right, kid."

I dug my chin into his chest a little. "Thanks for the help."

His chest rumbled as he swatted my chin off him. "Welcome. Now, sleep."

No problem.

CHAPTER 25

LENA

CASUALTIES

They know you're here.

Wilma's warning boomed inside my brain, pulling me out of a deep sleep. I jumped up, and fell, my legs not as awake as everything else. I elbowed Farren who snapped to attention and made it to his feet in under five seconds.

"What? What is it?"

He didn't wait for an answer and stomped to the window, touching the bottom right corner. The glass turned black, but didn't obstruct our view of what went on outside, which was nada. Definitely a good thing. He scanned the street anyway, craning his neck and pressing on the sill to get a better look farther down. "Well? You planning on answering me?"

I used the couch to help drag myself up and plopped on the bright orange cushions. Everything, from the furniture to the dishes in the kitchen sink screamed with vibrant reds, oranges, and yellows. Happy colors. Now, their lives were destroyed. I had to clear my throat a few times. "Um, Wilma. In my head. Said they know we're here."

"Shit." Farren left the window and bent to the sleeping woman whose little girl found her own way to breakfast. Farren whispered in the woman's ear, his tone gentle. She awoke confused at first, eyes wide. Then total devastation made her dark eyes endless, a sob escaping her lips. Farren whispered some more, my name coming up, while rubbing her shoulder. How he remained calm even though I knew he was wrapped tighter than a metal coil amazed me. After he finished, he gestured my way. "Lena, meet Cara."

I waved, and she gave a quiet smile.

Farren said a few more things, all the while continuing to rub her shoulder. Cara nodded, tears still lingering in her lashes, and wrapped one arm around his neck. He lifted them both and headed toward the back of the house. Without looking behind, he said, "We need to get away from the windows."

I followed. "But, didn't you push that button? They can't see in now, right?"

He pushed the bedroom door open with the tip of his boot and set the woman on the bed, which floated like the town. "Sure, but Guides can come right through the fucking walls in energy form. And I guarantee there's a recon mission ordered to find us. That's why the streets are so quiet." He tucked a blanket around the woman and smiled for her benefit as he continued. "They're trying to give us false confidence, make us believe it's safe to leave our hiding spot. Make it easier for those glowing balls of shit to feel static. Ah, no offense."

"None taken. I'm not a glowing ball of shit in this life."

He grinned. "Once a ball of shit...." His grin faltered and he bowed his head. "We need to leave. Staying here makes us easy targets. Trapped, you know?"

How the hell were we gonna leave, especially with Cara and her baby? If the answer would land right into my–

Stay put and wait until dark so you can see the Guides' lights. You're close. I can feel you. Stick to the alleyways. I'll meet you two blocks west from your current position. Don't be stupid!

Thank you, Wilma.

232

We'd still have to worry about our new responsibilities, but at least we'd have Wilma's help. I smiled and tapped my head. "Wilma said to wait until dark. She's gonna meet us."

"Tonight? Twelve hours…okay." He searched the room, checking the door for locks before tapping the corner of a tiny window too high for me to see out. He asked Cara something when the black didn't overtake the clear glass and she shook her head. Farren cursed. He came back to me, rubbing his forehead. "Here's the deal. Don't. Say. Another. Word."

I tilted my head and opened my mouth. No way did he need to talk to me like I was five.

"No, seriously, shut up. They'll have listened to a recording of your voice, mine too. We stay quiet. Period."

I nodded, finally getting it. Not liking it, but whatever. Unfortunately, no talking meant thinking, not what I really wanted to do. Tarek filled every corner of my mind. If he'd talk to me, find his way inside my mind, tell me how pissed he was. Anything.

I slammed the door on that part of my mind, which didn't help put a block on my heart. No amount of willpower could ease the pain brewing in there. Shaking my head, I rubbed my temples before pointing at Farren, the door…and finally to my mouth.

He shrugged with his hands out and a dumb grin on his face.

Stomping my foot, I made the motion of eating and drinking.

He mouthed *oh* and did some charades of his own.

My turn to hold out hands with a shrug.

Glancing at Cara, who looked at us as though we'd checked in from crazy town, Farren squatted, hesitated, and made what I'd consider an obscene gesture with his hands near his crotch before pointing back to me, a question raising his brows.

Ah, the bathroom…

I pointed from him to the door, mouthed *you first*, repeated his borderline porno moves, and scooped imaginary food into my mouth. He grinned again and left the room, thankfully understanding.

I sat next to Cara, trying to maintain a smile as I grazed a finger across her daughter's soft cheek. When I pulled away, Cara grabbed my hand and squeezed. She said nothing, gratitude and hope clouding her eyes. Responsibility for her safety overwhelmed me. I could barely take care of myself most of the time.

But…this place…

I straightened, clenching my jaw, and squeezed her hand in return. We'd give these people back their homes; give them a reason to fight. I might not be the strongest or the smartest, but goddammit, I had friends who were.

∞ ∞ ∞

Waiting gnawed at my patience. I managed to help Cara wash up and had the nerve-wracking honor of bathing the baby with a sponge that smelled like lavender and a carafe of water while Cara napped. This little person… I was in awe with her innocent face and delicate brown skin as soft as cotton. Fierce protectiveness flooded all my senses when her little hand found my finger and squeezed. That Protector, the bitch who pointed her gun, hopped back into my head, sealing her death. I'd find her. She'd pay.

They all would.

When the baby fussed, I tamped down the rage building long enough to coo and smile as I carried her toward the bed. Cara awoke as soon as I placed the baby beside her. Funny how a mother always knew. She opened her fresh, clean blouse, giving me a smile before feeding her child.

After making sure they were okay, I picked the spot on the floor beside Farren, who hadn't taken his eyes off the door since he sat down three hours ago. Waiting didn't seem to bother him at all. No fidgeting, pacing, nothing. Now that I didn't have the baby to occupy my attention, I had to sit on my hands to keep from pulling at the ends of my hair or tapping on my knees. Leftover dried fish and apricots Farren scavenged from the kitchen sat between us. Wasn't half-bad, actually. I picked at it to keep my hands busy.

I also waited for Tarek to invade my head. Wished for him to, more like.

Waiting.

Waiting.

Somewhere in those long, quiet eight hours, I fell asleep.

Static woke me up.

White noise pierced my temples until I screamed, though the static drowned out my agony even inside my head. Farren didn't have trouble hearing me. He gripped my shoulders as I slapped my palms over my ears, throat raw.

Farren shook me until I met his worried gaze, his mouth moving, but nothing coming out. At least, I didn't hear anything. With every bit of strength I had, I switched my screams to jumbled words I hoped he understood. "They found us."

He stormed to the window, grabbing a thick blanket on the way. Farren covered the glass until the room darkened– all except the twenty shining orbs glinting like stars.

I grit my teeth, their presence paralyzing me. One would've turned me into a drooling mess. Twenty held me on the ground like cement weights, the noise, and my attraction to them, more important than my life.

Farren yelled, though I could only read his lips. *"Move!"*

I tried, I swear, but those orbs...

Desperation colored his face as he glanced from me to Cara who had her mouth open in a scream. One second. That was all the time it took for Farren to scoop me up, fling me over his shoulder, and race from the room, leaving behind Cara and her baby. Orbs followed us through the house. The ten surrounding me created such a magnetic force I couldn't help reaching out to them. Farren stumbled under my weight as he tore open the front door. Ten others floated in separate directions, no doubt to alert their Protectors.

I struggled in Farren's arms, reaching for the lights, slowing him down. I needed to touch them, my arms stretching over his shoulders, and then pummeling his back, kicking him in the chest until he lost his hold. As soon as my butt hit the cobblestone, the orbs, now invisible in the bright sun, pulled me up and caressed me. They trapped me while I smiled, finally able to feel their heat. Static in my head lessoned as though they hypnotized me into loving the sound, craving it. I followed the lights in the opposite direction.

Farren jumped in front of me. As his fist flew toward my chin, and right before unconsciousness took over, I finally heard his voice. "Sorry, kid."

CHAPTER 26

LENA

SAVIOR

Fear cured most things. Hunger, thirst...hope. It filled me up until it ate my insides, burrowing deep into my psyche to remind me I was a piece of shit.

A failure.

I left them there, killed a mother and her child because I wasn't strong enough.

My eyelids, heavy and thick, refused to lift, forcing me to see their faces–Cara and her precious baby girl screaming for us, needing us. *And we just left them.* My mind replayed the same image of those lights swallowing them up, disintegrating them to ash.

Wake up!

My eyes shot open and pain lanced my brain. The static was gone, but the memories of it a dull, throbbing reminder. I tried to breathe, but panic forming in my throat made it difficult to do properly. Hyperventilating created clouds of dizziness. I tried to get up, but slammed back onto a floating surface as soft as velvet. When my movement made the swaying worse, I rolled to the edge of a bed and released all the dried apricots and fish from my stomach.

A bucket scooted under the vomit stream, the heaves so violent I almost fell to the floor. Warm hands held me up and pulled back my hair as I emptied the last of my stomach's contents, leaving a hole so big I wanted to disappear in it, escape everything.

Sobs filled the room, distant at first, but then blaring right inside my head, almost as loud as the Guides' attack. Moisture coated my face, coming from my eyes, my nose...my mouth. I couldn't do it anymore.

I couldn't.

"Shhh...I'm here, you're safe."

Familiar safety of soft arms held tighter, the smell of vanilla pushing past the pain.

Wilma.

I clung to her, not opening my eyes again, not wanting to face reality. Ever. She didn't force me and held on until the very last sob escaped. Until nothing was left.

I wanted to go home, forget everything.

I killed them.

My head stayed nestled in the crook of her arm. She rocked me, stroked my hair. Said words I didn't bother to try to comprehend. I cleaved to her voice. Too much. All of it had become too much. I couldn't deal anymore.

Take me home!

Oblivion rescued me again. This time, blackness gave me peace.

∞ ∞ ∞

The next time my eyes opened, I managed to hold onto my stomach, though nothing lingered there, anyway. Memories created raw pain, but thankfully, emptiness helped to combat the tears. Wilma still held me, gliding a finger up and down my arm, keeping me close.

I never wanted to leave her or this spot again.

"I killed them, Wilma." Tears I thought long gone flooded my eyes, and I pursed my lips to keep the sobs inside.

"No, you didn't. Don't ever think that." Her hand shook a little as she caressed my cheek, holding me closer. "There wasn't anything you could've done."

My fingers pressed into her forearm, and I curled closer to her. "The lights...they were so strong." The tears let go again and there wasn't a damn thing I could do about it. "Why couldn't I see them? *Why didn't I see?*"

She didn't answer, her chest hiccupping as her arms tightened around me.

"I couldn't move...I couldn't save Cara because...I..."

"Shh... Please, don't. They've killed so many, and not a single life they've taken has been your fault."

"But–"

"No, damn it, stop. I mean it. You have to stay strong, Lena. Stay strong."

I moved in closer, wishing I could crawl inside her and hide from everything. "I don't know how anymore."

Her voice trembled, something I had never heard. "Yes, you do. Remember, you're the strongest person I know."

I cried harder. "Tarek...he hates me. I-I can't live without..."

"That boy could never hate you! Trust me. He's in so much pain, I do believe he thinks the world is ending–and his dimension probably isn't too pleasant to be in, what with him moping like a teenager." She pulled away and made me look her in the eyes. "And you could most definitely live without him even *if* that were the case. You are not who you are because of him. You are who you are because in here," she pressed against my heart, "is fire and passion and courage. No one can take that away, understand?"

I scooted closer, now almost on her lap, and looked up. "Love you..."

She smiled, though I swear her eyes filled up, making the blue bright like the sea. "Right back at you, honey. Oh, which reminds me. You really think I'd waste centuries hanging out with an asshole?"

Heat crawling from my neck to my cheeks made me sweat. "He told you, huh?"

"More like yelled it inside my head for an hour. The big bastard gave me one hell of a headache."

"He defended her, even after I told him what she did."

She shrugged. "Well, of course he did! He loved her."

Damn, that hurt. I lowered my head, too empty to muster up any anger. "Yeah, well, he can have her."

"He does have her! *You* are her. Granted, she did let Exemplar defeat her in some ways, but she still had compassion. She wanted change, and just because she wasn't perfect–"

"She used blackmail. Against innocent people. That list..."

"Innocent? Honey, not a damn person on that list is innocent of everything. Neither was she. Neither am I. Hell, neither are you."

"But Winston said... He said..."

She shook her head and rolled off the huge bed, which was beautiful with bright green silk sheets in an elegant room with sandstone walls. "Winston cares about Winston. He also believes in every man for himself, or woman, if you prefer. You...the old you...never put herself first, not even for Tarek, whom she *did* love, mind you! Shitty thing to say to that boy, young lady."

The more she talked, the stronger I felt. Wilma's in-your-face reality checks always erased self-pity. "Yeah, well...well...crap. You have any idea what it's like being jealous of yourself?"

"Nope, and you shouldn't be either. Tarek loves *you*. He's in that damn hole for *you*. Old you had nothing to do with that, seeing as how she isn't…damn. This gets too complicated! Get over it."

I crawled off the bed, strength seeping in to remind me of who I am, not who I was. "Okay, okay, you win. I'll grovel, if he'll let me."

"*Let you?* I've been telling him to stay out of your damn head since you came here. Told him to let you cool off. He's going goddamn crazy."

"Well, can you tell him to talk to me now, please? I need to hear him."

She put her hands on her hips. "Maybe, if you act right. And why the hell didn't you wait until I said it was safe to come?"

I fidgeted with a blanket, feeling like an ass. "I-I was mad."

She slapped her forehead and stomped to the window. "Mad? *Mad?* Well, you being mad got Farren shot, missy."

Terror. News that created nightmares. *No. Not Farren.* "Why didn't you tell me? Where is he? I need to see him… please, God, don't let him be–"

"He's fine. Flesh wound to the leg. But that damn scratch will make him less effective in the fight."

Relief turned my knees to water. I held onto a nearby reading chair to keep from falling to the ground. "Why didn't you say that in the first place?"

"Say what?" Her innocent look didn't fool me one bit.

"Whatever, point taken. I'll listen from now on. Still want to see Ginger, though." I looked around the room, a fire lighting the area, giving the expensive gold and green furniture a soft glow. Night poured in, the breeze stinking of smoke and fire. "Where are we?"

"Not obvious?"

Teenesee's. "How did we…?" I rubbed my jaw, still sore. The memory of Farren's fist slamming into my face climbed to the surface. "That sonofabitch hit me."

"Good thing, too. I found him outside the gate, screaming his fool head off, ten Protectors hot on his ass. Brave kid. Dumb, but brave."

"He's not dumb."

She snorted and went to a dresser in the far left corner of the room and ripped some clothes from the drawers. A pair of pants, matching short-sleeved shirt, and tan sandals flew my way. I caught the pants. The rest landed in a clothes puddle at my feet.

"Get cleaned up." She pointed to a door, which I assumed was a bathroom. "All you're gonna do for a couple days is rest, and then Teenesee wants to see you. Zander, too."

The mention of Zander reminded me of something. "Wilma? The Guides...I couldn't see them. I can see Zander when he's...you know, but them? They were invisible."

She pushed the curls off her forehead and shrugged. "They're more advanced than Zander, like me and Winston, you understand?"

"Yeah, sure." More advanced assholes to wreak havoc on innocent people.

People like Cara and her baby.

I hesitated on my way to the bathroom. The hole in my heart ached, even though Wilma made it smaller. "Wilma?"

She sighed. "What?"

"Do you think they're dead?"

The irritated scowl left her face, replaced with compassion. I didn't have to tell her whom I meant. "I don't know. Farren said–it's killing him, too, Lena."

"The baby...I held her." I looked at my hands, the memory of her soft skin bringing back a fresh wave of tears.

Once again, I was in Wilma's arms. No smartass comments left her mouth. I felt love–and not the tough kind. "Listen, whatever happens, I promise to find out one way or the other."

"Yeah?" I rubbed my eyes on her red shirt, already stained with a night's worth of tears.

"Yeah."

"Wilma?"

"Yes?"

"Please have Tarek come to me."

She touched my cheek with a sad smile. "Soon."

Lynn Vroman

CHAPTER 27

LENA

BROTHER

The view from my window gave a clear picture of the devastation. Smoke plumes trapped burnt-out villages, claiming victory. The verdant fields I fell in love with the first time Tarek brought me here were now muddy and void of foliage, barren of glowing rocks.

All those bodies, strewn on the ground like trash...

They littered the field beyond the drawbridge. Protectors' bodies, useless without their energy–energy Wilma said had been collected by the Guides whose nest had yet to be found.

That was where I came into Winston's plan. Avery and Zander, too. We'd find the nest and burn it. Kill them so our side could collect the Protector energy from the bastards we planned on slaughtering. At first, I had reservations. After the other night, revenge replaced them. They'd die, and I was fine with that.

By the second morning, my body felt strong enough to leave the room. My mind wasn't quite there, but hey, some things weren't fixable with a few hours of sleep and dehydrated food washed down with stale water.

No visits from Tarek didn't help my head any, either. Wilma just kept saying, "Soon."

Our first stop was Farren's room. I insisted. Every other problem and person could wait until I saw for myself that he was okay.

We walked down the hall in silence, Wilma abnormally quiet until she stopped at a door about five away from mine. "He's in there." She studied her feet for a second before bringing her eyes to mine. "They killed Teenesee's daughters. She refuses to speak with anyone. We're hoping she'll talk to you."

Shock ripped through me, freezing my hand on the knob. "Why didn't you tell me?"

"I just did." She moved to the side, folding her hands in front of her.

"You–"

"Hurry up, Lena. This isn't the time." Her blue eyes shot daggers, but the sadness creeping in them silenced my retort.

I nodded instead and pushed open Farren's door. "Five minutes."

When the door shut, I adjusted to the dim light. A thick blanket covered the window. It may have blocked out the sight of destruction, but cries and shots, along with acrid smoke and rot, demanded entry. Forgetting wasn't possible, but I could ignore it for a few minutes, especially when I spotted Farren on the big floating bed, still asleep.

I ran to him, snuggling up to his side. As usual, his eyes popped open and he darted up, wincing when he put pressure on his leg. He turned to me and relief replaced the pain filling his eyes. He then fell onto the mattress and gathered me up in his arms, saying nothing. His chest moved erratically, breathing heavy, then not breathing for a few seconds before returning in a rush.

I cried with him.

Long after five minutes passed, and surprisingly no interruption from Wilma, Farren's breathing returned to normal, as did mine.

I cleared my throat a few times. "You hit me."

He laughed, pulling me closer, his voice shaky. "You're welcome."

"Leave it to you to get yourself shot." I pressed my fingers into his chest, making sure he was there next to me.

"Yeah, well, you're not exactly light. Slowed me down."

"Something you should never say to any girl."

He stroked a finger up and down my arm. "You're not *any* girl, kid."

My brother. Always. Forever. "Thank you."

"Just the truth."

I sat up, needing to see his face. "When Wilma told me you got shot…I almost died, right there."

He smiled, his eyes a little swollen, and brushed hair from my eyes. "Can't get rid of me that easy, remember? Besides, I don't think it's possible for you to live without me. Who'd teach you how to give a proper right hook?"

No, I couldn't live without him and not because of his skills in the ring. So many more reasons why bounced in my head, threatening tears. I swiped at my eyes and pasted on a smile. "I *would* have a tough time, what with Belva kicking my ass for not protecting you."

The mention of my friend caused his face to redden, his smile shining bright. "She's something, right? A goddamned Arcus ancient. Whatever the hell that means for the future."

I hopped off the bed after giving him a hug. "It doesn't matter because you'll be by her side."

He nodded, adjusting his bandaged leg. "You got that right. We'll all live happily ever after in Arcus, raising squid and swimming with elephants. One big fucked-up family."

I tried not to let Tarek into my mind, but not thinking about him was like asking my heart to stop beating. Neither possible.

"Guess we'll see."

∞ ∞ ∞

The last thing I wanted to do was leave Farren. I left anyway, promising to stop by as soon as I could. Wilma still waited. Miraculously, no irritation marred her round face. "Ready?"

I swept a hand down the hall. "Lead the way."

The walk took longer this time, going past room after room. Silence taking over the huge manse bothered me, so different from the pleasant chatter bouncing off the walls the last two times I'd been here. Like the house mourned Teenesee's daughters, too.

By the time we stopped at a set of large marble doors, I wanted to scream to create noise. Before Wilma opened them, she grabbed my shoulders. "I need you to prepare yourself. Teenesee…she's not the same."

"I'll be gentle."

Worry stained Wilma's cheeks. "That's not all. All the killing has weakened her, especially since the bastards are taking Empyrean energy too. She's using what she has left to protect this house."

Fear sizzled through my body, making my fingertips numb. "What're we gonna do? What if–"

She shook her head, palming my mouth and refusing to open the door. "See, that's not how I want you to react. Be strong, confident. Make her feel like we have a fighting chance, get her to see past her grief."

I swallowed, taking her hand from my mouth but keeping hold of it, needing to steal her strength. "Do we have a chance? Be honest. Can we win?"

She raised her chin. "Of course, we can. Those fuckers are idiots." She shrugged. "Idiots with large numbers and a lot of guns, but still idiots. And not one of them is stronger than me or Winston."

Man, I hated being a pessimist. "Yeah, but their numbers…"

"…mean shit. The plan is solid." She cracked open the door. "Now, go sell that to her. Make her believe her children didn't die for nothing."

I hesitated. "I'm not selling her snake oil, am I?"

"I wouldn't agree to any dumbass ideas."

"But–"

"Enough." She pulled the door wide and thrust me in, closing it behind her.

"Lena!"

I turned to find Zander rushing forward. I met him halfway, that familiar static filling my head. This fuzz was welcomed, unlike the potent, hypnotizing effect the authority Guides had. The dull buzz brought back memories–and not all bad. It reminded me of how I used to be a kid with the one goal of getting into college. Funny, how the new goal was trying to stay alive. When his arms wrapped around me, the desire to reverse time before all this and be with him in high school overwhelmed me. The feeling lasted seconds, but the impact, the urge, gave a residual ache.

I kept my face next to his neck, his familiar scent comforting. "Are you okay? I mean, you're not like screwed up or anything, right? No brain loss…except for the usual lack of cells?"

He laughed and pulled away to point to the bandage on his head. "Just a scratch, darlin'. Thanks for the concern."

That southern accent, the fake one he used when he tried to help kill me, made me smile now. His presence in my life then might have been an illusion, but it was a good illusion, and I missed it.

I smoothed a hand over his patched-up forehead. "I'm glad you're not dead."

"Likewise." His voice lost its accent as he guided me to the far corner of a room bigger than my entire apartment. He acknowledged Wilma, who followed us, and spoke in my ear. "She hasn't left that chair in days...since her daughters..."

I pulled on his hand, stopping. "You two stay here. Let me talk to her alone."

"You sure?" Wilma stepped up, her voice a raspy whisper. "You don't have to do it alone."

"Of course." I let go of Zander. "Has she eaten?"

"No, she—"

"I am in mourning, not deaf." Teenesee's honeyed voice, defeated and fragile, had all of us looking at our feet. Even Wilma.

Treating her like an invalid was stupid, despite her tattered heart. She still exuded power, even in her grief. Something I shouldn't have forgotten.

"Um...sorry." I cleared my throat and stood taller. "Truly, I am so, so sorry."

She sat in a high-backed chair, staring out the window, not barricaded like Farren's or bolted like the windows we passed to get to her room. The cries, shots, smells...everything deplorable, sinful, carried into the room with a breeze thick with the tinge of blood and death. She made sure her seat was as close as it could be without falling out the window. Her torture. Self-induced punishment.

Without looking behind her, Teenesee held out her hand. "Come, Lena."

I stumbled in the rush to her side, kneeling at her feet while taking her hands in mine. I wanted to reassure her, tell her we'd beat these bastards back to hell, and steal their energy. Restore her beautiful dimension.

None of that left my lips.

I held her cold hands and said nothing. Her ashen face stayed focused on the mayhem outside her window. She winced every time a scream–a final death scream–floated inside the room. When she winced, I squeezed her hand tighter, as if the pressure had the power to take away the grief.

She finally spoke, the pain in her voice reaching my soul. "They slaughtered them like lambs. Took them away from me as though they were trash for disposal."

I remained silent, squeezing her hands so hard my knuckles turned white.

"My beautiful daughters, so brave, now ash. Their souls taken."

The lump lodged in my throat made it difficult to breathe, but I couldn't do nothing, say nothing. My grief…specks of dust compared to hers, and it was about goddamn time I remembered that. Her daughters, Cara and her child, they needed to be avenged. Others hiding, hoping not to be next, needed saved. My people were the solution. If the Protectors Winston found hated me, so the fuck what? They'd get over it and help us fight. Exemplar's time running the universe was over.

I pulled a chair beside her and sat resting elbows on knees. "Look at me, Teenesee."

She refused, acting as though I hadn't spoken.

"Please."

Her topaz eyes closed as she bowed her head. "I have failed my people."

I leaned closer, squeezing her hands again. "No, you haven't. Those bastards ambushed you. They ambushed all of us. *Please, look at me.*" When she finally leveled her gaze with mine, I shook my head. "I won't let them win. *We* won't let them win. Tarek's going to open the lines, suck those bastards right in to play with the squid. And…and we have an ancient. Have you heard?"

A flicker, the slightest hint of faith lightened her eyes. "I have not."

I smiled, trying to transmit my confidence to her. "Well, we do. She controls the animals in Arcus with more precision than Tarek. We also have Winston Candell. You know him, right?" At her nod, I continued, "And I've spoken to Earth's Warden. He's in too. We'll find that goddamned nest and burn it to the ground. No more energy will leave here."

"How… How have you managed all this in such a short time?" Familiar strength seeped into her face, causing it to shine with that deadly beauty not many could fight against.

Finally.

"You believed in me before. Believe in me now because I believe in you. And I believe in your people. We *can* win, Teenesee."

Sadness tinged her eyes. "I am too weak to help you."

"That will change soon."

"If they kill me…"

I stood and palmed my heart like a knight in Arthur's court. Maybe silly, but that was how I felt and I was going with it. "They won't get a chance, I swear."

She breathed in and rose on shaky legs as she exhaled. "My brave Lena."

A snort interrupted the moment. "More bravery than brains, that's for sure."

I glared at Wilma, who came up behind us with a smirk. The pride shining on her face was the one reason I didn't snap.

Teenesee laughed. Damn, my Protector knew exactly what to say. Sadness had to be over. We needed to work.

I marched to a side table holding dried fruit and a water carafe. After pouring a glass and snatching a handful of dried apples, I went back to the Warden. "Eat something and we'll get down to business."

She accepted my offering after a hesitation. "To think I'd have you caring for me and not the other way around?"

"Just don't ask me to cook." I turned to Wilma and Zander. "What now?"

Zander shrugged with his hands out while Wilma crossed her arms over her chest with a grin. "Well, for starters you need to work on your groveling skills."

"Uh, what?"

"Winston's opening a portal now, right outside the manse drawbridge with thirteen new buddies." She tapped her head. "Sounds like he kept your presence a neat surprise."

Oh, shit.

Lynn Vroman

CHAPTER 28

LENA

DIPLOMACY

Having to apologize for shit I didn't do pissed me off. God knew Exemplians could hold a grudge–Mateusz proved that in the spring. I didn't grovel for him, and I sure as hell didn't want to bow down to the bad tempers of whomever Winston brought through the portal.

Fuck him for not warning them I'd be here. Christ, I left Arcus before they got there–he should've told them then, given them a choice to either fight or leave. I had to do all the convincing? When they all hated me?

Yeah, fuck him. No way would I lose sleep if those assholes hated me.

So why wouldn't the nerves stop jumping around long enough to confront said assholes?

Damn, I needed help–of the psychiatric variety.

Thankfully, I wasn't alone. Wilma and Farren flanked me with Zander and Teenesee walking ahead of us. Farren's subtle limp was the only indication his leg burned. After I left Teenesee's room, Wilma was kind enough to inform me that if the bullet had lodged in his flesh, the compound in it would have dispersed, killing him while pulling his energy inside. Since she told me, my hand hadn't left his. To think he'd come so close…

No. Nope. Not gonna go there.

We all filed into the room, Zander and I sitting on the sofa with Farren standing behind us–after he managed to yank his hand free. He bent down to whisper in my ear. "I ain't going anywhere, kid. Relax."

"Stop getting shot."

He chuckled, standing tall. "Stop making me knock you out."

"Fine." I gave Zander a quick reassuring smile that didn't show the chaos in my stomach. Man, I wanted to throw up.

Instead, I sat straighter, put on the bitch face, and waited. They weren't gonna see me scared. So what if my legs shook like leaves in a windstorm?

Wilma and Teenesee stayed in front of the sofa, as if not seeing me right off the bat would soften the blow. Sitting there, like a damn wuss hiding from the asshole brigade caused anger to eat up the nerves. Not that I wasn't grateful they decided to come.

Really.

But…assholes.

When heavy footsteps came closer, the nerve/anger cocktail wouldn't let me cower behind Wilma any longer. Zander tugged on my hand as I went to get up, which accomplished pissing me off more. "Let. Go."

"Lena, don't. These people…they're not going to react well."

Before I could tell him to shut up, Wilma pulled my hand from his and guided me to stand beside her. "If she wants to stand, let her stand, boy." She winked at me. "My girl's no coward."

I squeezed her hand, staring forward.

Footsteps stopped right outside the door, and…nothing. We all watched the thing, waiting for the marble and plaster to swing open. Leave it to Winston to create drama. But when not even the door's thickness quieted all the yelling coming from the other side, I figured out his reason for all the theatrics.

Great timing.

Sweat trickled down my spine and beaded on my upper lip. The sweating got really serious when Wilma bent a knee and balled her fists, while Farren came to stand beside her. Wilma glanced at him long enough to say, "Be ready."

Full-on Protector mode, Farren nodded, his attention centered on the door.

Teenesee, too weak to stand on her own, leaned against the sofa. "I'll not let petty grudges hinder my people's freedom."

I lifted my chin, even though my legs begged me to run and hide. "They accept the situation, or they leave. Their choice, but when the bastards invade Earth, whoever leaves won't get help from us."

Farren's voice, more like a growl, answered. "You're goddamn right."

My mouth went dry as soon as the yelling stopped and silence took over. As much as I hated the immediate confrontation, actually having them leave would screw us.

You got this, Tainted? Winston's voice, soft and mellow, bounced around in my head.

I clenched my fists, and whispered, "Yeah."

As soon as the word left my mouth, the doors flew open, Winston the first to enter. He gave a slight bow to Teenesee, who nodded, saying nothing. He then moved aside to let everyone else file in, Avery and Nicolette bringing up the rear. The thirteen newbies in the middle had my jaw dropping.

Like Winston said when I met him, I had a hard time with stereotypes. Another thing I'd need to work on if I lived long enough. Only one or two looked like Abercrombie from the gas station, a guy and girl.

Seriously. They could've been on those sexy billboards…well…without the present expressions scrunching up their faces. I, for one, would never buy tight jeans from people who looked like they wanted to tear out my throat.

The rest looked like everyday people. Average. Unremarkable. One even looked old enough to be my grandmother. A few resembled the stuffy librarian from high school, while others looked like they drove minivans and were in morning carpools. They did have one thing in common. The bullets shooting from their eyes, directed at me.

Sticky, wet heat drenched my armpits, soaking my shirt. No one spoke, so different from all the commotion a few minutes ago. There wasn't a need, though. Their eyes said all I needed to hear loud and clear.

I swallowed, wishing for some water, and took a step forward. I glanced at Winston. "Probably could've handled this a little better, huh?"

He shrugged, staying in between the Us and Them teams. "Eh, it's all good."

"Right." *Okay, who's the angriest-looking asshole…ah, supermodel boy.* "You wanna start, big guy?"

Wow, did he ever.

He lunged, fists flailing. He didn't get far. Both Wilma and Winston threw up their hands as Farren moved to tackle the guy. Ginger didn't get a chance to put Handsome on the ground because Winston had him slammed against the wall, immobile.

I tried not to flinch. Everything happened so fast. Farren pushed me behind him while Winston kept the guy hanging on the wall.

Wilma tilted her head, hands on hips. "Nice moves, but I had him."

Winston smiled and dropped his hand. The guy fell to the ground, but hopped back up, moving to come at me again. Winston waived toward Wilma. "He's all yours."

She froze Handsome in his tracks a couple feet from Farren. "Take it easy, hot stuff. We're not the enemy."

No one else tried to attack. Not that they could, with Farren's big body shielding mine and two of the strongest Protectors ever performing parlor tricks at the expense of the now furious Handsome. I moved within inches from him. "What's your name?"

He spit in my face.

"You sonofabitch!" Farren moved like lightning, his limp unnoticeable, and punched the guy square in the jaw. Shaking his hand, he gave me a wink before using his sleeve to wipe the spit off my cheek. "And that, kid, is the proper way to give a right hook."

Being angry would add to the tension in the room, but spit in the face…yeah, that really sucked. "Thanks, Ginger. Let's not beat our guests while frozen, though, okay? Not exactly fair odds."

He removed the last of the saliva. "Don't care. He spits on you again, I'll rip out his tongue." Farren said it loud enough for everyone to hear. Unfortunately, the confrontation headed in the exact direction I thought it would.

Sighing, I moved to put a hand on Wilma's arm, letting my thoughts flow. *I'm gonna have to show them they can trust me.*

Her subtle nod indicated she'd gotten the message.

Stepping toward Handsome again, his lip bloody, I crossed my arms, making sure to stand a little farther back, out of spitting range. "Let him go, Wilma."

When he regained control of his body, he wiped the blood off his face, hate pouring from his eyes. "Would've planned better if I had known you were involved."

I cocked my head to the side. "Yeah?"

His face was still pretty with the split lip. "Your death has topped the list for years."

When footsteps rushed behind me, I held up a hand and shook my head. I smiled, though I really wanted to fall to my knees and beg him not to kill me. "Well, someone beat you to it—over eighteen years ago."

He returned my smile, his blue eyes cold and lethal. "Good thing about knowing the truth is the possibility of killing people more than once."

My arms stayed crossed to avoid showing both the pit stains and the trembling. "You're not gonna get the chance...ah, name?"

He stayed silent.

"You want me to call you asshole, then?"

He raised a brow, the ice melting in his eyes. "Oren."

"Okay, Oren, here's the deal." I moved to stand in the middle of the furious thirteen. "I get you all hate me, and I also get that Winston not telling you I was here threw you a curve."

Oren stepped closer to the older woman, as if I had plans on dropping her to the ground.

Hmm....interesting.

I moved in their direction, his body going rigid, and instantly felt the static. A Guide. His Guide, for sure. I continued while watching her expression, not filled with rage like everyone else. "I'm only gonna say this once. *I* am not the person you despise. *I* didn't blackmail you. And we all know what will happen if Exemplar begins to wage a war on dimensions, seeing as how you've made a pit stop in Arcus before coming here."

I paused, giving them all a chance to let that sink in. They were Exemplians, and so they should get how serious the situation was without me going into gory detail.

When shoulders relaxed and the death stares dimmed, I cleared my throat. "I might have been your enemy before, but I'm your ally now. We can stop them—as long as we can be civil enough to trust none of us will cut each other's throats."

Oren piped in, his voice hard. "If you think the small lot of us has a chance in hell at taking down Exemplar, you're delusional. They'll keep coming until they get what they want."

"Maybe so, but we can win *this* battle. We'll worry about each attack as they come." I smiled at the older woman. "And now that we have four Guides, finding the nest will be easier."

Oren stood in front of her before she could answer. "Grace won't be joining the fight."

"She can't speak for herself?"

He took a step forward, and no amount of convincing with my hand gestures prevented Wilma from coming to my side. "You touch Lena, I hurt you. Simple." She moved to stand beside Farren, who rocked a death stare. "Listen to what the girl has to say and maybe you'll learn something."

Oren clenched his jaw, the left side developing a tic. He then moved back to the older woman, grabbing her hand. "Like I said, she's not helping."

The woman pulled her hand from Oren's before patting his forearm. "It's fine, Ore. I can speak."

I nodded, not taking my eyes off Oren's angry face. "Yeah, *Ore*. Let her speak."

The older woman wagged a finger in my face. "There isn't a need to antagonize. He's trying to protect me, as are the people who love you."

Ah! She had me. Lowering my gaze away from Oren to acknowledge Grace, I smiled, though my face burned. "Sorry. You're right. He's your Protector, I take it?"

She folded her hands, fingers bending with arthritis, and returned my smile. "That's what he tells me, anyway."

My insides froze. "What do you mean?"

"Oren landed on my doorstep one day, and I decided to like his company. To be honest," she tapped her forehead, "I thought he was a might touched, you know, in the head? Never really believed his stories until your friends came to us."

Holy... So, she was like me.

I found Avery in the crowd. "Care to explain?"

She fidgeted, her tiny hands combing through her hair and fussing with the front of her robe. "I-I made a deal...with Oren, eighteen years ago."

"You're full of deals, aren't you? What'd you promise him?"

She opened her mouth, but Oren beat her to it. "She promised to help me find my Guide in exchange for my promise to not find you."

"*What?*"

Avery rushed forward, grabbing my hands, her eyes pleading. "Grace chose retirement and was living another cycle in Earth. She was his Guide through three cycles in Exemplar, and he needed...um, in order for him not to seek you out, I told him where to find her."

I shrugged my hands from her grasp, my whole body shaking and ready to explode. "So, what's Earth? Your dumping ground? How many Exemplians have retired there?" I narrowed my eyes, so wanting to hit her. "Better yet, how many recycled Exemplians are you *hiding* there?"

She blinked a few times. "Umm...I–"

"That many, huh? Why would you do that? Earth's, what? A hotbed of unassuming recycled Exemplians? All that energy–all that power–easy pickings for those bastards! And we don't have magic rocks there to help us! They'll... Christ, they'll burn it to the ground!"

She cried. "No, the dimension is too large, the largest. They'd be insane to attempt–"

"A takeover? Didn't you tell me Earth was the next target?" I stepped closer. "Guess they're pretty fucking insane, huh?"

Nicolette came to wrap her arm around Avery, but she stayed silent. Maybe she thought the idea as stupid, regardless of how much she cared about her Guide.

"I never thought... I assumed we'd have a plan in place. A way to defeat them before they found out! I needed," Avery grabbed my hands again, "*we* needed to make sure there was enough concentrated energy in one place. Please...our intentions were good. They–"

"No. No more. Your voice makes my ears bleed." I moved away before I gave in to the temptation to practice my right hook. "Everyone, please, who she's talking about, who I used to be, I'm not that person. Not anymore. I want what you want. Peace. A chance to live my life without Exemplian interference."

When a few grumbled, I held up a hand. "Wait, I get it, trust me. What happened to you, I'm sorry, truly. But who I was... Damn." I looked at my hands. "Who I was wanted Exemplian control to stop." After a deep breath, I met every gaze. "And I agree with her."

A collective roar resounded, and some of the soccer moms rushed me. Surprisingly, before Wilma had to throw anyone else in the air, Oren spoke up. "I agree with her, just not with her methods. Prove you're different."

"How?" Anything. I'd do anything to prove it.

"We fight if, and only if, we do it together. No secrets. No blackmail. If someone wants out, we let them out."

I couldn't nod fast enough. "Yes, yes, definitely. I agree."

His baby blues shifted solely on me. "And if those we fight want to join us, we let them."

Almost anything.

"Are you insane? We're gonna trust a bunch of murdering bastards to help us? Besides, we need their energy to repair this dimension. No way."

"We'll kill plenty to help Empyrean." He folded his arms across his chest. "Those are my conditions. Accept them, or Grace and I are gone."

Avery jumped in as I opened my mouth, more than prepared for him to leave. "He's right, Lena. Many Exemplians do not wish to be here. There is no choice for them, either fight or be marked Tainted. What would you do?"

No answer for that so I kept my trap shut and listened.

"We can figure out a way–there has to be *some* way–to reach those tired of Exemplian control," Avery said.

I looked from her to everyone in the room. "Does everyone agree to these terms?"

Most nodded, some did nothing.

"Fine." I bit the inside of my cheek to prevent spewing any more reservations. They could save all they wanted, but whoever turned on us would become squid food. "If you don't, you're free to leave, though I wouldn't go back to Earth."

A woman, the librarian look-a-like, stepped forward. "Some of us have families there. People who have no clue how the world truly is. We can't leave them to suffer for our decisions." She looked around. "And you know they will all be made to suffer because of us."

Well, finally a situation we could fix. "We can get them to Arcus. They'll be safe there."

Librarian pinned me with a glare. "Arcus? So they can die of starvation? Or maybe shock? Did you not hear me when I said most do not know of us?"

Stomach acid churned. Any more confrontations and I might run away crying. "We have an Arcus ancient on our side. Her presence makes the environment safer. My family's been staying there and is doing fine. So has Winston's." Time for the dig, I'd think about my diplomacy skills later. "And maybe it's time you're honest with people you claim to love, huh? Let them know who you are?"

Her face reddened. "I'm leaving. If you all choose to stay, so be it." She waded through the small crowd to the doors. Before storming out, she turned to me. "I have no trouble with the truth, Tainted. It's you who had the problem, and I'd never *ever* trust you."

"*Had*." I shrugged, but her words had the intended effect. They cut. Deep. I cleared my throat and addressed our small army one more time. "If you choose to stay, we will help collect your families and bring them to safety once the battle is over. Anyone else wants to leave, now's the time to do it."

I hadn't expected anyone else to go, but two others left. A guy who could be an accountant and the gorgeous girl. Shit. That left ten newbies. I glanced over at Winston, a grin curving the left side of his mouth. "Don't worry about it."

Yeah, sure, whatever.

I went to Grace and hugged her. She looked like she needed it. "I'm sorry, and believe me when I say I understand if you want to stay away from the fight."

She patted my back and pulled away. "I'd do anything for Ore." She gave him an adoring look, which turned his bad attitude to mush.

His face softened as he squeezed her hand. "I don't need you to put yourself in danger."

Her dark brown eyes, so young in a wrinkled, aged face, brightened. "I will do whatever I please, and you'll be fine with it." She turned to me, keeping her hand in his. "Of course, I'll help. But I warn you, the only time I've ever felt the static he always spoke about is when I met her." She pointed to Avery. "Now I can't seem to shut it off."

I smiled, loving her immediately, and gestured to Oren. "We'll help you."

"Good." She yawned, hiding it behind a hand. "I do need some rest, however."

I jumped, ready to do whatever she wanted. "Absolutely! Um…" *Okay, forgot this wasn't my place.*

Teenesee strode to the door, showing no signs of weakness. If the people in the room knew her, they'd wonder about her silence during the whole conversation. Her secret was safe, though. No way would we mention how frail she'd become. "Come, everyone. My home is your home. Rest tonight. In two days' time we will begin to take back my world."

Everyone filed out, some with a shell-shocked expression. Hopefully, no one would have a change of heart once sleep helped clear their mind.

Before Avery left, I called to her. "I expect you'll have an answer to how we're supposed to find the sympathizers soon? If not, I don't see any other option but killing them all."

Her face paled, and it looked as though a small breeze could carry her away. "I will come up with something."

Nicolette glowered at me before the two escaped through the doors.

Oren spoke up when Wilma, Farren, Winston, and I remained in the room. "So, we start the nest search in a couple days?"

I kept my eyes on the door, not bothering to look at him. "If everything goes right."

"We'll all probably die before finding it. Not a doubt in my mind they're watching our every move."

My gut dropped to the floor. The way he said it, as if the outcome were inevitable, scared the living shit out of me. "You always a pessimist?"

Oren sauntered toward the door. "No, but I'm always a realist." He looked behind him. "We aren't the first to go against Exemplar, and we won't be the last." He disappeared up the stairs, taking a huge chunk of my confidence with him.

I turned to Wilma with a snort. "You believe that guy?" I made my voice deep and curved my arms like a gorilla. "*We aren't the first and won't be the last… Prick.*"

She didn't give the reaction I wanted. No, "screw him," or "he's a dumbass." Instead, she hugged me until I could barely breathe. "I love you more than anything or anyone, Lena. Always remember that. Whatever happens, as long as I'm breathing, no one will touch you." She hurried to the door, letting it slam shut.

Shocked, I stood there with my hands out staring after her. "Winston? We're gonna be fine, right?"

He hopped off the edge of the couch. "Nothing's ever guaranteed. But what you're doing…how you handled those people…I'd be proud to die beside you. Have a little faith. We got pretty good odds." He kissed my cheek, his lips warm on my cold skin, and left after a wave to Farren.

The pain in my chest squeezed and ripped until I swore my heart would explode. The way Wilma reacted… So not the confidence she'd been feeding me lately. My complete gullibility up until that moment surprised me. I could die, and I'd never see my family again.

Oh. God.

If I only had a couple nights to live, I wanted to spend at least one feeling alive, remind myself I had something worth living for–and worth dying for.

As if he could hear my thoughts worlds away, Tarek's voice penetrated my brain. *Come to me. Please.*

Yes, yes I would.

"Let's get some rest." Farren grabbed my elbow and led me to the door.

All the color drained from his face, his fingers cold and shaky on my elbow. I stopped, refusing to take one more step. "Wait. Just wait for a second."

He bent his head, rubbing the bridge of his nose.

I moved his hand away from his face and made him look at me. "We can leave. Right now. Go to them."

He tilted his head. "But everything you said...now you want to run?"

"No, not run. Escape for the night. One night. I can't... If I die... Please, Farren. Don't you want to see Belva? One more time?"

A little bit of color came back to his cheeks and his eyes brightened. "Wilma won't let that happen."

"We won't tell her. Anyway, she'll know I'm gone as soon as I go through the portal."

He shook his head. "She'll be pissed."

"She'll understand." I ran to a large map in the corner of the room sitting on a marble pedestal. Our light came from the raging fireplace. Thick iron shutters blockaded the bay window. The soft glow was enough.

"Look, right here." Dimension coordinates appeared where my finger touched the thick paper.

I enlarged the area. "We'll open a portal in the field beyond the drawbridge, where no one is, and return at this spot here. I'll have Tarek tell Wilma when we're coming back, and she'll make sure nothing happens when we return." I tried hard not to start sobbing, my desperation bubbling up and threatening to consume me. "Please, we–"

Farren silenced my hysteria with a finger to my lips. "I'm convinced."

Tears blinded me. One last time. If I had this one time, I'd take it. "Thank you."

"Guess we deserve a day." His serious tone didn't quite pull off the flippant remark.

I grabbed his hand, pulling him to the door. "We're taking one, even if we don't."

We raced through the manse, trying to be as quiet as possible. Farren struggled a little, but his leg didn't seem to bother him much. More than likely thanks to some magic Empyrean meds, the same that Wilma used to mend my hand. In our rush, I ran into a bronze bust sitting on yet another marble pedestal. The head of some obviously important guy would've toppled if not for Farren's quick hands.

Stupid. Bronze clanging on marble floors would boom like cannon fire.

"Sorry." My thin whisper echoed through the empty hall, bouncing all the way down to the opposite end.

Farren shook his head, motioning for me to keep my mouth zipped.

I nodded, feeling like an ass, and kept moving. All it'd take would be for someone to scream or accuse us of going AWOL and alarm bells would start ringing. Well, not so much alarm bells as Wilma yelling while she dragged us to our rooms.

Every time we passed a window, the acrid smells and faint sounds of agonizing screams tore at my heart. Cara slaughtered next to her child raced through my head. The thought almost changed my mind. I did want to save them, all of them, but no way would I be any good if I didn't leave for the night. Farren, I'm sure, felt the same. My reasoning was selfish, but I stuck to that excuse, replaying it inside my head until it rang with truth.

By the time we made it to the thick door leading outside, relief made me giddy. A few more steps, and–

Static.

"Where're you going?"

Lynn Vroman

CHAPTER 29

LENA

FORGIVENESS

Zander's voice poured into my ears like ice water. The urge to jab him in the throat and run almost won over being mature.

"If you say a word, I'll take you out. Swear to Christ." Okay, mature might have been a stretch, but hysteria causing my voice to sound like a soprano also skewed my better judgment.

"Damn, Lena." Farren elbowed my side and grinned.

Zander looked as though I killed his dog. "I-I won't say anything. Just be careful, okay?" He turned in the opposite direction, head bent and kicking an imaginary can down the hall.

Really? Not even a fuck you? I felt like an even bigger shit. Swallowing the crazy, I jogged after him. "Zander, wait."

When he stopped, he didn't bother turning around. I had to circle to the front of him and lift his chin to meet my eyes. "I'm sorry. God," I ran a hand through my tangled hair, getting fingers caught in knots, "I've had to say that a lot lately."

His face, so deceptively adorable, made the guilt fester. "You don't have to be sorry, Lena. Not with me."

Ugh! Didn't that make the guilt happy?

"Yes, yeah, I do. It's... I need to see him."

He smiled that same smile that melted my heart in the past–and maybe a little now, too. "Always knew *Him* would come between us."

When he used my name for Tarek before I knew he was more than a dream, tears threatened. Memories whipped through my mind. Again, simpler times flashed through my brain, when I was just a girl and he was just a boy. I wrapped my arms around his neck.

His fingers kneaded my back, taking the tension and hysteria away. He let go and wiped the tears from my cheeks. "Don't be long, or Wilma will blow a gasket. I don't know about you, but I wouldn't want to be on her bad side."

I laughed even though the tears still came. Man, I'd cried more in the past few days than I had the last six months. "Yeah, I'm sure everyone will know I'm missing when she starts throwing stuff."

"I'll make sure to duck."

I smiled. "Good plan."

Then he did the unthinkable.

Zander leaned in and kissed me–and I let him. His lips were soft, almost imagined when they found mine, but the brief touch reached a tiny place in my heart. "Hurry back."

I nodded, tingling spreading to my fingertips. "I will."

He brushed my cheek and continued down the hall, never looking back.

∞ ∞ ∞

Hail smacked our bodies as soon as the portal dropped us close to the castle. The sky, so dark it blocked our path, kept beating us with precipitation, the golf-ball-sized ice bombs stinging my back, knocking me to the ground. As Farren bent to help me, his face twisted in a pained grimace, the door swung open. Tarek hauled me up and kept me in his arms, the ice hitting him going unnoticed.

Farren barged past us when we didn't move to get away from the storm. "You guys can get beat up all you want. I got stuff to do."

Tarek didn't even acknowledge him. He held me with trembling arms and cupped the back of my head as he turned to protect me from the ice. The storm ricocheted off the stone walls, piercing my eardrums. Still Tarek didn't seem to notice, holding us there, letting the storm attack him.

I stood on my tiptoes and found his ear. "You need to calm down. The ice, it's gonna kill someone."

He buried his face in my neck and breathed in deep. The storm let up, though the pelting ice still smacked hard against his back.

One thing left to do–my favorite thing.

I pulled away far enough to capture his lips with mine.

There was the fire. The blood-heating kind that proved exactly who held my heart. When his tongue pushed past my lips, and the kiss deepened until I swore even my toes melted, the deadly ice disappeared with a whimper. The sky transformed to its normal silver-gray–the same intense gray as his eyes.

His shaky hands pushed through my hair, the kiss going on forever.

Forever was never long enough.

When we came up for air, I finally noticed the bags circling his beautiful eyes. Guilt waltzed back into my conscience, jumping around and getting cozy. I did this to him. Not only did I do this to him, I put my family in danger because of stupid jealousy.

That didn't help alleviate seeing green, though. I still had to share him with a ghost.

Damn. Maybe it was time I learned how to share.

"What I said... I didn't mean it." I held his cheeks, hoping he'd see down to my soul. "How could she not love you? And, I'm so sorry for... I let anger at her–my jealousy–hurt you. Christ, I put Farren in danger because of it, too. I should've never left. I've seen what real devastation is," Cara's face swam in my mind, "and what I did... So stupid."

He grabbed my hands and kissed each fingertip, saying nothing. His face, pale and sunken, made me want to crawl inside him and attack the pain. The pain my words caused.

"I-I understand why she did what she did. I don't like how she did it, but I get it. I do. She...she tried to do the impossible and lost. Lost everything. Lost you."

He leaned in, touching his forehead to mine, holding my hands to his chest. "You were right, Lena."

"No, no, I–"

"Yes. She lost herself, a long time before her death. I never wanted to admit it. She...she blocked me out, barred me from her life, what she planned. But you...you're so different. So passionate, never hiding anything. With you it's so raw, so real." He smiled. "I need to learn to adjust to, ah, actual emotion. Anger. Pain. And I'm more than willing because the way I love you–*you*–scares me. I like it. A lot."

"Yeah?"

His dimples appeared, making all my problems go away for a second. "Yes."

He bent to kiss me, and I reveled in the explosion bursting in my heart. He loved me. Me. Now all I had to do was deal with my own pettiness.

What the hell do you think you're doing!

"*Ah!*" I bent forward, Wilma's voice blaring like a bullhorn in my head.

"What? What is it?" Tarek grabbed my shoulders and pulled me up.

"Wilma."

"Shit."

Get your ass back here! Are you insane?

I clapped my hands over my ears as if that would quiet her down. No such luck.

You're putting yourself and everyone else in danger. If I have to come get you...

"Tarek, tell her...tell her to knock it off."

He nodded and closed his eyes. His facial expressions went from angry to contrite to plain wincing as he had a conversation with her inside his head.

After what seemed like hours, one more blast wrenched through my tender brain. *If you're not back before everyone wakes, I'm coming to get you and it ain't gonna be pretty. These people are looking to you as a leader, and you failed!*

Oh, damn. Nothing like giving the guilt party extra fuel to get it really rocking.

I cleared my throat and took my hands from my ears, feeling like a glob of crap. "I have until morning."

He grabbed my hand, heading to the cabin. "Then we should make the best of it."

"Wait. My mom."

Confusion clouded his eyes before understanding made him smile. "Right. She's worried about you. Jake too."

"Yeah, I've been a shitty daughter lately."

He switched directions, heading toward our main room. "No, you've been busy. Big difference."

Once we made it into the room, a roaring fire blazing to combat the now quiet hailstorm, Mom jumped from the couch, yelling what sounded like my name. Jake followed, taking us in his arms. Sandwiched in between Mom and Jake, I gave Shaina a nod, who returned it while staying on the couch. She didn't look worried or scared, which confused me. Belva and Farren were long gone, more than likely spending the stolen time in one of the rooms upstairs.

After all the "I love yous" and "everything will be fines," I sat next to Winston's girl. "You're not scared?"

She smiled, making her pretty face shine. I mean, the crazy weather Tarek's emotions created, her man about to go into a battle, not to mention sitting on a sofa in an entirely different world, and she grinned as if we were hanging out at a coffee shop discussing *Teen Vogue*.

"Winston promised to come back to me, and I believe him."

"Just like that, huh?"

"I have faith in my man. He'll be back for me."

Wonder if she charged for optimism lessons.

I hugged her, hoping that positivity would rub off on me.

∞ ∞ ∞

The walk to the cabin was silent except for the moaning squid, who obviously were tired from weathering what amounted to a tropical storm in the warm sticky part of Arcus. The forest's weather the exact opposite of the hailstorm near the castle, but raged the same. Christ, I hoped they'd have enough time to recuperate before Tarek bled the lines. Belva's pink, squishy friends were important for the plan to work right.

I broke the silence, pointing up. "You think they'll be ready?"

"I've been such an ass." His face flushed as he opened the cabin door.

I pulled him in, kicking the door shut. "It's not like being Arcus's Warden comes with an instruction manual. You'll learn to control the place–even when I'm being a bitch."

He wrapped me into his arms, tugging me close. "Now, that's no way to talk about the woman I love."

Woman. *Huh? Weird.*

"She *can* be a bitch sometimes, especially in the morning." I reached to kiss the tip of his nose before going to the stale granola stash.

His laugh followed me. "Well, since I haven't been around you much during the morning, I'll take your word for it."

My fingers froze, the granola wrapper going unopened. Clarity sucked. He hadn't been around me much. Ever. In the past five months, our conversations were all one-sided. I knew a ton about him, but…not exactly the best way to get to know someone.

I swallowed, opening the wrapper and breaking the bar into pieces, trying to find words. I faced him, his face brighter, though the bags still lingered. Little things weighed on me. All those tiny little things that made me the neurotic person I was.

Like how I had hated granola since puking it up one night after a tough track practice.

"Hey, um, can I ask you a question?"

His brightness dimmed. "Of course."

Whatever I asked, his emotional wellbeing came first. The squid probably wouldn't have been able to take much more. But I had to ask one thing. Just one. "What's my favorite color?" The question didn't matter. What mattered was his answer.

His shoulders relaxed and he took the few steps to me, leaning down to touch his lips to mine. When he pulled away, he said, "The color of sunset, deep orange with hints of gold."

Stunned, I smiled, smoothing his silky hair from his eyes. "Yeah, it always reminds me that–"

"Tomorrow you can start over."

"How'd you know?"

He grinned. *Ah, dimples.* "Wilma."

"Huh?"

"What do you think we talked about every time she came here?"

"Hmm, well..." Feeling a little self-conscience, I looked down at his feet. "So you know everything?"

He tilted my chin. "Every. Single. Gory. Detail."

"Like wh-what?"

He smoothed a thumb across my lower lip. "Like you cry every time you watch…ah…*E.T.*, I think she said?"

My face heated. "It's a good movie."

He kissed one cheek and then the other. "So good you made her play it over and over when you were little, every time you'd go to her house for peanut butter and fluff, your favorite sandwich."

His warm fingers and roaming lips made it hard to concentrate, but with every detail he gave, another fear evaporated. "What I wouldn't give for a peanut butter fluff right now."

Full lips skimmed my face to hover above my mouth. "I also know you sleep with my shirt wrapped around a pillow."

My face went from hot to burning. "It smells like you."

"Like sweat? Dirt?" He grinned, his lips touching mine as he spoke.

My breath came out in sharp intervals, his touch never failing to stoke the flames. "No…apples."

"Apples?" His warm chuckle vibrated off my mouth, melting my knees.

"Yes…" Big hands trailed down my back, forcing everything but his touch from my mind. "Please."

"Please, what?"

"Shut up."

His smile turned a little dangerous, his warm breath turning my blood to fire. He kissed me, deep and long, until my knees gave and he had to hold me up.

I wanted more. More than his lips. I wanted everything. This could be the last time I ever saw him. After I left...I might not come back from Empyrean. Not alive.

I wouldn't ask him.

I'd show him.

I stepped back and lifted my shirt over my head.

His breath hitched as he stared at me, his trembling hand wiping his mouth. "What are you doing?"

He didn't move.

So, I went to him.

Keeping my eyes locked on his, I slowly pulled his shirt up, revealing his tight stomach. He closed his eyes and stilled my hand. "Lena..."

I wouldn't take no for an answer, not this time. No reasons to stop separated us. He was mine and I was his. As crazy and bizarre as our relationship had been, I loved him. Who cared about all the reasons people might throw at me, claiming it wasn't possible? *Five months? Not enough time...*

To hell with them.

Why?

As Tarek always whispered in my ear during those five months: *Your energy was the reason why mine was made*, and with everything in me, I'd love him forever. At that moment, I knew it, maybe for the first time.

Standing on my toes, I touched my lips to his until his hold on my hand went lax. Our lips drifted apart long enough for him to yank his shirt off, his shaking hands finding my cheeks after. I guided us backward, toward the bed, willing the spell to remain unbroken, needing him. Like he needed me.

As he pressed me against the mattress, his body fitting perfectly to mine, he searched my eyes. "Are you sure?"

My hand, strong and steady, touched his face, my heart bursting. "Yes."

He smiled and glided a hand across my collarbone. Lower. Nerve endings that must have remained dormant ignited in a thousand little sparks as if they waited for his hands. Waited for this moment. "You're beautiful."

After that, there were no more words.

∞ ∞ ∞

In the darkness, we lay on that narrow bunk, bones and skin preventing me from getting as close as I wanted. I settled for resting my chin on his bare chest to watch him sleep.

After a minute, his dimples flared. "It's not polite to stare."

I ran my fingers over his chest, memorizing every muscle, cementing it in my mind. I always thought I'd be nervous my first time. No. This…this was heaven. "Admiring my man is all."

Keeping his eyes closed, he drew me closer, his smile soft. "Carry on, then."

I kissed his heart. "Tarek?"

"Hmm?"

"What's your favorite color?"

He opened his eyes, his smile deepening as he pulled me up until we were nose to nose. After brushing knotted hair behind my ear, he cupped my chin. "Green."

Perfect… He was perfect. "I love you."

"You'd better."

Fear picked that moment to interrupt. If the worst thing happened…I had to ask for his word. "You have to promise me something."

He played with my hair. "Anything."

I captured his fingers in my hand and squeezed. "If I die, do whatever needs done to make sure my energy is sent here to you. Keep it safe until…until we can figure out…I don't know…what to do next?"

His eyes hardened, along with the rest of his face. "Nothing will happen to you."

"Come on, you know that's not realistic…please."

His eyes slammed shut, his jaw tightening as he worked to control his emotions. The wind picked up outside, though no storms erupted. When he spoke, his voice was soft, deceptively soft. "You have Wilma."

"Great. Wonderful, but there's always what-if." He shook his head, and I grasped the sides of his face, forcing him to look at me. "Maybe there's only a slight chance, but there's a chance. Just make sure I end up here."

He inhaled, blowing it out in slow intervals. Then he kissed me until I almost forgot what I asked.

Almost.

But yeah, he definitely had moves.

We broke apart, both of us working on catching our breath. But I wouldn't let it go. Not until he promised. "Promise me."

He slid a finger down my cheek, sadness dulling his eyes.

"Tarek?"

A pause, the silence I loved and hated, stretched between us. He finally leaned up to speak right against my lips. "Wherever you are is where I'll be. Always."

Lynn Vroman

CHAPTER 30

LENA

WAR ROOMS

As soon as the portal opened, the drawbridge came down far enough for us to leap onto it. We ran full-bore to the big double steel doors as the bridge moved to close up again. The right door flung open when we were feet from it, Wilma there waving a frantic hand to hurry.

The door slammed behind us while Farren and I gasped for breath, mostly from the rush of adrenaline, both of us used to a little exercise.

Wilma glared while we heaved and coughed, her hands planted on hips. When I caught my breath, I managed to find every cobweb woven in the hallway ceiling. I counted twenty before glancing at Wilma again, who still tagged us with her famous sneer.

Speak, dumbass!

It wasn't clear if Wilma or I blared the command in my head, but we were probably thinking along the same lines.

Farren braved her wrath first. "Umm…Wilma? This was my idea. Don't–"

"Save it." She raised a hand to him, keeping her blue glare on me. "There's not a damn thing you can say to convince me you didn't let a kid talk you into being stupid."

"Hey! I'm not…" My face burned when her eyes narrowed. "…a kid."

I so wanted to sound more mature than that.

She didn't acknowledge me, not with words, anyway. I still got the stare that'd turn Hell into an ice rink. She pointed to Farren. "Go get some sleep. You got two hours before we figure shit out."

Under normal circumstance, he would've told the person talking to him like that to fuck off. Wilma wasn't *any* person–and she never would be. "Yeah, okay. Ah…sorry, Wilma." He nudged my shoulder before taking off down the hall past Wilma, doing a run/walk trot before disappearing around the corner.

Wilma tortured me with her condemnation a few minutes longer. I wouldn't say sorry, though. No matter how much my knees shook, I kept my chin lifted, staring right into her shark eyes. Finally, she let me have it.

"Do you realize how dangerous that was?" Her voice grew quieter with every word, way different than her usual yelling. That flat tone made me wish I'd went to the bathroom before coming back.

"I-I had to go. The plan wouldn't have worked, if not."

The calm she exuded wasn't fooling anybody. "Is that right?"

I swallowed, fighting the urge to cross my legs. If I pissed myself, well, that'd suck. "Y-yes. Tarek…he was so upset…the weather." Spitting out this excuse before Farren opened the returning portal sounded so much more convincing. I dropped my gaze, shaking my head. The energy it took to talk my way out of the mess became exhausting. I went with good old-fashioned honesty. "I had to see him, one more time, in case I didn't make it back."

"Oh, you'll make it back. I'll make sure nothing–ah, damn it." Her raspy voice hardened, but there was no denying how it quaked.

I glanced up to find her anger gone, replaced with unshed tears. "Wilma?"

She yanked me down into a fierce hug, taking me by complete surprise. "Don't ever leave without telling me again. Ever. I promise never to stop you, but... I can't protect you if I don't know where you are."

I squeezed her hard, my own tears soaking her neck. "Deal. Sorry." Okay, fine. I said it. But this Wilma had a stronger impact than angry Wilma.

"Me too, honey. For everything. Your life, *this life*, wasn't supposed to work out this way. I wanted you to be happy for once."

I buried my face deeper in her warmth, wanting to absorb all the stress I caused her. "I *am* happy–if you don't count the 'dimension wanting to kill us' problem."

She laughed. "That's a pretty big problem."

"Yeah, but there's no place I'd rather be than right here with you."

Snorting, she patted my back. "Well, you're a dumbass."

Awe, there she was, and man, I loved her.

∞ ∞ ∞

Sleep never came. Granted, two hours wasn't exactly enough time to take a sponge bath, remove the crud from my hair and pull a brush through it, eat, and nap. Something had to give, not that my nerves would let me sleep, anyway.

Did these people really think I could lead a goddamn recon mission? Wilma said they were looking at me as a leader. Hopefully, she meant that in the most metaphorical way possible. The only thing I'd ever led was a track team. We won states last year, but still. Never had to kill anybody to do it.

After the last knot came loose, I pulled my hair in a bun. When the knock on the door rang through the hollow room, I was more than ready to get everything in motion–so it could end.

Expecting Farren or Wilma, I yelled to come in, busy figuring out how to tighten the waist on the way too fancy Empyrean pants. Having trembling hands didn't help matters. Frustrated, I yanked a little too hard, breaking the leather ties.

"Damn it! How can I pretend like I know what I'm doing in front of those people if I can't even figure out how to work my pants?"

Then the fuzz registered.

I looked up to find a sad smile painting Zander's face. "Oh. Oh, um, hi."

"Hey." He moved to the dresser and pulled out another pair of pants made from fabric I didn't recognize.

Recognize it or not, all the clothes here were made from the same stuff, and when on, they felt like being wrapped in a cloud. If it weren't for the damn ties…

He handed them to me, grinning. "Here, try again."

I hugged them to my chest, my face burning. Crazy I let him kiss me.

Can't believe I felt something.

"Ah, thanks." I sprinted behind the dressing screen by the shuttered window. The ties on the second pair weren't any easier. "Aren't there any with an elastic waist?"

"Afraid not."

"Shit."

His footsteps echoed on the marble floor, coming closer. "Let me help."

First instinct was to tell him to back off, but I swallowed that in favor of not having my pants end up around my ankles. I stepped from behind the curtain, holding them up to avoid a scene. Unfortunately, I couldn't find any cloudy-soft underwear. "Just…watch where you put your fingers."

"Damn, Lena. I'm not a perv." His deft fingers had no trouble lacing the blue fabric together. "There. You ready?" He headed toward the door.

"Zander?"

He stopped, not turning around. "Yeah?"

I concentrated on my fingers, cataloging every new scratch. "About last night, I–"

"No, don't. Don't say it." His shoulders sagged. "I'll never have a chance with you, and I'll never be able to make up for what I've done, but…let me have last night, okay?"

Nothing I could have said would've made it easier, and so I did the next best thing. I moved to circle his waist, resting my cheek on his back.

He folded my hands in his. "When this is over, if you don't mind, I want to go to Arcus with you. You'll need my help for when…for when they attack again."

There was no *if*, only *when*.

I turned into his shirt and smiled. "I'd like that."

"Come on." He squeezed my hands. "There are a few more people you have to meet."

Great. We might as well add to the tally of others who potentially hated me.

Zander took us through hall after hall until the whole place felt like a rat maze. The more halls we trekked, the deeper we went into the manse. When I finally had enough marble and empty space, Zander opened a door–to stairs.

"You've got to be kidding me," I said.

He grinned, yanking a torch from the hand of one of many statues decorating the halls. "A little farther." He grabbed my hand. "Stay to the right."

I snorted. "Or what? We fall into the dragon's lair?"

"Nothing so dramatic." He flashed the torch on the stairs, the stone crumbled and chipped. "The right side's in better shape. Lights went out a few days ago."

"What's down here?" I held his hand so tight, my nails dug into his skin.

"Ah! Ease up, will ya? It's kinda like a bomb shelter, I guess. We've been using it as a military room lately."

"Military room?"

We reached a platform, and Zander guided us to the left. "You think Empyrean wouldn't have an army?"

"By the looks of things outside…"

He nodded. "They haven't been winning any battles. Their numbers are low, maybe a hundred. Most are residing here in case Teenesee can't keep the shield up. If they take her–"

"We're screwed."

"Pretty much, yeah."

We stopped at a set of iron doors that put doors in gothic insane asylums to shame. Zander handed me the torch and pulled out a key hanging from a chain around his neck. After a few tries, the lock clicked. Zander shouldered the heavy door open. Wouldn't you know it, another long-ass corridor. "Really, Zander?"

He took the torch back, the flames flashing on his grin. "Almost there."

Thankfully, we only walked another few minutes before the fuzz in my brain magnified. Avery and Grace were down here, or we wouldn't have to look that far for the nest. Since Zander didn't panic, I assumed the former.

We turned one last corner, and the hall bled into one single, enormous room. Large groups of people, including Winston, the Protectors he brought with him, and Wilma and Farren crowded around the biggest table with map holograms glowing above it. The sole person to glance our way was Wilma, who motioned us over.

Zander hooked the torch on an iron holder cemented in the wall, its flame no longer necessary. A cache of those ultra-green orbs encased in a cell-like room took up the entire left wall, putting out enough energy to light up New York City. "Holy shit."

He tugged me over to the table, smiling. "Cool, huh?"

Cool. Sure, we'd go with cool.

I moved to stand beside Winston and Farren as some really tall, really dark, and really handsome man explained the dimension's terrain, pointing at certain spots marked with a bright green *N*. When he looked down and noticed me, he smiled and extended his hand through the hologram. "It has been a while, Lena." His soft voice carried.

I reached for his hand, his grip firm. "Um, I take it we knew each other? Before?"

He nodded once. "Pit, Commander of Teenesee's guard."

"Nice to meet you, again." Our odds were getting better and better.

He gestured to the map. "As we were discussing, we will begin the hunt tonight in order to avoid Guides in their purest form." He brought the two marked spots closer by touching them. "These two areas have the highest Exemplian activity. The nests are more than likely in the vicinity."

I squinted, taking a closer look at the terrain. "How can you be sure?"

"Because I trust my scouts. The wooded site has less traffic, but there is still activity." He straightened, a small grin lighting his face. "They have become overly confident, not leaving many Protectors there to guard that nest." Pit's calm washed through my brain, infecting me. "We will be rid of this plague by morning."

His confidence, quieter than Winston's but as strong, made everyone in the room lift their chins a bit higher.

The thought of being anywhere near a cluster of Guides in energy form caused my skin to prickle, though.

Last time, their attack made me useless. But I wouldn't share that. No, I had to act as if I knew what to do next.

I pointed to the two marked spots. "Okay, so we split up, Winston with one group, Wilma with the other. Better to communicate through minds. Who knows what devices they have, bad enough they got the screens."

"I'm impressed, Lena. I see a new life becomes you." Pit folded his hands in front of him.

My face heated, but his compliment gave my beat-up ego a boost. I kept focus on the map. "Yeah, well, almost getting killed a couple times makes you quick on your feet."

Winston jumped in. "My group'll scout this area." He pointed to the main village. "Wilma can check out the woods."

Knowing I'd be with Wilma, I didn't like that idea much. "No. We'll check that one out. You take Grace and Zander. We'll take Avery."

Winston shook his head. "You take Grace and check out the woods. The villages are crawling with Exemplians killing off the population."

I closed my eyes to keep from rolling them and clenched my fists to prevent punching him in the face. No way would I waste time arguing. "Each group needs an active Guide if one of us…" Didn't need to finish that thought. "I'm going to check out the village site. Period." I opened my eyes and pegged him with a look I'd practiced after getting it from Wilma for years. "There isn't gonna be any debate."

He opened his mouth, but Wilma interjected, her tone leaving no room for argument. "We're taking the village." Her promise drifted in my head: *I'll find out, one way or another*…

Farren slung an arm across my shoulders, thankfully no longer fangirling around Winston. "I'm going with her."

He nodded to Soccer Mom and Accountant. "Take a few of them to help protect Zander and the old lady."

Oren perked up, irritation tightening his face. "Watch it."

I held up a hand, so not wanting to deal with testosterone. "Enough. Farren, ease up. And, Oren? Stop making that face. Anyone ever tell you it might freeze like that?" I turned to Pit, who though calm, had tension narrowing his eyes. "Sorry, continue."

"Right." He cleared his throat, focusing on the screen. "As soon as the fires are blazing, I will need to be informed." He touched his temple. "We will then stage an attack. However," he glanced at Winston, "you must inform Arcus's Warden when the enemy screams render the air. That is our surprise–that is how we will beat them."

Winston nodded, concentrating on the map. "We need to do anything and everything to kill as many as possible. The more energy, the better."

Oren crowded the table, pushing a few Empyrean soldiers out of the way. "Wait. We had a deal."

I sighed, looking at Avery, forever hiding behind her Protector. "You come up with anything?"

She stepped forward, face ashen and looking about ten pounds lighter than when we first met. "The only way is for Zander and I to go into the camps in energy form, sense the reluctant participants, and convince them to leave with us."

I palmed the table, leaning forward to make sure she didn't miss my anger. "That's it? That's what you came up with?" I looked at Zander, who shook his head, and pegged her again. "Your plan will eat up precious time. Time we're not gonna have when they figure out we're around." I stood back. "No. It's too risky."

Oren's face turned a bright shade of red, almost purple. "So, you're willing to kill innocent people?" He sneered, throwing a finger in my face. "You talk about change, a new life? Different ideas? No. Death hasn't changed you."

All right, that did it. I slammed a fist on the table, making the hologram's pixels scatter. "Every goddamned person out there is fucking guilty!" Not even Wilma tried to calm me down. "Have you seen what they've done to these people? Because I have. The real innocent people are covered in bloody sheets and thrown on the street like trash." I narrowed my eyes. "Do you know they killed Teenesee's daughters? Do you even care?"

His face paled. "They're here under duress. It's fight or death."

"So you want to save people with a 'better them than me' mentality? Is that it? They've killed children," my voice hitched before I could swallow it, "babies."

From my peripheral, I noticed a few Protectors shaking their heads. Soccer Mom had tears pooling in her eyes.

Oren pursed his lips–and kept on arguing. "I'm saying we should at least try."

"Fuck that."

I nodded to Pit before heading to the hall. Who knew if I'd find my way back up to my room, but when Wilma, Farren, Winston, and Zander followed me I stopped worrying about it. If that sonofabitch thought throwing the past in my face would change my mind, well, he didn't know *me* all that well.

I yelled over my shoulder as we rounded the corner. "Tell you what, anyone who grovels–no, begs–for mercy might get a chance to live another life, but trust me when I say this, they won't get to finish this one."

CHAPTER 31

LENA

THE CALM BEFORE

I needed to puke. Seriously. I even had to swallow the regurgitated diet of dried fruit and fish a couple times. Talking about killing people as if I'd done it before, like it wasn't a big deal, made me sound like I belonged in a psyche ward.

Sociopath, anyone?

They followed me to my room, none making any moves to leave once I opened the door. I shuffled my feet, wishing for alone time. All I wanted was to let my stomach have free reign over the toilet in private. "So, um, I guess I'll see you all tonight?"

Winston shrugged and stuck in his earbuds before taking off down the hall. "Sounds good. Later."

Christ, if I thought of myself as the perfect case study for sociopathy, well, the way Winston acted he'd have been any psyche major's wet dream.

Zander scratched his head. "Yeah, I'm gonna go too, get some sleep." He bent to kiss my cheek, and whispered, "See you tonight." He left, going in the opposite direction as Winston.

Wilma steam-rolled past me and barged in my room. "I'm staying with you." Her gravelly voice left no room for argument.

I grinned despite everything. Upchucking by myself would have to take a rain check. "Great. Now I have to deal with her snoring."

Farren smiled and squeezed my shoulder. "You okay, kid?"

"No, yeah, well–" I swiped at my cheek. "No, I'm fine, everything's fine." I found my feet, studying the way the leather weaved over my toes. "I've never, you know, killed anybody."

He chuckled, lifting my chin. "No shit? Hmm…learn something new every day"

"Not funny."

He pulled me to his chest, patting my head as if I were a Golden Retriever. "No, it's not. But listen, you won't have to worry about that, okay? As soon as the bad and ugly goes down, we're going to get you out."

"So you want me to be a hound dog, sniff out the nest, and hide while you guys put your lives at risk?"

"Yup!" Wilma's voice reverberated off the walls, echoing down the hall.

Farren pulled away and traced my jaw with his thumb. "Yup." His soft whisper was as convincing as Wilma's yell.

"But I can fight. Isn't this why you've been training me?"

"We got this now, kid. Don't worry."

I'd let them win this battle. We'd see what would actually go down. "Fine. Guess I'll see you tonight."

He glanced in my room with a grimace, not leaving.

"Ah, your room's that way?" I waved a hand down the hall.

His fingers tapped his thigh as he looked down the hall then back into my room. "You know what? No." He swept past me, jumping on the floating bed. "This bed's big enough for ten people. Don't worry, I don't snore."

I laughed, shutting the door. Private puke fest would definitely have to wait another night. "Whatever. I get the left side."

We settled in, Wilma taking the middle and Farren on the right, not keeping his non-snoring promise. I grabbed her hand, holding it to my chest, needing her close. As my eyes drooped, I squeezed her fingers. "Wilma? Could you tell Tarek to…?"

She closed her eyes. "It's already done. Relax, he'll be along soon." In minutes, she snored along with Farren.

And I waited.

He didn't make me wait long. *Hey, you.*

Silent tears tracked my cheeks, soaking the pillow. "Hey."

∞ ∞ ∞

None of us spoke much. There wasn't a lot to say. Farren grunted something about getting his suit and left before I climbed off the bed. Wilma was already up, not even acknowledging him when he left as she washed her face with the basin of water on the dresser.

After all the time spent preparing for what so many others failed to do in the past, it finally hit home. Exemplar had proven it could annihilate worlds, Arcus being the poster child. In essence, our little rebellion was like an annoying ant problem. They'd spend the time exterminating us and go on about their business.

Damn, not a good mindset to have. But that thought was all that rushed through my mind as I crawled from the bed to put on my contego suit. The calm Tarek gave me today, singing a lullaby in the most off-key voice possible until I fell asleep, flaked away. Tension squeezed my heart, causing my lungs to work overtime. My lips grew numb, and if I thought lacing the pants was tough, trying to lace up that goddamned suit with fingers that shook like Jell-O was near impossible.

I tried to ask Wilma for help while she stuffed herself in her own suit, but words couldn't make it past my tight airway. Instead, I crumbled on the nearest cushioned chair and used my eyes to plead with her.

When Wilma finished with her suit, she finally glanced in my direction. Her eyes widened before she closed them, along with her open mouth, and motioned for me to stand.

If only it were that easy.

I groped for the couch's arm and pushed up on unsteady legs. "I don't think I can do this."

Her fingers were rough as they laced me up. "Well, you're gonna do it whether you think you can or not." The color drained from her face, making her gruff words less Wilma-like.

"What if they feel us coming?"

"These suits are Empyrean, better than what they have when turned on. Keep your suit turned on! They help deflect attention, like a static camouflage, plus those damn bullets can't penetrate them."

"What if they know our plan already?" Sweat poured from my skin, making the suit sticky and uncomfortable. "What if they send the authority to Arcus?"

She tightened the laces until the fabric pinched my sides. "They don't know."

"But what if they do?"

"They. Don't."

"Yeah, but how do you know?"

She rolled her eyes, the laces getting tighter. "I just do."

"But–"

"Stop. Please."

I grabbed her hands. "So many people are gonna die tonight, Wilma."

She bowed her head, clutching my hands. Her mouth opened and closed a few times, but nothing came out. No "shut-up" or "quit asking questions" left her lips. Only a little sob, which she swallowed as soon as it escaped.

For some reason, as soon as her desperation reached through to my own panic, all my nerves calmed. Acid roiling in my gut settled, and the need to puke dissolved like a cloud after a storm. I slipped my hands from hers to pull her close. Sometimes I forgot she was human, too. I'd always considered her Superman's tougher big sister.

When a few minutes past, she leaned back, a rare sad smile on her face. "I wish I could tell you everything will be fine, that this will be easy, like I used to when you were a little girl. But this–I can't tell you that now."

She had always wiped my tears, told me to stop feeling sorry for myself, and made me a peanut butter fluff–and held me until I fell asleep. Somehow, I had awakened in my own bed and never realized how. The last year explained that well enough. But she did, you know, make everything okay. Though at that moment, she seemed helpless, and I couldn't let her feel that way, even with fear dancing on my spine.

"You don't have to say it, Wilma. I'm not a little girl anymore." I brushed a stray tear from her cheek, causing more to flow from her blue eyes.

"Yes, you are. You're *my* little girl, always have been."

That almost had me blubbering on the floor.

She was right.

Clearing my throat, I moved to look in the tall mirror, watching her through it. "So, how do I look? Like an ass-kicker, right? I could totally kick some ass."

She scrubbed her cheeks, the smile returning. The quick subject change didn't bother her in the slightest. I could be strong for her. Hell, at that instant I could be strong for myself.

Shaking her head, Wilma stomped over, elbowing me out of the way. She situated her suit over her ample chest, pushing up her girls. "Now, *this* is an ass-kicker image. You look like a twelve-year-old boy."

I laughed. No way could my ladies compete with hers. "All right, you win."

"Damn right, I do."

A sharp knock echoed, and Winston barged in looking lethal in his glowing green suit with all his muscles straining against the fabric. The only skin showing, his neck and hands, showed off those awesome tattoos. Man, if I were the enemy, I wouldn't want to fuck with him. Who knew he had all that going on under those baggy clothes?

He shot me a bored glower and raised a brow as Wilma still fussed with her chest. "Don't know if y'all got the memo, but we're going to be fighting, not clubbing."

Wilma rolled her eyes, giving herself a final adjustment before waving me to the door. "You try stuffing curves in tight fabric. Definitely didn't miss these damn suits. They don't let me breathe." She snuck past him like a ninja and barged down the hall, expecting us to follow.

Of course, we followed.

As we trudged to the basement room, I caught Winston sneaking glances in my direction. After about the sixth time, his little covert peep show grated my nerves. "What, damn it?"

He chuckled and nodded his head as though earbuds were permanently attached to his ears. "You ready for this, Tainted?"

No. "Of course." I moved a couple paces ahead as we rounded the never-ending hallway. "I've been in plenty of wars."

He laughed, coming up to my side. "It'll all be over before you know it, especially with your man opening up what most of them assholes consider Hell. Chances are they'll be on the first portal back to Exemplar before shit gets real serious."

I worried my lip. Sounded good, but… "With everything they've taken from here, Exemplians will be next to invincible." Shit. Just…shit. "They're gonna keep on coming after this."

He shrugged. "Guess we'll worry about that later."

So not what I wanted to hear.

We headed into the room, everyone wearing glowing suits except Wilma and me. Until Winston touched a spot under my right arm. The slick black fabric came to life, buzzing on my body with electricity that hummed through my skin. Felt nice, actually, like a force field or something.

"You turn this off, the bullets can come knocking on your skin, you heard?"

The second person to warn me tonight.

"Yeah, got it."

Wilma turned her suit on, too, as she went to meet Pit at the map table, holograms blazing.

Our Protectors and a few Empyrean soldiers crowded the table talking strategy while some men were busy collecting the orbs from the cage. They molded them until the snow-globe-sized spheres were as small as pebbles and stuffed them into rows of satchels. Some were loaded into clips and locked into what looked like pistols you'd find on *Star Trek* or the SyFy channel.

After a quick look at Winston, who nodded toward the gun table with a half-grin, I went to pick one up. The smooth, warm metal fit perfectly in my hands. I'd never shot a gun before, and the thought of shooting one now wasn't exactly pleasant. I went to put it down, but one of the men shook his head saying something in Empyrean.

"I-I don't know… Do you speak Desis?" I really had to brush up on foreign languages. I didn't have a nifty chip in

my brain to translate like all the Exemplians in the room–
another tidbit of information Tarek shared during our
nightly one-sided talks.

Farren came into the room when the man said it a
second time after I tried putting the gun back. "He said to
keep it and take a satchel of ammo, too." Farren listened
again as the man spoke. "He also said to be careful with
what you have. It's all the power Empyrean has left."

"Oh." I slung the offered bag across my shoulder.
"Thank you."

The soldier smiled, handing off weapons to both
Winston and Farren before everyone else tending to them
went to dole out the only resources Empyrean had left.
Winston checked his weapon before holstering it in his
belt. He gave a half-salute to us before heading over to
everyone else.

Farren slid his gun in the same place after giving it a
little twirl around his finger.

Rolling my eyes, I turned in a circle and gave a mock
bow. "Well?"

"Eh." He waved a hand toward my torso. "Too
skinny."

"How 'bout you bite me, 'kay?"

He winked. "Wouldn't want to make Tarek jealous.
You might like the way I bite better."

"Ugh, gross, Ginger."

Laughing, he yanked me to his side. "Agreed. Listen,"
he veered off to a corner and lowered his voice to a
whisper, "Cara's place isn't far. Wilma agreed to take a
route that passes by. We'll have maybe a minute tops to
check if…if she…"

I nodded when he didn't finish. "Okay."

Farren grabbed my gun and pointed to a small button
by the trigger. "Turn off the safety and shoot." He yanked
out a clip carrying at least a hundred tiny glowing orbs

then locked it back in. "And pull out and refill with the ones in your bag when empty."

"Great. Thanks. But that still doesn't help with my aim."

He grinned. "Shoot real close."

I snatched my gun. "Best instructor ever."

"One more thing," he tilted my chin, his face turning serious. "Those guns with the mercury bullets, they're what we in the authority affectionately call soul-stealers. If a bullet lodges in your body, you die. Forever. No take-backs or redoes, understand?"

"Wilma told me." I panicked. "Jesus, so if you'd have–"

"My energy would be powering a fucking toaster or something on Exemplar right now."

My arms whipped around his waist and squeezed like the contact could erase the memory. "Avoid soul-stealers. Check."

Lynn Vroman

CHAPTER 32

LENA

CARA

Fear used to be something I chased. Not fear, really, but how I reacted to it. Proof, when fight or flight kicked in, I still felt like having a go at the whole life thing. When a door off the military room opened to an underground tunnel leading into the city, I was never more positive that I craved life. Not that I had any doubts lately.

Winston and his group took off in the opposite direction, toward the fields. He said nothing to me before leaving–just gave that cocky nod and led his team. Zander hugged me, kissed my cheek, and made me promise not to be stupid.

Always hated making promises I had no intention of keeping, but whatever.

My group remained quiet, maneuvering around puddles of stagnant water and trying not to gag when it became obvious the tunnels were underground sewage passageways. Avery held a perfumed rag to her nose, which pissed me off. After I stepped in a brown puddle that smelled like ass, I put that blame directly on her shoulders, too.

"Why the scowl, kid?" Farren held my elbow, leading me away from the others. "Someone shit in your Cheerios? Or on your boots?" He pointed to my soaked hikers. It didn't make matters better when the moisture seeped through the thin material, soaking my socks.

"I'm fine. Thinking about people who annoy me is all." I said it loud enough for everyone to hear and emphasized with a thumb shot at exactly whom I found irritating so no one misunderstood.

Wilma snorted and said something about subtlety, while Nicolette consoled Avery, who even managed to weep annoyingly. When I glanced over, Nicolette made sure to narrow her eyes and mouth, *Watch it.*

Whatever.

I turned around, flying the bird behind my back. *Watch this.*

Farren shook his head, but smiled as we evaded the deeper slushy brown puddles. "Lighten up."

I kicked a little muck on his boots. "Nope."

He jumped, unsuccessfully dodging the brown sludge. "Ah! You'll pay for that one." He stomped his foot, the stubborn filth refusing to let go. "When you least suspect it. I'm like a shit ninja. You'll wake up one morning with squid crap all over your face."

I snorted, kicking a little more his way. "Sure, if I live past tonight."

His smile disappeared as he came to a dead stop and clamped his meaty palms on my shoulders. "Stop being so goddamned doomsday, Lena."

"I'm just saying–"

"You're not going to die. I won't let you."

I glanced back at Wilma because Farren's intense eyes made me squirm. She had her arms crossed with a smirk on her face. "You'd best listen to him."

What?

I turned to face Farren's angry glare again. "Okay, fine. I won't say it again. Maybe *you* should lighten up."

His eyes closed, lids squeezed shut before they slowly opened, all the serious gone. One big hand drifted to my elbow, while the other dropped to his side as we continued down the tunnel. Nothing was said for a few seconds, the plop and drip of smelly condensation leaking from the walls to the ground keeping us company.

He switched his grip from my elbow to clasp my hand. "I'll never lighten up. Not when it involves your life."

The rest of the tunnel trip remained quiet.

Wilma eventually took the lead, guiding the way with a small, oval device that gave off enough green light to blind somebody. We could've done without it thanks to our glowing suits. But when the orb switched to red, and she stopped to look up, the thing turned out to be a high-tech GPS.

"This is where we get off," Wilma said.

Above our heads, the ceiling revealed a manhole cover the width of maybe Farren's shoulders. Not too big, but enough for us to squeeze through. Black slime oozed from it, either hiding a latch or maybe eating it. From the smell polluting the tunnel, the plausibility of the crap coating the cover being alive leaned toward the high end on the more-than-likely scale.

Wilma tossed Farren the device and climbed the equally slimy iron brackets leading up to fresher air with as much stealth as a Navy Seal. Still amazed me how graceful she moved considering her…um…voluptuousness.

Any concerns about how the cover would let us free flew out the stinky crap tunnel. When she made it to the top, Wilma flicked a few fingers, and the thing shifted to the side a few inches. She listened with her eyes closed a few minutes before waving at Farren. She then used her skills to move the cover the rest of the way. Before Farren began to climb, Wilma had already squeezed through the opening, disappearing from sight.

He latched onto the brackets, the squishy sound of skin touching slime as cringe inducing as grinding teeth. He took a few steps upward and glanced down to Nicolette. "You next. We'll make sure it's clear before these two come up."

"Got it." She guided Avery to stand next to me.

We watched them disappear, the awkward tension as thick as the shit smell that would forever stain my nose hairs.

"I am so sorry, Lena." Avery's soft voice snaked through the filth.

Breathing deep through my nose–and gagging because, you know, shit–I shook my head, still focused on the opening, and hoped for cleaner air. "Don't worry about it."

"Well, I do. When I came to you..." She paused. "I should have never..." She didn't finish.

"Should have never what?" My hand moved to push the hair from my face when I glanced down at her, but stopped right before my dirty fingers had a chance to give me an outhouse makeover.

She wrung her hands, tears coating her eyelashes. "Told you Cassondra sought revenge."

"So I could be blindsided when she came to kill me? Gee, thanks."

Her whimpers turned to sobs. "She was not seeking revenge, Lena."

Rage, blinding and black, made my hands shake. The only reason I came to Empyrean was the imminent threat from Cassondra. I'd have stayed away and ignored Avery's desire to close the lines–lived by the goddamn rules! Because of a lie, an entire world suffered. "Why would you..."

"Because I needed your help! The lines, they must be–"

"You should've told me what you really wanted." I stepped closer to her whimpering form, wanting to hit her. Worse. "Or stayed the fuck away! *This*, all of it, is your fault."

"I'm so very sorry."

My hands raked through my hair anyway, an action better than tearing her face apart. "Everything that has happened could've been avoided if you told me the goddamn truth."

Tears tracked clean paths down her dirty face, which did nothing more than strengthen the urge to slap her. "I was so desperate."

"*Desperate*?" I backed away from her. "Teenesee, her people, they don't deserve this. All these deaths are on your shoulders. Live with that." I shifted my satchel and concentrated on the opening. "Stop crying."

She didn't respond, and I didn't expect her to.

A few more minutes ticked by before Wilma stuck her head in to give us the all clear. I waved for Avery to go first, in case her weak arms couldn't pull her up. The long drop would probably do her some damage. Hard to admit, but we needed her. After this? Well, she and her watchdog would need to find somewhere else to hide.

As soon as she made it up about five feet, I started to climb, prepared to stop a fall. She slipped a few times, but finally made it to the top. Nicolette bent down to help drag her out. As soon as she was out of the way, I scaled the brackets quickly, jumping out into a pitch-black alley, except for our glowing suits.

I whispered, "What's next?"

Wilma swooped over and grabbed my elbow. She held a finger to her lips, shaking her head.

I nodded, swallowing hard. Even though darkness blanketed us, it couldn't hide the crying and distant screams. The smell… Worse than the sewer. Smoke stung my eyes as the stench, like road kill on a sweltering August day, slammed into me. I slapped a hand over my nose, my eyes watering.

They were burning the bodies.

I stumbled until I found an object to lean against, trying hard not to double over or crawl back into the sewer. I had no clue what I held onto, but it was metal and cool, a relief from the hot, suffocating smoke. The town's buoyancy didn't help matters either, the swaying ground cheering on my roiling stomach. Wilma grabbed my shoulders, her eyes pleading with me, her lips a thin line. I locked on her face, the smoke squeezing my lungs. Horror softened to revulsion until blessed shock kicked in. After raising my thumb, Wilma let go, motioning for everyone to gather around.

In quick, sharp hand gestures, Wilma told us to go to the left, make a right, and stay quiet. She jabbed a finger at Farren, indicating he'd bring up the rear. At his nod, Wilma pointed to Nicolette, flattened her palm, and used two fingers to show her flanking Avery and me. When everyone nodded our understanding, she took the lead, sliding against the wall of some shop. Drawing our guns, we moved forward.

We slinked to the end of the alley, our boots soundless against the cobblestone. Wilma waved for us to stay against the wall as she peered around the corner. Her head whipped back, and she turned off her suit. We followed her lead and reached under our armpits as Protectors waltzed by, joking like they were out for a night of clubbing. One stopped right by the alley, scratching his head. As he turned toward the entry, searching with a small light, Wilma waved her hand in front of his face.

Another came up to slap him on the back. Wilma waved her other hand. "Hey, what's the deal, man?"

"Don't you feel that?"

The other guy stopped for a second, looking straight at us. "Nope. We gotta go. Cassondra wants everyone back in fifteen."

They both gave one more direct look at us, causing my breath to hitch. I wanted to scream, run…shoot them, but I stayed as quiet and still as everyone else. As the group moved on, Wilma dropped her hands, only to bend and grab her knees, breathing heavy.

I rubbed her shoulder, feeling her tremble underneath my fingers. "You okay?"

Shit, how'd she do that? From what I knew, persuasion didn't work on Exemplians, retired or otherwise. She was stronger than I thought.

She looked up at me, face pale and sweaty. "Yeah, give me a minute."

I waited for her to catch her breath. If my heart refused to slow down, there was a good chance I might keel over.

Once Wilma straightened, she brushed a shaky hand through her hair and looked past me to the others. "You all hear what he said?"

"We got problems." Farren squeezed his gun tighter, his fingertips white.

"No shit." Wilma gestured toward Avery. "Why the hell are you smiling? You miss Cassondra, do you?"

Avery, who up to this point acted like a helpless kitten, shook her head and stood taller. "I do not miss her in the least. On the contrary, I'd as soon gut her with a fishing knife. No, there is some good from her being here."

Wilma rolled her eyes. "Such as?"

"No one is monitoring the screens. Oh, I'm sure this dimension is under scrutiny, but Arcus and Earth are safe. Synod elders worry about this war, not what might be happening in places where Lena dwells. They do not seek personal revenge."

Lynn Vroman

That... Well that actually made me happy. Not happy enough to forgive her for starting a war, but relieved, nonetheless.

Wilma turned on her suit, and we did the same. "Okay." She pointed left. "One stop and we move on to the nest. Lena and Avery should start to feel it at about a half-mile from this point."

Avery gave her Protector a quick glance. The exchange made me nervous. She hid something else, and whatever it was, it'd be bad. When this was over, I'd have a hard time not killing her. Yet, after I told everyone what she'd done, I may have to wait in line.

As we walked through the deserted town, the once quaint and pretty shops now burnt warned us to stop and turn around. The screams died down, but crying echoed within the recesses of the buildings. These people lost everything and now had to suffer by watching the mounds of sheet-covered bodies burning right there on the sidewalks. The stench coming from the charred remains became too much, and I couldn't make it to a more discreet place before my stomach gave up. I fell to my knees. Dry heaves attacking after nothing else came.

Wilma scooped me up and didn't let go until I could stand. "Keep it together, damn it."

All I could do was nod as I wiped the leftover vomit from my cheek. She continued forward, and I let Avery and Nicolette go ahead of me. Farren still took up the rear, prodding me if I slowed down.

Just... Damn.

All that talk, all that shit I said to the Protectors and Teenesee, all the confidence I faked... I couldn't fake it here. Not with dead bodies reminding me of how totally scared I was for their surviving families. *My* family.

Then Cara pushed through the fear.

Please, please, please, let her be alive.

I covered my nose as we kept to the shadows. When we got closer, I recognized where we were. The same area Farren opened the portal. Which meant one of the lookalike homes lining the streets in Empyrean's main village was Cara's. I searched my brain, trying to remember exactly which house she lived in, but didn't have to wonder long. Farren took the lead, running in a direct path to her doorstep.

I jogged up behind him, shirking Wilma's hand when she reached out to stop me. She wasn't that serious to hold me back, though. One flick of her hand and I'd have been a pissed off statue.

Farren used his sleeve to wipe the dirt from the window. When I looked through the spot he cleared, my heart raced. There she was, reading a hologram book on that bright orange couch, smiling.

"She's okay!"

Farren shook his head.

"Of course, she is. Look." I tapped on the window, but she didn't look up. After the second tap, I noticed her body flicker–like a hologram. A man walked in from the kitchen, holding two steaming mugs. His body flickered, too.

"The window blockers are still up," Farren said.

As fast as the elation came, it flew away, forcing me to hold onto the sill before my knees gave out.

Farren stalked to the door to find it unlocked. He disappeared through the entryway, and in seconds, his face met mine through the glass. When he shook his head, face drawn, I stumbled backward until I tripped over the burned heap in front of her house. The mounds on this street were not complete ash. Careless Protectors didn't stick around to make sure fires took. But the pile grew larger. Kneeling, I lifted the half-burned sheet.

"No, Lena, don't." Wilma's hand covered mine.

I lifted my chin, pleading with her. "I have to."

She stared at me for a while before pulling her hand away. As Farren came over and hunched beside me, I lifted the fabric, sobs choking me. What I found brought me closer to the ground as I fell to the cobblestone slicked with ash. Charred bones and skulls with melted strings of hair. Tarnished jewelry wrapped around cindered wrists and blackened rings melted around fingers whose skin had not quite disintegrated. One ring I recognized, the delicate design not yet burned away.

"Oh, God." On the inside, I screamed, but my voice remained a whisper. I tore my blurred gaze from the ring to what Cara held clutched in her arms. The screams inside echoed out, filling the quiet streets, matching the heartache in the distance. Her little girl wrapped in cloth, and by some miracle not touched by the fire, lay on Cara's concaved chest.

I covered my ears and shut my eyes. "No, no, no, no, no…"

Someone clamped a hand over my mouth and dragged me against a solid chest. Hot breath smacked against the hand over my ear. "Quiet, Lena. Please. I'm sorry…please."

Farren's plea cut through the torment wreaking havoc on my brain. I wished the shock would come back. *Please come back!* His hand didn't leave my mouth until I stopped whaling.

I hated it, the influx of pain, misery, defeat. "We should've never went in there. We killed them…We killed them…We killed them."

"No." His voice hitched, cracking.

I searched the faces in front of me. All had despair radiating from their eyes. I found Wilma and reached for her. She rushed to me, picking me off the ground, and keeping me wrapped in her arms. She whispered unintelligible words until the first waves subsided.

Wilma pulled away, her face an angry mask. "Do you feel it?" She flattened a hand against my stomach. "In here, can you feel it bubbling?"

Ripples of pure rage, the need for revenge, circulated through me. I nodded, my tears drying, my eyes gritty. I felt it. Hate. So raw, so potent, I could live off it, be sustained by it.

"Use it. Own it. And let's go get those bastards."

The hatred took over, sealing off my heart, making me stronger. I didn't care anymore about black and white and the gray area in between. Farren was wrong. Black and white...there was nothing else. I now understood who I used to be and why. No doubts remained. I knew her, and I wanted what she wanted.

Tarek once told me living the same life over and over again turned most Exemplians hard, immune to feelings. Past Lena's apathy prevented her from doing what I knew in my heart she wished she would've done.

I didn't have that problem.

I would kill every single one of them.

Lynn Vroman

CHAPTER 33

LENA

EVERYTHING

Avery felt it before I did. Static didn't cloud my brain until we were almost on top of the nest, which happened to be the only building not charred or ransacked.

Nest.

Right.

I didn't know what I expected, but a building wasn't it. A building that took up an entire block. From the statue of Teenesee–broken and crumbling–gracing the tiny yard, I assumed it to be the equivalent of the courthouse. A few Protectors patrolled the outside, some sitting on the stone steps leading up to the main doors. Others took their job a bit more seriously, walking the perimeter.

We hid a block down, inside what used to be a tavern with upturned tables and chairs, whiskey bottles broken on the floor, the shelf behind the bar empty. Funny how the bastards didn't burn this place, only trashed it, taking what they wanted.

All *I* wanted was to set the courthouse on fire. Torch it and listen for the screams. I stared out the window, waiting. The one thing keeping me sane was the image of them paying for killing Cara and her baby.

The. One. Thing.

We had to wait for Winston to come back from destroying the nest in the woods, since he had to help

Tarek keep the lines open. The nest we found was too big for us to handle, another hiccup in the plan. It had to be destroyed before the lines opened, though. For that, we'd need Winston and the Protectors with him, as well. The static was almost enough to send me into a coma.

Almost.

The lines bleeding had revenge salivating in my mouth. Desire to see their fear, feel it when they saw Arcus coming to get them, actually had a laugh escaping. Wilma looked over, her brow scrunched.

I shrugged. "What?"

She pursed her lips, crossing her arms. "You gonna make it?"

"I'm fine." I returned my attention to the window. "Fine…fine…fine."

"You don't sound fine."

I tapped my fingers against the glass. "Leave it alone."

She stayed quiet–for about thirty seconds. "When Winston gets here, you and the rest of the Guides stay behind."

That got my attention. I pushed away from the window and stormed to where she stood, not giving two shits about repercussions as I stared down at her. I pressed all my hate through my voice. "I'm not staying here."

Wilma's eyes flickered. "Zander and Avery might have to collect energies; their bodies need protection."

I bit my lip to keep from screaming–or laughing. Whatever swirled inside my head grew dark, thick, and heavy. "Don't do that. Don't act like you're giving me a job when all you want to do is lock me away. Give the babysitting duty to a couple Protectors. I can fight, damn it."

Her eyes narrowed as her finger jammed into my chest. "You will stay–along with some Protectors. If anything happens, they're to cart your ass outta here. That's nonnegotiable. Understand, girl?" She jabbed my chest again with a little more force, propelling me backward. "*You* don't give orders to me." Another jab. "*You* do what I say." And another. "And if I hear one more stupid thing come out of *your* mouth, I'll take *your* ass far away from here myself."

For the first time in my life, I wanted to hurt her. She made me powerless, impotent.

No, she reminded me of how powerless and impotent I really was.

I staggered back to the window, shaking my head. "You're not my mother, and you're not my ruler." My attention returned to the distant guards, picturing their bodies in flames. "You're not my anything."

Her breath hissed in the silence. Through the reflection of the glass, I saw Farren's big body stalk toward me. "Stay away from me." My eyes met his in the window. "Both of you."

He froze, his mouth forming a thin line. Farren turned to whisper with Wilma, and to be honest, I didn't care what they conspired together. I'd do what I wanted. They couldn't keep me in here.

Avery spoke, cutting through the thick tension. "I must use the facilities." When no one answered her, she added, "I believe I noticed a restroom upstairs."

Still, no one even gave her a glance. Farren and Wilma were undoubtedly too busy lamenting about my attitude. Me? Well, those guards weren't gonna imagine their deaths themselves, were they?

Time crawled as if in a repeating loop, never moving forward. The more I stared at the walking corpses down the block, the stronger the urge became to run outside and test my aim. Cara's melted flesh and her little girl bundled in her arms fought through the hardening shell surrounding my heart, further solidifying my desire for blood.

Wilma and Farren's whispering continued. Their voices like sandpaper against my brain. No doubt, they planned a way to keep me in here, but that would only happen if someone stayed with me. Or maybe they planned to take me away before the party started. If they tried, I'd never forgive them. Never. I'd–

Oh, shit.

Static, thick and potent, rushed past me, leaving me breathless before the feeling faded. One thing I'd come to realize after spending time with Exemplians was each Guide I came across had a unique effect on me. Once I felt it and met the source, I couldn't forget.

I knew exactly to whom that energy belonged.

I ripped up the stairs, taking two at a time, not getting to the room fast enough. "You bitch!"

Stomping feet followed me up. I tried to force the door open with no luck. Wilma thrust me aside, and waved her hand, the door exploding from the hinges. There was Nicolette, gun drawn, guarding Avery's body.

"What have you done?" Wilma's face paled and her hand twitched right before she waved it, picking Nicolette off the ground, and tossing her against the brick wall.

Nicolette struggled to stand, her gun wavering as her pointer finger reached for the trigger. Before she could shoot, I kicked the weapon from her hand. She swept my feet from under me, flipping me into a chokehold, backing up against the wall. Her grip was tight, but I could still breathe.

Nicolette's entire body trembled. "Don't make me hurt her."

Wilma stepped forward, and Nicolette's grip stiffened. I held up a hand as Wilma waved hers. When Wilma lowered it, I swallowed. "You know you won't win this fight."

Nicolette sobbed, though her hold remained. "I asked her not to, begged her, but..." She hid her face in my neck, her tears soaking through my suit. "She swears there are innocent people in there. She had to give them a chance."

"Fuck this." Wilma flashed her deadly hand, ripping Nicolette's grasp from my neck and pulling me to her side. "You know what you two assholes managed to do? We no longer have the element of surprise. In seconds, that whole goddamn building will know we're here."

Nicolette stumbled over to Avery and draped herself over the Guide's body. "I tried to tell her. Don't kill her, Wilma. Please don't kill her."

Wilma's hands shook, and there wasn't a doubt in my mind she wanted to do exactly that.

I wanted her to. The bitch betrayed us.

They both did.

But Wilma closed her eyes and lowered her hands. Farren glanced over her head at me, and I shrugged, about to whip out my gun and do it myself. Then Wilma's eyes opened. "Winston's here."

She left the room, turning her back on the crying Protector and her traitor Guide.

No. Not good enough. I reached for my gun.

Farren grabbed my hand. He pulled me from the room as Wilma flung a hand behind her, shutting the bathroom door. Well, lifting the door off the ground and slamming it against the entry.

Winston barged into the tavern, Zander, Oren, and our group of Protectors behind them. Grace nowhere in sight. He didn't waste any time with chitchat. "They know we're here."

Wilma moved to the window. "No shit. Avery went in, blew our cover."

For the first time since I'd met him, Winston flipped, whipping tables and chairs around the room. No one, not even Wilma, tried to intervene. When the room lay in even bigger shambles, he seemed better, breathing slow with his eyes closed. "Okay, change of plans."

"Well, you better make it fast because there's a light show over there." Wilma pointed to the window with the courthouse view as the sky burst with a firework display of red, blue, green, and white orbs while Protectors stormed from the building waving their soul-stealers.

Winston clapped his hands and rubbed them together. "Imma open the lines in here. Let Pit know it's time to bring the fire."

Wilma nodded, and as soon as she closed her eyes, the roofs came to life with Empyrean soldiers. Pit's army swarmed the streets, firing their weapons, killing the Protectors like flies. Unfortunately, the orbs swooped in every time a Protector fell, absorbing their energy, which meant Teenesee didn't get an ounce of it. Empyrean soldiers fell, too. Soul-stealers hit their marks while orbs swooped down to steal more energy.

Still, Winston concentrated as if nothing went on outside. He raised his hands toward the bar, sweat beading on his forehead. The fight came closer to our sanctuary, but he didn't move. We all stood tense, and I knew every single person in the room itched to join the fight as we watched Empyreans fall. Some even tried to leave the bar, but Wilma froze them. "Don't give our position away. He needs to get the damn lines open."

Winston struggled, his arms straining as he yelled.

The enemy drew closer. Orbs infiltrated the bar, paralyzing me. Their beautiful light swirled around Zander and I, suffocating us.

"They're coming." A Protector pointed, the soccer mom, who now looked like a warrior, deadly and fierce.

I wanted to lift my gun with the rest of them, but the lights… I needed their heat, their touch. Farren swooped in, taking Zander and me under an arm and ramming us into a darkened corner, his grip tight. Lights continued to swirl around us, diving into our opened mouths. The heat they produced made my lungs burn, and by Zander's screams, they did the same to him. Still, I didn't care. I craved it, needed it.

"Hurry up, Winston!" Farren's booming voice cut through the heat, and I managed to smile at him even as I screamed.

I wanted to reassure him, let him know I was fine dying this way, but the heat wouldn't let me. Nothing mattered. Death. Not so bad. Not so–

I'm here, love. Open your eyes.

Tarek.

I concentrated on the power his words always had, struggling to lift my lids. The heat eased as I opened my eyes to find the bar transformed. Boards and bricks broke off, flying into Arcus's vibrant forest. No longer were there empty shelves and broken glass. My giant stood with Belva next to him, her squid an intimidating army taking commands from their mistress. Like a vacuum, the orbs swept across the lines, releasing Zander and me from their hold.

I bent forward and Farren caught me, the excitement on his face palpable. "Ready to kick some ass?"

Oh, hell yeah.

When Farren released us, Winston yelled again as he blew the front of the building away, meeting the surprised enemy head-on. Most back peddled when their eyes landed on what waited for them inside.

Tarek remained deadly calm, his circling palms forming a clump of blue, green, red, and white light. Whatever he did, the Guides weren't able to escape his hands.

Farren took off into the fight, a war cry escaping his lips. Wilma, already in the fray, threw Protectors toward Belva's squid, and at my friend's command, thick pink tentacles reached for the flying Exemplians, curling them into their bodies and silencing their cries. Winston stayed, his muscles straining, but he managed to drag Protectors toward Belva's cephalopod army while maintaining the open lines. Tarek sucked up every Guide who dared to come near, the mass of light he held hostage growing larger.

Not one Protector dared to cross the lines voluntarily, the squid, vicious and snarling, hungry for the kill. As more enemies disappeared across the lines, the less stress registered on Winston's face.

When ten more Protectors met the squids, Tarek yelled to Winston, "Go, I got this."

Not needing any more prompting, Winston gave him a salute, and rushed out into the melee, but not before turning to us. "Do. Not. Leave. You heard?"

My eyes shifted to the ball of light Tarek wielded while strength and anger seeped back into my body. Those Guides might have been powerful, but they couldn't make me forget the hate for long.

"Lena!"

I jerked my attention toward Winston, my mouth dry and bitter with revenge.

"You heard?"

When I nodded, he jumped in, a lethal whirlwind of fury as he dodged bullets like a samurai while throwing Protectors into Arcus. Everyone fought hard, but those orbs swooped in, collecting energy, giving many more Exemplians another chance at life while ending the lives of brave Empyreans.

The answer to the problem lay hidden in that building, almost certainly under heavy protection. The Guides had to die, or all this was for nothing.

I grabbed under Zander's arm and lifted him from the ground, Exemplian bullets whizzing by us. Not willing to take chances, I led him to the alcove under the stairs. Once we were relatively safe, I pointed outside. "We're not gonna win if we can't get rid of the Guides."

He squatted, pulling me down with him when a few stray bullets lodged into the wooden planks. "What's our plan?"

I glanced up, not expecting him to volunteer himself but grateful all the same. "We make a run for the building, find the bodies, and stick with the original plan."

He grabbed a stair, his face determined. "We burn them."

"Yes."

His fingertips whitened. "On our way here...I saw what they did to people I knew, cared about." He pursed his lips. "We'll need help."

There wasn't time to ask about what happened with his group and the nest in the woods, but by the hardened expression that hadn't left his face since he came through the doors I assumed the experience left him...well, a little like me.

I squeezed his hand before scouting the bar. The only people of ours left were Soccer Mom and Oren. "Looks like they're our babysitters. Guess we should tell them where we're going, huh?"

"They'll get the hint eventually." Zander got up and reached for my hand. I clasped it, pushing off the ground. He gave a grin that didn't reach his eyes. "Ready?"

"Wouldn't matter if I wasn't."

We ducked out from under the alcove. They'd follow us–hopefully. I gave Tarek one last glance. As if he knew, he turned his attention to me, shaking his head.

Don't do it. His voice vibrated inside my head, pleading.

I pulled the gun from my belt, and mouthed, *I have to.* Then I was gone.

Lena!

Tarek's command matched Oren's as his boots smacked the cobblestone behind us. Of course, Zander and I kept going, staying to the edge of the fight, making sure to avoid Wilma, Farren, and Winston, who all fought as savagely as berserkers.

We ran hard, Zander struggling to keep up with me. In seconds, Oren matched my pace, which would've colored me impressed under different circumstances. He didn't try to yank me back to the bar, though. He didn't need to be told where to go, either. Any Protectors who noticed us, Oren handled, with his gun or fists, no one who tried able to best him.

As we hit the courthouse's marble stairs, Zander's wheezing cough informed me he caught up, along with Soccer Mom. We took the steps two at a time, Oren and Soccer demolishing any detractors with skill that would've impressed Jet Li.

What stumped me as we breached the entry was how hardly any Protectors stayed behind to defend the nest, which punched me in the gut as soon as we were about fifty feet down the wide, cavernous hallway. The static tingled through my body, making me light. With effort, I tamped down the craving to sit and enjoy it and trudged forward.

Doors marked the walls every three feet or so, running the length of the hall, all shut and locked. As we rounded the corner, more doors appeared for us to choose from along with about ten Protectors blocking the door at the end of the hall. From the buzz amplifying in my head, I knew what they protected behind that door.

None moved to attack, remaining in a solid line, protecting the nest. Oren didn't feel so inclined to do nothing, and neither did Soccer Mom. They blasted the guards, taking down four before the others had time to aim their soul-stealers.

As soon as they fired, I yanked Zander into a doorway, standing flat against the wall. My gun in hand, I couldn't shoot. As much as I desired to kill them a short time ago, when the moment came I couldn't. Every time I tried to aim, my hand would shake and my conscience would freeze my trigger finger.

Zander had no such issue.

He stayed in front of me and shot with as much precision as Oren and Soccer. Sweat dripped into my eyes and my hands quaked even more. The fear pissed me off, the hate running scared when faced with action.

Oren planted his body in the entry directly across from us, Soccer a few doorways down. When the blasts from the opposite side ended, Soccer ripped down the hall. The remaining Protector, another woman, ran out of ammo. Before she could reload, Soccer leapt, giving the Protector a scissor kick to the head. When the bitch fell to her knees, Soccer grinned, sauntering behind her, watching her prey suffer. She then put one hand on the Protector's chin and the other across her forehead. In the silence, a loud crack echoed before the Protector slumped to the ground.

Soccer opened the door, peered inside, and waved us forward. Fear turned to shame, my face heating on the jog to the door. Yet again, someone had to save me. No one commented on my lack of help, which made the shame crawl deeper into my brain. But once we ended up in a stairwell, determination stomped on the disgrace.

Static in the well overwhelmed both Zander and I. He held onto the railing, breathing deep, seemingly better able to ignore the pull. Even without their energies, these Synod Guides could turn me into a co-dependent moron. But the attraction didn't control me as wholly.

My trembling hand swept damp hair from my brow. I glanced at Zander. "Up or down?"

He shook his head, keeping his eyes closed and his hands clenched around the metal rail. "Don't know. Both, maybe?"

"Okay, um…" Shit.

Oren cleared his throat after looking out the door. "Whatever we do, we need to do it now."

I glanced over his shoulder to find two people headed our way. When Zander's attention followed mine, he gasped, his mouth slack. "Cassondra."

Panic ripped through me, but by some miracle I tamped it down, my voice as calm as bathwater. "You and Soccer Mom go upstairs." I already began racing downward, Oren following.

"It's Erin, Tainted." I looked up to find Soc–ah, Erin grinning down at me. "Never stepped foot on a soccer field in my life."

I nodded and kept moving. We jumped down flights of stairs, Oren landing with more finesse than I. Funny we never heard the door swing open, or anyone chasing us. Maybe they didn't see us? And maybe the dead Protectors disappeared, too, right? The hairs on the back of my neck stood. Why didn't she follow us?

As soon as we reached the ground floor, Cassondra left my mind. Oren peered through the glass window while the static screamed so loudly in my head it brought me to my knees.

His hair, soaked with sweat, plastered the sides of his face. After swiping it from his forehead, he searched again.

"At least three hundred bodies are in there and not one Protector. Easy fucking targets."

I pressed onto the cool ground, trying to block the desire to run, flee from responsibility. These people, who lay defenseless, lined up head to toe, helped massacre hundreds of people, maybe more.

We had to do it.

I couldn't.

"Oren?"

He hunched to meet my eyes, his bright with sympathy. "I was wrong about you, Tainted." He brushed my cheek. "You have changed. Good."

"I don't think… I can't kill them."

He sighed, biting his lower lip. After a second, he jumped to his feet. "But I can."

An explosion rocked the building, shaking the already floating ground. Dust landed on my head, scratching my eyes, and clogging my throat.

Coughing, Oren said, "And it sounds like someone else can too. Two nests, no protection. Callous motherfuckers."

I gasped for air, pulling in more dust. The building trembled, the dust turning to chunks of debris. Oren pulled me from the ground, shoving me back up the stairs at the same time snatching my satchel from my shoulder. He took his off, too, and threw both into the room, shooting at them until they caught on fire. "Go! Go! Go!"

I raced up the stairs, my lungs burning even as the building tumbled around us. The light guiding our way was our glowing suits, now flickering. Another explosion ricocheted through the well. I fell backward.

Oren caught me by the armpits, just to throw me forward again. "Move!"

Steps crumbled underneath our feet as we climbed, our progress too slow, like ants swimming in honey. My legs grew heavy, but adrenaline refused to let them give up.

Smoke–the ever-present smoke polluting Empyrean–clogged the stairwell, attacking us.

I tripped, and Oren scooped me up, dragging us both until we hit the door. Zander and Erin met us in the hall and we all raced to the exit, the walls crumbling in our wake. Another boom crashed through the building, knocking us the last few feet outside and down the marble stairs.

Zander lay motionless next to Oren, who sputtered and gagged. I crawled to him, leaning on his chest. "Zander!" I shook his shoulder when he didn't respond. "Wake up! Please! Wake up… Wake up."

He coughed once. Twice. His eyes fluttered open as he floundered, searching the streets. "Did we do it?"

I laughed–and cried. "Yeah, we did."

The streets looked like a scene right out of a WWII movie, bodies strewn everywhere. But most were Exemplian bodies, and the only light shining on the once beautiful town came from the orange sunrise. No more orbs. No more control. Portals opened as the surviving Protectors left, some devastated, no doubt because they left without their Guides, whose energies stayed here. For Teenesee.

My legs wobbled as I struggled to my feet, Oren behind me helping. Relief cleared away the pain, both physical and mental.

We did it.

We won.

Hopefully Teenesee would find a way to heal herself and her people.

"You!"

I snapped my head to the right to find Wilma rushing toward me. Rage fired through her blue eyes, her suit turned off and unbuttoned in the front. Oh, man. I had a lot to apologize for, but I'd do it with a smile on my face. For starters, I needed to make sure she knew exactly how much she meant. What I said to her before... No, she was everything.

I grinned with a shrug. "I–"

A bullet skated past my head.

Surprised shined on Wilma's face before the blue sphere slammed into her chest.

Her eyes widened.

She fell.

"*Noooooo!*" I dropped to my knees, cradling her head...rocking.

Rocking.

Rocking.

Rocking.

"Wilma?" I covered her wound. Blood seeped through my fingers. "*Wilma!*"

Blood leaked from her mouth.

So much blood.

"*Please!*"

Her whitened lips moved, but no sound came out.

More blood.

"*No...*" My face buried in her neck as her body stiffened.

Life drained away.

"Oh, God, no! Please. I'm sorry...I'm sorry...I'm sorry...I'm sorry."

Sorry.

Sorry.

Sorry.

Yelling, screaming, cursing rendered the air. Wave after wave of screams.

My screams.

Zander's. "Stay away from her!"

A woman, as colorless as Casimir, stood above us.

Cassondra.

She smiled and held out her hand. Wilma took one last breath as the bullet lodged in her chest came loose, flying into Cassondra's palm. I felt a whoosh, and a hole punctured my heart. An empty space. Gutted.

She held the glowing blue pellet for me to see. "You took from me, and now I'll take *everything* from you."

Her other hand flew in the air as Farren and Winston came running behind her.

They were too late.

The portal swept her up, took Cassondra away.

Took Wilma away.

Forever.

CHAPTER 34

LENA

REVENGE

Fall was always Wilma's favorite season. She'd bitch about the leaves scattered on her porch and the bears getting into the garbage, but she loved it. A long time ago, she told me fall reminded her of second chances–when the old fell away to let winter cleanse the heart. She was poetic when the mood struck.

She was a lot of things. Everything.

We spent the summer collecting Protectors' loved ones willing to stay in Arcus. Many nights were spent having long conversations explaining reality to shell-shocked husbands and wives, boyfriends and girlfriends, even a few children.

We also collected supplies, mostly from Earth, to help rebuild Arcus's villages. Belva's squid worked to tear down trees, dragging logs to the surrounding fields so Tarek and others could shave them down, turn them into cabins.

My mom became *the* mom. Grace volunteered as her sidekick. Everyone acted happy, despite the threat of the now more powerful Exemplar looming, planning the next attack.

Normal.

No.

Nothing would ever be normal again.

Winston led what he called our foraging missions to Earth. He didn't do it to be nice, but to give Shaina a chance to say goodbye to her family and friends. He even fixed the whole mess Exemplar made for us before…before…she died.

Police stopped looking for Farren, Mom, Jake, and I. The guy in my apartment went from a murder victim to a suicide. Unfortunate, how that homeless man found his way into our apartment–the story Winston drilled into the heads of those who mattered. We would have the chance to go back. Someday.

Belva's parents believed she ran off with the circus. Seriously. That was the story Winston gave them when he rang their doorbell one night. He even added she fell in love with a redheaded clown.

Belva would disappear with her redheaded clown as soon as the day's work ended. They were in love. They found their happy ending.

Cassondra stole mine.

Zander became my rock, my verbal punching bag…the unconditional friend he pretended to be before. He didn't leave my side most days, and I liked having him around, especially if the rage took over and needed an outlet. Maybe he stuck around to punish himself for the past. Regardless, I'm glad he did.

We trained every day, too. Oren helped Farren with that, along with Tarek. Not just boxing. I wanted to be able to kill.

I wanted to be able to pull the trigger next time.

Avery and Nicolette vanished, never coming back to Arcus. Don't know if they died, but for their sakes, they had better never show their faces again. I'd kill them both. There wouldn't be any hesitation–my conscience died with Wilma.

Every night Tarek and I would hide in his cabin as soon as the sky darkened over the village. I didn't sleep much. The nightmares...her face...her blood... my final words to her... none of it would let me.

In the mornings, Tarek would hold me and stroke my hair, while sobs wracked my body. Every day took her farther away.

But not today. Today, the blackness held on through the morning, giving blissful emptiness. It did that sometimes–allowed me to feel nothing. On the crisp fall morning, the leaves crackling under my feet, I held onto the nothing as I opened the trailer door to find my dad still alive. Still scared. Still sitting in that chair in front of his wall.

I wouldn't be coming back here after today. We had too much to do. Too much to prepare for. This would be his last chance to come with me, the last time he saw me if he again refused.

"Dad?"

He jumped and pulled the afghan closer to his chin. "I ain't going. You can't make me."

I went to kiss him on the cheek and ignored his flinch. "This is the last time I'll ask. I won't be back."

His face paled. I wished he were still the monster under my bed and in my nightmares. Easily conquered. Easy to escape. "I'm gonna be all alone?"

"Yeah, I guess so."

"Well, then." His muddy eyes found his chief.

I sighed and went to the door, not bothering to say anything else as I shut it behind me.

Walking through the woods brought back memories, like the first time I met Tarek. The night my life changed forever. My heart used to skip every time I passed the stream's edge. Now all it did was function, pumping blood to vital organs, keep me living. It only lay vulnerable in those early morning hours with Tarek. The hours when death felt like a better option.

Winston met me by the river alone, leaning on his crotch rocket.

I rolled my eyes. "Really?"

He stood, grinning. "Tired of all the exercise I'm getting."

I nodded, not quite able to muster a fake laugh.

Come home. Tarek's voice, gentle and soothing, echoed in my dull brain. My heart didn't skip then as it used to, either.

I glanced at the gray sky. A small purple slash sat above the trees. Since Empyrean, Tarek managed to open and close the lines for short periods without worlds bleeding permanently. Winston showed him. I never bothered asking how. It didn't matter.

I sighed. "Time to go." I held Winston's waist while he lifted a hand to the sky, his other on his bike's handlebar.

"Hold on tight, Tainted. If I have to choose between you or my bike, you'll lose."

"Whatever." I cinched my arms tighter, anyway. The man never made promises he didn't keep. Thank God.

Before the portal took us, I gave my life there one last thought—and erased the memories for good. The past...it didn't matter anymore.

Only one thing did.

Revenge.

GLOSSARY

Arcus- A world deplete of humans, with an evolution that falls behind many others. This world's highest evolved species is giant tree squid. Also, the vivid color permeating the world is "contagious" and transmits to those humans who happen to go there.

Contego suit- An Exemplian uniform that protects from dangers found in all the worlds.

Cycle- Each life a person lives is considered a cycle.

Desis- A common language spoken in many worlds, including Earth.

Dimensions/Worlds- Dimensions are worlds connected to each other with dimension lines. Each dimension is in a different stage of evolution, with some more advanced than others.

Dimension lines- Intangible lines, akin to electrical currents, separating each world. Only Protectors have the ability to open these lines to other worlds. In some cases, when a Warden is strong enough, the lines can be bled between worlds, or erased, for short periods of time.

Empyrean- A world more evolved than Earth but not as advanced as Exemplar. The villages float over lush fields and streams. This world is as close to utopian as possible.

Energy- The soul

Exemplar- A world that is more evolved than any other world known. Humans from this world are more advanced, as well. Exemplar is responsible for manipulating the energy circulation throughout the entire universe. Only the most "privileged" energy is brought to Exemplar to live a cycle.

Guide- An advanced person from Exemplar who has the ability to read energies and transport them to other worlds. Also, their energies are able to leave their corporeal form and travel to other dimensions. Some are more advanced than others, depending on how many cycles they have lived in Exemplar.

Pairing- The act of one Guide and one Protector being matched together in Exemplar. The Pairing helps Protectors know if their Guides are in danger.

Protector- An advanced person from Exemplar who has the telekinetic ability to open lines between worlds. They are able to travel across world lines in their corporeal form, unlike Guides. Their duty is to protect Guides as they collect energy from other worlds. As with Guides, some Protectors are more advanced than others, depending on how many cycles they have lived in Exemplar.

Synod- Exemplar's governing branch

Synod authority- Exemplar's army

Tainted- 1. (n) An Exemplian traitor

        2. (v) To be treacherous

About the Author

Lynn Vroman

Born in Pennsylvania, Lynn spent most of her childhood, especially during math class, daydreaming. The main result that came from honing her imagination skills was brilliantly failing algebra. Today, she still spends an obscene amount of time in her head, only now she writes down all the cool stuff.

With a degree in English Literature, Lynn used college as an excuse to read for four years straight. She lives in the Pocono Mountains with her husband, raising the four most incredible human beings on the planet. She writes young adult novels, both fantasy and contemporary.

FRACTURED ENERGY

COMING 2015

Book 3 of the Energy Series

Coming Soon From
∞ UNTOLD PRESS ∞

ANOTHER GREAT NOVEL
YOU'LL BE SURE TO
LOVE

by
Another Amazing Author

OTHER WORKS

BY LYNN VROMAN

Young Adult Contemporary Romance

Macy Diaz has managed childhood friend Jeb Porter's crush for years. However, his infatuation turns to obsession, even putting a kid in the hospital just for hitting on her. In the past, Macy brushed it off, explained his bizarre acts away. But now she harbors a secret. She's in love…with Jeb's sister, Rachel.

By some miracle, Rachel loves Macy back, and despite the small minds polluting their sleepy southern town, they're sticking together. Unfortunately, making sure Jeb never grows suspicious proves harder every day—until everything falls apart.

As a sick, unstable Jeb starts to threaten all Macy values, she is reminded of what has always been perfectly clear. Macy belongs to him, only him, and he won't let her go. Ever.

If only Macy could've loved Jeb, she wouldn't have to worry about surviving him now.